Praise for *Spin Doctor*

'Michael Shea knows all about political
intrigue and makes fine use of his expertise in
Spin Doctor, which dashes enjoyably around
the corridors of influence. What gives *Spin
Doctor* its cutting edge is the fact that Michael
Shea has been a spin doctor himself. His fiction
bears a disturbing resemblance to fact.'
Sunday Times

'A gem – a taut thriller of political intrigue and
skulduggery that fairly belts along. A chilling
portrait of the Machiavellian world that lies
behind the corridors of power in Westminster
and Whitehall.'
Today

'An entertaining romp.'
The Times

'This suspenseful and highly readable tale of
political intrigue and conspiracy is very revealing about what goes on behind another of the
nation's "thrones" – the political one that is
based at 10 Downing Street.'
Manches... ...ening ...

MICHAEL SHEA

THE BRITISH AMBASSADOR

HarperCollins*Publishers*

HarperCollins*Publishers*
77–85 Fulham Palace Road,
Hammersmith, London W6 8JB

This paperback edition 1997

1 3 5 7 9 8 6 4 2

First published in Great Britain by
HarperCollins*Publishers* 1996

Copyright © Michael Shea 1996

The Author asserts the moral right to
be identified as the author of this work

ISBN 0 00 649323 8

Set in Linotron Sabon

Printed and bound in Great Britain by
Caledonian International
Book Manufacturing Ltd, Glasgow

To Mona, Katriona
and Ingeborg

Between the idea
And the reality
Between the motion
And the act
Falls the Shadow

from *'The Hollow Men'*
by T. S. Eliot

Saturday 26 November 1966

The last faint light in the western sky brought an end to the short Norwegian day. A disconsolate, solitary gull perched in precarious warmth on a rusting steel stanchion by a vent near the wheelhouse door. Ahead, a crust of ice anchored the larger, broken floes until the reinforced steel bow of the ferry ploughed and shredded everything asunder. From where he watched by the rail, the resultant slivers were overwhelmed then submerged by the relentless grey waves that swirled below him.

He was almost home, almost happy. In the distance he could just make out the shape of the high, snow-covered mountains lining the fjord with, here and there, the faint lights of some remote farm or fishing township. To an outsider it was a bleak and inhospitable prospect, but, like any Norwegian, he was proudly patriotic, and he knew that warmth and love awaited him nearby. An hour at the most and he would be at the door of the pretty painted wooden house amid the snowdrifts on the outskirts of Bergen. His wife, his seven-year-old daughter, the new spaniel puppy he had heard about but had never seen: they would not be expecting him for a few days yet. He would surprise them. His wife would be overjoyed and only a little upset. She would have preferred to have had an appointment with the hairdresser before he arrived; there would be little festive food and wine in the house. She would fuss around and quickly rustle up a meal worthy of the occasion, washed down with too much beer and aquavit. Then there was his daughter . . . He could hardly wait.

His wife would be in even more celebratory mood when he told her the best news of all: this was to be his last trip. No more urgent, stomach-churning calls in the middle of the night; no more unexpected departures; no more tearful farewells; no more weeks of uncertainty, of her not knowing where he was and whether he was safe. No more pointless, pleading telephone calls to the contact at his 'office', asking how he was and when she might expect him. His sole foray into anger had been when he heard later that she had been doing that, but he soon forgave her because he loved her.

Even when he had come home in the past – and she knew enough of his work to realize that his was the most dangerous of all professions – she expected, from long experience, that he would say next to nothing about where he had been or what he had been doing. Only once, when he had returned with severe frostbite in his feet and some of his blistered and blackened toes had had to be amputated in hospital, had he whispered something of having had to lie hidden for days in a makeshift bivouac somewhere in the unforgiving tundra of the north. When she had asked why, he had laughed and said that it was better to lose a few toes than to be shot, or, worse, tortured into some sort of confession before being thrown into an anonymous Soviet gulag to rot for an eternity.

A bearded crewman in thick fisherman's jersey, bareheaded and with no gloves on his huge hands, who seemed totally oblivious to the cold, appeared and manhandled a crate of tinned fish towards a cargo hatch. He left it there, ready to be unloaded, then disappeared down a companionway to the oily warmth of the quarters below. That was where all sensible travellers were, away from the relentless, biting wind.

The two thick-set men, in leather coats with fleece-lined collars and knitted woollen hats, had boarded the ferry at Ålesund. Each carried a heavy suitcase; too heavy, a percipient observer might have thought. They came, still with their suitcases, to flank him as he stood alone by the ferry's rail. He paid little attention to them. He was safe in Norwegian territorial waters. He was home.

A thin strand of piano wire, strung almost unnoticed between the two suitcases' handles, strangled his cry before it was uttered. Three heavy splashes passed unheard on the now abandoned deck. The wire and the weights would hold the body until it disintegrated in the ice-grey winter sea.

1

'You're much better informed than I am about current Anglo–US tensions, Ma'am.' He hoped he did not sound condescending.

'Suppose one ought to be. After all, one's been reading Foreign Office telegrams for well over forty years. A horrid thought ... It would be a bit remiss ... don't you think?' The Queen flashed a quick smile.

Sir Martin Milner struggled for a suitable response. Should he perhaps be drawing the audience to an end or would that be against protocol?

'What do you think of the President, Ma'am?' he ventured.

'Bit difficult to make a judgement after only one or two highly formal meetings. Wife seems bright enough. I suppose ... like everyone else ... one gets most of one's impressions from his television image.'

'Television's a great equalizer; makes small men great and humbles some of the would-be great,' Milner responded.

'I was saying to the Prime Minister the other day – not mentioning any names of course – that some of his colleagues would better serve their party if they kept *off* the box.' The Queen laughed out loud, a wicked glint in her eyes. Milner thought, once again, how much her subjects underrated her intelligence.

Reaching down for her handbag which had been strategically placed by the side of the gold lacquered chair, she rose to her feet and hooked the handle of the bag over her arm. The audience was at an end. Sir Martin Milner, his wife, Annabel, beside him, stood and moved back a pace. He was aware that a footman, an elegant, gold-braided equerry and a formidable lady-in-waiting, whom they had met earlier while they had been waiting for their audience, had suddenly reappeared through the double doors of the Bow Room.

The Queen came forward and formally shook first Annabel's hand and then his own. 'Good luck,' she said, rather lamely. Then, 'You may have us descending on you, you know. A state visit's on the cards . . .'

There followed bows, curtseys, a retiral towards the doors, then a final bow and curtsey. The ceremony of Kissing of Hands by the new British Ambassador to Washington was over.

Shown out through the Grand Entrance, they said their good-byes to the members of the Household, then were whisked out and away in the drab Foreign Office cars, through the quadrangle, out past the guard changing by the Privy Purse Gate, and into the bustle of real-life London.

After a few moments Annabel turned to him. 'Wise old bird,' she said.

'Seen it all,' responded her husband. 'Sharp political mind.'

'What did she mean by the *other candidate*?' asked Annabel suspiciously. Her steel-grey hair was meticulously styled and tapered; she may have begun giving way to ever more matronly habits, her body expanding from the lithe figure he had married some twenty-five years earlier, but her mind was still as sharp as a scalpel. Wherever they had been posted she was more respected – and feared – by junior embassy staff and their wives than he was.

'Something let slip that I am not supposed to know about,' Milner muttered.

'I thought you were going to tell me everything when it came to future postings.' Her voice was suddenly shrill. He read the danger signals and played it cool.

'Don't know all the details but office gossip has it that when Robinson had his heart attack and I was meant to be going to Ottawa, the Party pushed hard for a political appointment. According to a source not a million miles away from the Head of Personnel, the PM and the Foreign Secretary actually agreed that Vincent, the former Party Chairman, should get the job. Then in stormed the Chief Whip. They looked at the size of their

Commons majority, the risks of losing a by-election in Vincent's constituency and at the long-term uncertainties over the next election, and decided on the soft option. Me.' Milner paused, waiting for his wife's reaction. When none was forthcoming he went on. 'I gather Vincent – or more correctly his pretentious wife – is pissed off. He was looking forward to a couple of glamorous years in Washington. Then his peerage.'

'Pretentious ... is that what they say about her.' Annabel sniffed in a way that was less than approving. He waited, expecting a further barb ... and it came. 'And us, Martin?' His wife turned in the seat to stare at him. He looked away. 'A couple of glamorous years in Washington, or are you all set for your usual workaholic act once you get there, leaving me as social asset and nanny to the young embassy wives?'

'I am what I am.' It was one of his full-stop phrases. Milner was not going to allow her to draw him into a spat, especially with the Foreign Office chauffeur eavesdropping. Husband and wife lapsed into their customary, hostile silence.

The car turned from the Mall down past Horseguards Parade towards Birdcage Walk. The traffic was heavy in Parliament Square but they were soon into Whitehall, King Charles Street and the sanctity of the Office itself. It was twelve-thirty. A lot had happened, but the day was far from over.

In a bleak little changing room he slipped out of his morning coat and striped trousers, the accepted dress for Buckingham Palace. How he hated the stiff white collar, though it was, he supposed, a shade better than struggling into diplomatic uniform as he had had to do in the past. Annabel had left him at the door. They had brushed each other's cheeks with a formal kiss but neither could wait to escape from the other's presence. Had it not been for the need for such a senior ambassador to appear to have a stable, happy marriage, and because their partnership suited them both well in terms of his ambition and her liking for the glamour of diplomatic life, they would have divorced long since.

Annabel was meeting her sister for lunch. He, by contrast, had a demanding afternoon of briefing meetings ahead of him, arranged by the Heads of Mission Section, to prepare him prior to his departure for Washington. He knew much of the background already. In Brussels, his last post, he had seen most of the important telegrams, knew several of the key people, was familiar with the major crisis points. Once he got to Washington he realized only too well that much of the work would be far from glamorous. It was not just the core diplomatic tasks; it was all the protocol and entertaining that went with being an ambassador there. Outsiders thought it must be fun. Sometimes it was, but little did they realize what a high degree of physical stamina was needed to wine and dine the great and the good for Britain, and to act as a first-class hotelier to the constant stream of official visitors, royalty, ministers, MPs and others, who treated the Washington residence as a home from home. Half of any ambassador's life was either that or acting as a postbox for other people's ideas. The other half, the work that he relished, was adding his expert touch to lubricate the business of what was modern international diplomacy.

Sir Martin Milner also knew that, this time round – he had served there as a junior diplomat – Washington would be very different. The last time, as a mere First Secretary, he had dealt largely with one subject: NATO and the Western Alliance in general. He hadn't needed to know much about US internal politics, trade, cultural or consular matters. This time there was nothing that the embassy and its staff were involved in that he could ignore. In those days he had analysed and given advice to his seniors. Now he would be in charge. There were real problems to solve, minor disputes threatening to suppurate into major crises, as weak political leaders on both sides of the Atlantic dug themselves into ever deeper holes, posturing themselves into ever more intransigent positions. Each problem that arose was inflamed by the media, not because the newspapers and television were particularly malicious, but because they were there not only to seek out truth but to look for cracks, to identify scandal, to unearth dispute and division. The media thrived on bad news, and current Anglo–American relations offered a lot of that.

He changed rapidly into his business suit, packed away the

morning dress in its hanging bag, then went through to the temporary office he had been allocated. He had half a dozen telephone calls to make, including arrangements for a lunch with his son, David, later that week. He would take him to the Travellers Club. He was looking forward to a heart-to-heart with David. The young man's life seemed to be a bit unsettled following an uneasy move from the freedom of university to the disciplines of a City desk, and maybe a reassuring, fatherly word would be helpful, particularly as they would see so much less of each other now that he was Washington-bound. David: the clone of himself, in looks, in build, in character. David: Annabel's darling.

Was that really true? Was David a clone of himself? Certainly they looked very much alike. He, the father, tall, fair hair turning to grey at the temples, with a long taut face, slightly hooked nose, and lips that Annabel had once called sensuous. Now she was more likely to brand his look as contemptuous. To outsiders, his clear blue eyes were his most fascinating feature. Unlike many intelligent people, he looked intently at others when they spoke to him and they felt almost hypnotized by the strength of his gaze, the eyes under their heavy hooded lids, staring at or through them. In his youth he had had as powerful a body as David's, but now it was slightly stooped as a result of his habit of bending down to talk to people of lesser height. That, along with his half-moon reading glasses that seemed always to be perched halfway down his nose, gave him something of an academic look.

Yet under his clothes, he was proud of the fact that he had not let himself slip, as so many of his colleagues had done, into middle-aged overweight. His waist was as trim as it had been twenty years earlier. He took sufficient exercise to keep his figure that way but, more importantly, he knew how to resist the temptation to overindulge in the best wines and the superb cuisine that were constantly on offer in the diplomatic circuit. He was not an out and out aesthete though many thought him so. But he was highly disciplined, and, as Annabel had complained on their drive back from the Palace, was also something of a workaholic. He took some time off, but did not believe in letting work pile up around him. He had one rule: he liked to see a day's tasks properly completed before he retired for the night.

Of his other physical attributes, perhaps the most noticeable things about him after his eyes were his hands. They were long-fingered, finely formed with carefully manicured nails. There was something almost feminine about them, about the way he would carefully pick up a pen and meticulously amend a draft, or write a letter. His handwriting too said much about him: a firm italic, clear, precise with almost no errors. He thought carefully before tracing any line of ink on paper. And it always was ink. He abhorred biro. Yes, as Annabel had said, he did work too hard. Yes, he still had ambition and knew he was going to have to be relentless in Washington in order to succeed. Yes, he was what he was.

He made a couple of telephone calls, one to arrange to see the Defence Secretary on current problems with the Americans about the NATO Rapid Reaction Group and another to the Department of Industry to arrange to brief himself on protectionist moves in Congress that threatened to disrupt the progress on the new GATT agreement. Those completed, he pushed all his papers into his briefcase, took his coat from the hook behind the door and was just about to leave the room when the telephone rang. He looked at his watch, sighed briefly since he would be late for his next meeting. He hated keeping people waiting. Reluctantly he picked up the telephone.

'Sir Martin Milner?' a female voice asked.

'Who's speaking?'

'It's not necessary you should know.' The woman sounded unidentifiably foreign.

'I don't accept anonymous calls. I'm going to ring off.' He was uneasy and abrupt.

'You will listen when I tell you. This is a warning. I . . . we now know about you. We may hate you for it . . . But they . . . they are people who like to cut the strings. All the strings.'

There was a noise in the background and the line went dead. Milner slammed the telephone down. Damn it. What the hell was that about? He looked again at his watch. He *was* late. He had more important things to do and would force the unsettling telephone call out of his mind.

Alexander was not one of the great lights of the British diplomatic service but he had an inbuilt cunning which made him an effective Head of American Department. It was at a meeting with him that Milner was due next. In his shabby office Alexander rose to greet him with a grimace. 'Just when we thought everything bad on the Anglo–American front had hit us, along comes today's hassle.' He flapped a telegram in Milner's direction, somewhat nervous of his distinguished colleague. Alexander was much the junior of the two men even though he would draft the instructions that the ambassador would later have to act upon when he got to Washington. As a defence mechanism against his nervousness, Alexander adopted a light-hearted approach to the difficult political decisions that his department currently were having to deal with.

'What this time?' he was asked.

'Pulling their contingent out of the peace-keeping force. Like next week.' Alexander draped himself in what he believed was a relaxed posture over his office chair.

'We expected it.' Milner pulled up another chair and sat opposite, upright and still.

'Yes, but they could have had the courtesy to warn us when. We sent a gentle protest; they more or less told us to get stuffed.'

'Too gentle . . . That's our problem. We're too nice. Our political leaders smile too much. Thatcher didn't go around grinning and people listened. When she and Tebbit smiled, grown men shuddered and crept away. We need more steel.' Milner knew the office style: kid gloves and not a steel fist in sight.

Alexander laughed. 'The President's a bit of a smile nice, talk nice, do nothing man too. Except when it comes to us . . .'

'What's biting him?' It was a question that Milner would ask many people.

'The Brits appear to be public enemy number one in the President's eyes. It's all in that file.' Alexander pointed to a brown-covered folder on his desk. 'It gets thicker and thicker by the day.'

'A personal thing? The President, I mean.'

'That's your reading; that's my reading. To the media, thank God, it's still the Americans lashing out at everyone to take attention away from their own domestic inadequacies.'

'What was Robinson's guess – before his heart attack, I mean – of what drives the President?' Milner was genuinely curious.

'Never have had it our own way. Special Relationship . . . always a bit of a myth even with Reagan and Bush . . . then with Clinton. But, by and large, there were far more ups than downs. Now this guy comes along.' Alexander was flailing around.

'He's part Irish.' Milner volunteered a prompt line while knowing the answer.

'Nobody's ever suggested that as a reason. There are packs of people far more extreme than him on Irish issues, in the Senate and in the House, and, in any case, everything's looking rosy on that front. Gone through his past with a tooth comb, but we've never come up with serious anti-British comments on that score.'

'So what moves him?' Milner kept pressing his colleague. He wasn't going to get the answer of answers from Alexander but it helped his own thoughts to develop.

'That's why they appointed you ambassador. To find out.' Alexander paused, wondering if he was being too cheeky. But what he had said was true enough. The department and Sir Martin's predecessors had all drawn a blank. 'Nevertheless . . .' he went on hurriedly. 'Before you settle down with these files, let me take you through some of the other big headaches . . .'

Extract from the Court Circular in *The Times*, Wednesday 23 April

Buckingham Palace, Tuesday 22 April.
Sir Martin Milner had the honour of being received by Her Majesty The Queen and kissed hands on his appointment as Her Majesty's Ambassador to Washington. Lady Milner also had the honour of being received by The Queen.

Somewhere in north London, where neither buying *The Times* nor paying attention to the Court Circular was common, the announcement was read out loud by a man to a woman. The man affected an upper-class accent; his audience of one shivered involuntarily.

'Kissed hands. Can you believe . . . ?'

'What else should he be kissing?' the woman asked nervously, not quite understanding.

'The coffin lid,' said the man with a chilling sneer.

*

Like most people he had a view of himself that was not shared by others. Martin Milner thought of himself as astute, hard-working and approachable. The last of these he was certainly not. He had never been someone a junior colleague would rush to in search of solace. If it was not his intention to be remote, it was how he was universally perceived to be.

Between the public and the private man there was a void. There was no in-between with Milner. He would have been shocked to be told, if anyone could bring himself to tell him, that he had few real friends: there were plenty of acquaintances of course, but not many too close. He was, to the outside world, a deeply reserved man, fired by his professionalism and his personal resolve. Those hooded blue eyes of his, according to one less than sympathetic colleague, were like darkened windows on a limousine, allowing him to see out but preventing outsiders looking in. For a diplomat, his background was impeccably correct. Good middle-class professional family, public school, and New College, Oxford. His file in the Personnel Department charted a high-flyer's rise through his career, helped by a mixture of talent and good fortune. It noted his admission to being a slave to the Protestant work ethic: nothing should be left undone at close of play; a tidy working style was the mark of a tidy mind; sleep was a just sleep only when the day's tasks were well completed. That was his self-assessment and it was too kindly; to colleagues who had to work with or for him, he had an over-pernickety attention to the minutest detail. Admittedly his preference for official technocracy over politics as a means of getting things done had served him well throughout his career. Additionally, on the up side, he did not harbour grievances. Once he had told a junior diplomat off for some misdeed or omission, he moved on to other things. He was a present and future man; he talked little about his past. He did not reminisce. Small-talk did not come easily to him.

Yet to mere acquaintances he was not perceived as being totally arid, because he forced himself, as his profession demanded, to socialize, to make merry in a disciplined sort of way. He was good at networking. He was a smooth diplomatic host. He made amusing, pungent speeches; he was clear and fair in his dealings with his staff; and in social conversation he worked hard not to be boring or to talk shop all the time. With his wife, Annabel, as in so many marriages, the end of sex had come early, and now, with various highly emotional lapses, they were more business partners than man and wife. In public she too was efficient and hospitable if not warm, in a world where high entertaining, placement and protocol, were still of key importance. Her only openly expressed and justifiable complaint was that in Washington it would be non-stop: constant formal meals, VIP guests, receptions, the day-to-day work that equated itself more to running a five-star hotel than operating a diplomatic establishment. In private she was very different: in turn moody and demanding, and a constant thorn in his flesh. But both hid their conflicts well and few guessed at the stresses and strains that tore at the hearts of this outwardly successful couple.

For this and for other reasons, from time to time even the self-sufficient Sir Martin Milner needed someone else to turn to. It was not that Dr Mark Ivor was his guru nor one who strived to find out much, though he might have guessed, about the strains of the marriage with Annabel. Neither man would have claimed that the one depended on the other except in the comradely way of men with similar intellects and goals. But Mark Ivor was the better listener, a man of reasonable integrity who offered wise advice. To outsiders, they were lifelong friends, though both had gone their very separate ways. Ivor, whom the British media had branded the Modern Machiavelli, the spin doctor supreme, had a largely justified reputation of influencing the minds of more men and women in apparent authority than any other in British political life. He was someone who shared many of Martin Milner's ideas and aspirations, but who acted behind the panoply of state rather than on the public platform as his diplomat friend had done. Ivor read and understood the passions of British domestic politicians, their whims, their transitory views, their fickleness. He knew how to work the London Establishment, that small matrix of people who exercised power through their social connections as much as across a boardroom table or desk. He knew because he was part of that élite.

Physically too they were very different. Milner, tall, fair, stooping, like an ill-placed Oxbridge don. Ivor was darker, shorter and more naturally gregarious. To alert outsiders, both men displayed their strengths through their shared sense of vision coupled with the body language of the powerful. What at a less elevated level the two men enjoyed most, however, was basic political gossip, the plots, the verbal assassinations, the scheming, the tactics, the making of decisions that the tribal leaders of the various political packs appeared to take. Martin Milner and Mark Ivor, so different but both so successful in their chosen fields, had dinner, *à deux*, that late-April evening at the Garrick Club.

Throughout the meal, at a small side table in the dark, portrait-hung Coffee Room, and later, at Mark Ivor's flat in Westminster, as they made considerable inroads into a bottle of vintage Macallan, the spin doctor adopted a style of catechism. He asked; Martin Milner responded. He prodded; the other explained. He interrogated; the newly-appointed Ambassador to Washington expounded. Ivor was Milner's catalyst; both men recognizing and relishing their separate roles as evening wore on into the early hours of the next day.

'The diplomatic profession is not what it was.' Ivor opened the game.

'Cliché.' Milner shrugged, sipping cautiously at his glass.

'You are now well-paid postmen. The work is done by fax, E-mail and phone, from head of state to head of state, from capital to capital.'

'You've been reading the *Spectator*, or the *Daily Express* more likely.'

'The scribbleati have it in for you, I agree. But they're almost right. Most diplomacy is now of the shuttle variety: ministers and top civil servants flying in and out. Or it's done multilaterally in Brussels or the UN.' Ivor was trying to provoke his friend. It was an old battle.

'Who lays the groundwork? When the Secretary of State arrives in some capital, you don't think he starts negotiating then, do you?' Milner was aroused.

'Sure: a lot of preparatory work has gone on behind the scenes.'

'*All the work* has gone on behind the scenes. The Secretary of State has been negotiating, via the ambassador, long before he arrives. He's put his *imprimatur* on the document, on the treaty or whatever, before he steps off the plane. The rest is window-dressing.' Milner stood, stretched his legs and helped himself, unasked, to a refill of Macallan.

'My point precisely. All you're doing is fixing.'

'That's what diplomacy is.'

'Is it going to be any different for you in Washington?' Ivor began adding more bite to his questioning.

'Depends on the personalities. On me, I suppose. Some ambassadors *are* mere postmen. Smile warmly, dress well, have attractive wives who choose good chefs and deliver good dinner parties. We impress by attending all the right receptions and shaking the right hands. We don't put a foot wrong. We don't say a word out of place. But that's not enough in real international life. Some, like you, Mark, make things move. As in all societies, all governments, all diplomatic services, it depends on the individual. Take the present government . . .' Milner gestured with a theatrical sweep of his arm to the otherwise empty room.

'You can take the present government as far as I am concerned.' Ivor laughed.

'Be serious. It's weak. It drifts into crises without knowing where it's heading. It's not got a proper roadmap . . . nor agenda . . . With the present bunch of inadequate ministers, impelled by the system rather than directing it, the people behind the scenes make all the running. People like you . . .' Milner gestured again, this time at his host.

'It certainly makes our tasks easier, we puppet masters, not having our devious plots and ploys interfered with by real people.' Ivor again laughed out loud at his own remark.

'What's true in internal British politics at the moment is also true in American politics.' Milner injected a different note. 'Look at Washington's constant battle between domestic policies and foreign issues. Again and again in the Foreign Office files I see reports from our embassy of how those round the President try to manipulate him in one direction or another . . .'

'The Secret State runs things. Everything is all really governed by civil servants. And by us spin doctors of course.' Ivor stared up at the other man.

'To a great extent, true. Occasionally political figures like Margaret Thatcher emerge who do actually have an agenda, who do actually take decisions, though even she was largely run by her kitchen cabinet . . . Charles Powell, Bernard Ingham, Tim Bell and so on. Just as you, Mark, are reputed to mould the Prime Minister, Michael Wilson's mind . . .' Milner said slowly.

'Is that what they say? Come, come, Martin . . . The PM has a mind of his own.' Ivor glanced down at his empty glass.

'Of course he does. It's just that he gives too much free access to it. Like a rudderless boat he swings with the waves. No stout hand on the helm and all that.' Milner began pacing the room.

'Sit down, Martin. You make me nervous. Back to your American President. Tell me all about him.'

Milner crashed back into his chair. He knew he was getting a little drunk. 'At first, when I started reading all the speeches and telegrams about him, he seemed like an empty suit if ever there was one. I felt I would have to examine the team behind him to know what was making America tick. Then . . .'

'You know what makes America tick? At the moment? If you do you're the only one,' Ivor interrupted.

'Which is what I'm getting at. I don't pretend to understand what's got into the White House, particularly its anti-British stand. That's what I've been asked to find out. Who's pushing the President?' Milner sounded almost plaintive.

'Are you sure he's being pushed? He may be a simple man on the surface, but simple men – remember Ronald Reagan, and Michael Wilson for that matter – often have simplistic agendas which they stick to like limpets.'

'You know that Wilson is completely programmed, Mark. Which is exactly why I want to look at the inner team in Washington. Some of the White House staff are top quality; when they're running things, they really are running things. Take Antonio Delgadi, the Secretary of State . . . There are plenty of placeholders of course, but the good people like him make things happen.' Milner was now more than a little flushed in his enthusiasm.

'And you? You're going to make things happen?' asked Ivor. He was at least two drinks behind his guest.

'My reputation often frightens me.'

'You don't like your advice being ignored,' Ivor prompted.

'Who does? You?' Milner pointed a finger at Ivor.

'A lot of people put up with it. Like me. My advice is often ignored. But they pay me for giving it. I agree on one thing: you and your image match each other. You're a go-getter, Martin. You'll have your effect on Anglo–American relations . . . for good or ill. Which is why . . .' Ivor paused and watched as Milner stood up and went back over to a sideboard and picked up the bottle of Macallan. 'Do you really need another?' he asked gently.

'It goes down well. One for the journey.' Milner paused, then replaced the bottle on the tray. 'No, perhaps that's enough for tonight,' he said remotely. Then . . . 'Which is why what?' he asked.

Another man might have prevaricated, would have held his peace. But Ivor had lots of reasons why he wanted his friend to know what he had done. 'Which is why I pushed your name on the PM. You are the best.'

Milner looked to see whether the other man was joking. 'You're serious,' he said eventually. 'You got me this job? You're the bloody king-maker? Thanks . . .'

'King . . . Ambassador . . . Once your name was in front of him, the choice was obvious.' Ivor shrugged.

'Well, well,' said Milner. 'I do owe you a favour.' It put his friend in a very different light though, and through the haze of alcohol he was not altogether happy. He began to say something but Ivor stopped him.

'Yes, I put your name forward. I trust your ability after all – and value your friendship. Known you a long time, though I still feel I don't . . . know you.'

As he spoke Ivor wondered if he now had gone too far. Emboldened by his own, lesser, quota of alcohol, he decided to press on. It was true what he had said. He did not know this other man, this Martin Milner. Of course he knew what he had achieved, his successes and the way he went about his business. He liked the cut and thrust of their discussions together. He revelled in the other man's acerbic wit: the way he would build up and destroy the reputations of political figures with a smile or a word. But there was another side to Milner: his obsessive industry, his secretiveness, his aloofness with others which, though it might have been initially born out of shyness, was off-putting to many. Had he been a psychologist, Ivor would probably have gone for some theory about anal retentiveness. Yet there was more upside to his friend – he called him his friend to others – than there was downside. Milner was successful in everything he had ever done in his career. If his family life was not everything that the career managers might have wished, that too was, to a large extent, a private matter. It had been the one shadow when he had proposed his friend's name for the Washington embassy, and it had not seemed to matter.

'Who knows anyone?' Milner slurred his words a little.

'You know what I mean,' said Ivor. 'I still don't know what

17

pushes you, what motivates you. It's no longer ambition: you've got all the rewards, reached all the pinnacles you could wish for. After Washington, probably the House of Lords, but as you know you're bound to get that in the end, you've stopped trying. No, it's not ambition. What makes you tick?'

'Same thing as most people: job satisfaction; comfortable life; not too much hassle; duty-free booze; the knowledge that one can sleep well without worrying. And talking of sleep, I must . . .' Milner was beginning to mumble with a mixture of alcohol and tiredness.

'Balls.'

'If you say so. But no different from anyone else.'

'There's something deeper, Martin. If I were a conspiracy theorist, I would guess that deep inside you there's a secret.'

'Murdered my grandmother?' Milner allowed himself a tired smile. 'Come to think of it, I was tempted. She was a bad-tempered old bitch . . .'

'No joking. I don't know, but I don't think it's anything sexual. You may have fantasies, I suppose, but you keep yourself under control. I'm talking about something else . . .' Mark Ivor hesitated. 'Something more brutal . . .'

The other man was silent for a long time. He stared down at his glass of whisky, hands cupped round the glass. Then eventually, without looking up, Milner said, 'Why did you say that?' He suddenly sounded alert and very sober.

'I don't know. The whisky, I suppose. Forget it.'

'Can I forget it?' Milner insisted.

'Is it true?'

Again there was a long pause. 'I don't think so. No,' said the diplomat.

'You remember Marlowe's *Dr Faustus*?' Ivor asked.

'A bit . . .'

'He's sold his soul to the devil . . . eventually the devil came for him . . . You remember? What was the Latin? "*O lente, lente currite noctis equi*" – "*Run slowly, slowly, horses of the night*". He's working late. At midnight, Lucifer comes for his soul.' Ivor smiled a hesitant smile. He suddenly felt ill-at-ease with his analogy.

'I remember something . . . Had to learn it at school,' Milner muttered.

'I can't quite recall how it finishes but there's another line where he pleads for "*a year, a month, a week, a natural day that Faustus may repent and save his soul*".'

'What are you getting at?' said Milner irritably, rising to his feet.

'Have you a soul that needs to be saved, Martin?' Mark Ivor paused, looked grim for a moment, then smiled. 'Aw, forget it,' he said again. 'Have one last one. Then I'll go order you a taxi.'

At lunchtime two days later Sir Martin Milner stood at the door of the Travellers Club in Pall Mall waiting for his son David to arrive. He glanced at his watch: David was late. He had taken the day off from his City job, borrowed his father's car since his own old banger was in for repair; he would be stuck in traffic somewhere. Milner greeted one of his Foreign Office colleagues, currently British Ambassador in Riyadh, on home leave, who came bounding up the steps towards him.

'Hello, Patrick. Good to see you. How's Saudi Arabia?' They shook hands warmly.

'Same as Saudi always is. Dry, dry, dry. And you? It must have been a whopping surprise getting Washington instead of going to quiet old Ottawa?'

'A bit.' Milner stared beyond him, down Pall Mall, looking for a familiar figure.

'Nasty time to be taking over. Beautiful residence though . . . Lutyens and all that.'

'It's bound to get better,' Milner suggested.

'Why?'

'Things always do.'

'You haven't been in Jeddah recently.' His colleague nodded and made his way on into the club.

Milner looked at his watch again, went inside and beckoned to the hall porter. 'Sure there are no messages for me?'

'No, Sir Martin, nothing.'

'Damn.' He went back towards the door. In the distance, the air was filled with the sounds of screaming sirens and hooting cars.

'It's getting worse, sir,' said the porter, coming out to join him. 'All these roadworks . . . Driving, were they?'

'My son. Borrowed my car. Hellish area to find a parking place. Should have been here ten minutes ago,' grumbled Milner.

'Can't judge how long any journey is going to take these days. Bloody marvel anyone gets anywhere any more,' said the hall porter.

An hour later, having tried without avail to reach David at the family flat or, because he might have changed his mind about going into work, his office, he had lunch at the centre table sitting beside the ambassador home from Saudi Arabia, then made his way back to the Foreign Office. He was not too concerned; David was usually so prompt and there was doubtless some very good reason for his non-appearance. There would be a message waiting back at the office.

At around three o'clock he was thinking of trying to get hold of Annabel to ask if she had heard anything, when the phone on his desk rang.

The voice at the end was hesitant. 'Sir Martin Milner?'

'Yes. What is it?'

'Foreign Office Security, sir. Somebody to see you, sir. Can I bring him up?'

'Who is it?'

He heard other voices in the background, then: 'Sir . . . I think he'd better explain himself, sir, when he comes, sir.'

An unusual sense of apprehension engulfed Milner. He was someone who was always totally in control of his actions, of his feelings, of life's events. He was not one to believe in premonitions but, on top of the strange phone call the other day, there was something not right ... He waited. After some moments there was a firm knock on the door.

'In ...' he ordered.

Two men came into the room. One was a police sergeant in uniform, the other had policeman stamped all over him, but was younger, leaner and fitter; at a guess, a plain-clothes detective. In the background hovered the Foreign Office Security man.

'Sir Martin?'

He stood up. 'What is it?' he asked, suddenly afraid.

'Some bad news for you, sir.'

'It's my son. It's David, isn't it?'

'Sir. I'm afraid so, sir.'

'How ... where is he? He's been in a car accident, is that it?'

'No, sir. A shooting, sir.'

'A shooting?' Milner gasped, uncomprehending.

'He's been shot, sir. As he was getting into his car.' The younger policeman was surprisingly nervous at being the bearer of the dramatic news.

'My car ... Is he ...? Is he ...?'

'No, sir. Still alive, bad injuries ... Punctured lung. Other wounds in the cheek, shoulder and groin.'

'Groin ... Oh, Christ! Where? When?' Milner's words spattered out.

'Outside your flat, sir. Before lunch.'

'I was waiting for him, you know,' he said inanely.

'I gather, sir.'

'Where is he? Come on, let's ...'

'In emergency, sir. St Thomas's. We'll take you over now, sir.'

'What the hell's happened? Who would shoot ...?' His voice broke as he spoke.

'As far as we can make out, sir, he was getting into the car ... your car ... He was shot several times by a man who was riding pillion on a motorcycle. They didn't stop. Got clear away.'

'Who would shoot my David ...?' Why didn't the stupid policeman understand his simple question?

'That's the point, sir. It has all the hallmarks of a very professional hit,' came the shattering response.

2

Someone had made an attempt to brighten up the waiting room. There were several vases of wilting flowers and cheerful prints hung on the walls. In one corner a pinboard carried faded notices about AIDS, the dangers of smoking, and alcohol abuse. There was another sign asking people to be alert to strange packages. A middle-aged couple sat in the distant corner, sobbing. A nurse was overheard explaining to a colleague that their child had been killed in a motorcycle accident.

In the opposite corner, Sir Martin and Lady Milner sat on shabby, plastic-covered chairs. Beside them hovered a birdlike woman from Heads of Mission Section, while outside somewhere, a man from Protocol Department was with the police holding some sort of preliminary enquiry and helping keep the press at bay. Milner attempted to put an arm lightly around his wife's shoulders but she pushed him away roughly. She was weeping openly, eyes bloated, make-up long gone.

'It's too late for that. Why him . . . ? Oh, why on earth . . . ?' she muttered. She had always lived for David.

'I've no idea,' he responded, realizing that, if she kept to character, she would soon collect herself enough to start apportioning blame: the police, the hospital staff, or, most likely, him.

It was not that he wanted to talk to her. He did not wish to be distracted from his own sense of shock by anticipating her likely reactions. He wanted to think . . . think it out. David was a straightforward type, not someone to get into trouble or pick up the wrong sort of friends. David, in his first job after college, was popular and would have no enemies. So . . . it was some sort of mistaken identity. That had been reinforced by the plain-clothes

23

policeman's remark as they drove to the hospital: David and his father looked so alike, with the same features, same build. 'He was coming out of your house and getting into your car, sir.' The policeman left him to draw his own conclusions.

'Mistaken identity . . . me and David? How could . . . ? Why should I . . . ?' Until that moment Milner had, unbelievably, put out of his mind the unpleasant telephone call that he had received a few days earlier. It had not occurred to him till now, so battered was he by his son's condition. But suddenly, though his reactions were still confused, there came the realization that it must have some significance. What had they said? 'This is a warning . . . we know about you . . . they are people who like to cut the strings . . .' But how could it have significance? Why would anyone want to harm him? He had just been appointed as British Ambassador to the United States. They were not at war. He had no enemies. He struggled to remember. In the old days the IRA perhaps, but they had long ceased doing that sort of thing, nor could he surely be a target for any of the fundamentalist extremists, from the Middle East and elsewhere, who occasionally caused mayhem in the streets of London. Drugs . . . organized crime . . . Such people were not interested in diplomatic functionaries like him. It had to be someone else's identity that had been mistaken.

A young doctor strode purposefully into the waiting room, stethoscope dangling from the pocket of his white coat. Milner was aware that the policeman and the man from Protocol were standing watching from the doorway. He stood up anxiously as the doctor approached them.

'Well?' he asked.

'He's going to live, Sir Martin . . . Lady Milner . . . A lot of damage but most of it superficial.'

'How is he?' Annabel asked. 'Can I see him? Can I see him? Is he conscious?'

'He's heavily sedated. It won't be advisable for you to see him for some time. The good news is that he . . . his lung . . . should be OK. The groin wound . . . well . . . we'll have to wait . . .'

'Have to wait . . . ? Christ,' Milner burst out.

'It's too early to say . . .' the doctor said softly. 'Now I suggest you both go home and try and get some rest. We'll let you know as soon as he's able to receive anyone. It may be some days.'

In the background the two policemen stood watching the scene. Had Milner been able to overhear their conversation, he would have heard the plain-clothes man say, 'I can't tell him now.'

'He's got to know some time, sir,' said the sergeant, bluntly.

'Not now. He won't run away. He's going to be under heavy protection from now on. How many witnesses?'

'Several. We have vague descriptions but both men were dressed in leathers and helmets and no one saw the registration number.'

'He'll hear some other way and there'll be hell to pay,' said the plain-clothes policeman.

'Yessir,' said the sergeant, which was why the plain-clothes man, against his better judgement, came up to Milner and clumsily blurted out: 'We have two witnesses, sir. A couple walking their dog. A clear lead, if you like. They heard one of the bikers calling out, "Sir Martin, Sir Martin . . ." Your son started to turn round, of course. That's when they shot him.'

It was in many ways fortunate that Annabel, overhearing this new piece of information, immediately collapsed. The alternative would have been some terrible outburst from her. It also forced Milner into action which temporarily removed this new horror from his mind. He caught her as she fell and, together with the doctor, they laid her out on one of the waiting-room couches. The doctor pressed his bleeper and a nurse came running.

'My bag. Bring it and a stretcher. And some water.' As the nurse disappeared, Annabel started stirring. Her eyes slowly opened and she gazed emptily around her. Milner noticed that something was wrong with her pupils. They appeared vacant and unseeing. He bent over and whispered.

'You'll be all right. David will be all right. I promise you. I promise you.'

'Away . . . Go away . . .' Annabel murmured.

'What, my dear?'

'Go away . . . Go away . . .' She made a weak gesture of dismissal.

'You both need some rest. I can arrange for a bed here, if you like, for your wife,' said the young doctor efficiently as the man from Protocol and the girl from Heads of Mission bustled around arranging cars.

'No, no. I'll see her home. She'll be fine once I get her home.' But somehow Milner knew that something had changed fundamentally and that it would not be like that at all.

That evening, at the big American oil company dinner at Claridge's, where security was especially tight, the talk was all of the shooting. Martin Milner should have been there, joining the two hundred or so men and one woman – Lady Thatcher – at one of the most power-filled occasions of the British political year. Apart from the oil company men, every face was a famous one. The guest speaker was a former President of the United States, two other former Presidents were seated along with three British ex-Prime Ministers, half the Cabinet, ten of the greatest captains of industry, permanent secretaries, members of the Royal Household, editors, proprietors, publishers – the cream of the great and the good of British public life.

Before dinner, as the champagne flowed, Dr Mark Ivor worked his way around the crowded anteroom, making his presence felt here, establishing a raincheck for a future meeting there, avoiding the bores and those whom he could meet on other less grand occasions. He was in his element, and because he was known to have the ear of Michael Wilson, those who wished to lobby the Prime Minister lobbied Ivor as much as he did others. The influence game was being played to the full by the man the media called the Modern Machiavelli.

It was by no accident that Her Majesty's Principal Secretary of State for Foreign and Commonwealth Affairs, Trafford Leigh, manoeuvred Mark Ivor into a relatively quiet corner of the room. Leigh was an old-style, old-Etonian figure who, according to conventional media wisdom, added a touch of class and dignity, qualities that were in short supply in Michael Wilson's Cabinet.

'Tragic business,' he began. There was no need to explain what. 'I gather . . .' he had to raise his voice above the noise, 'that you had dinner with Milner only the other night . . . at the Garrick.'

'You're well informed,' responded Ivor cautiously. He wondered what was coming.

'Old friends, I gather.' Trafford Leigh used 'gather' a great deal in his vocabulary.

'We go back a long way.' So far this was not game-playing of a high order. Trafford Leigh would be perfectly well aware that he, Ivor, had put forward Milner's name for the Washington post to the PM in the first place.

'How was he?'

'Bit academic that question – after today.' Ivor was blunt.

'You know exactly what I mean.' Leigh's lips pursed into something approaching a smile.

'In good form. Looking forward to Washington. He was . . .' Ivor hesitated.

'Will he still go?'

'What d'you want me to say?' In other circumstances Leigh would have known all this from his officials at the Foreign Office.

'Have you talked to him . . . since his son . . . David, isn't it?'

'This evening. He's in deep shock. Annabel's worse,' Ivor added.

'Will he pull out?'

'Washington? I don't know . . . Hasn't he indicated?'

Leigh shook his head. 'Your guess?'

'If you push him. No.'

'No need to disinter Vincent?' asked Leigh.

'I don't think so . . .'

'You know the PM's mind . . .' The Secretary of State glanced cautiously round the room, then deliberately turned his back on a Cabinet colleague who was advancing on him. He did not want this particular conversation interrupted.

Ivor grimaced. Trafford Leigh was not believed to have much respect for Michael Wilson's mind. 'He listens to me. Let's not beat about the bush. What d'you want me to feed in, Trafford?'

'We, the Foreign Office that is, want Sir Martin to continue to go to Washington. It would upset a lot of things . . . plans. Our relations with the White House are at a rocky stage . . .'

'I read the papers,' said Ivor dismissively.

'You're in a unique position. You proposed him in the first place. It would be helpful . . . You can push both sides – Michael and Martin Milner. It's in his own best interests, you know.'

At that moment a tail-coated toastmaster banged his gavel and announced dinner. Above the increased bustle and noise, Mark Ivor nodded his head, 'I'll do my best,' and shouted: 'My guess: you can stand Vincent down.'

Sir Martin Milner hated being at the cottage on his own. It was cold, it was unfriendly, and the garden needed too much attention. He was making a desultory attempt to sort out some papers and books that he had intended taking with him to the States. But now? It didn't matter, and, anyway, how could he concentrate with his son critically ill in hospital and his wife giving every semblance of having had a stroke or breakdown? Having refused to see a doctor, she was now at their flat in London with her sister, Sheila, looking after her. The only understandable statement she was reported to have made and kept making was that she did not want to see him and was absolutely adamant that she herself was not going to Washington.

He had gone through more emotions than he realized he had over the past few days. He was not someone who believed in feelings, least of all those that were publicly demonstrated. Emotions were signs of weakness, enemies of rational thinking and reasoned action. They interfered with the smooth running of lives and events. They should be controlled. Yet here he was, like lesser men, going from deep grief and shock through to blinding anger at the unknown assailants who had maimed his son. Yes, David was going to live. But in what condition? He, so healthy, so fond of sports, so fond of girls, so fond of everything that gave life its meaning. He was just beginning to settle to a well-paid City job.

At best his lower body was badly shattered. Milner was also still seething with fury at the stupidity of the policeman who had blurted out, in front of Annabel, that they had called out *his* name before firing. The bullets were meant for him. So Annabel, in her strange mad way, was now blaming him totally for David's injuries. She was right. He was the reason. But . . . why? Why?

He eventually quelled the most extreme of these feelings, forcing himself to think rationally, to try and work out what it was that could have made him a target, and his son a victim. Only yesterday he had attended an emergency meeting at the Foreign Office with representatives from MI6, MI5 and Special Branch. As a mark of the importance of the meeting, it was chaired by the Secretary of State, Trafford Leigh, himself, and, along with officers from the Metropolitan Police and the Anti-Terrorist Squad, the Prime Minister's personal security adviser was also present. Milner's only contribution was to repeat the story about the anonymous telephone call, but that added little to the store of knowledge. They seemed more interested in forensic reports about the type of bullet used. What did he learn from the meeting? That they knew nothing. They had no idea at all what could be behind it. All they knew was that the gunmen had been looking for him. The telephone call added sparse additional evidence in terms of its intelligence value.

That everyone was taking it very seriously was demonstrated by the fact that, like it or not, Milner was now accompanied everywhere by bodyguards – personal protection officers – who never let him out of their sight. Even now, there were two men sitting in the next room, guns in their shoulder-holsters, reading his magazines and drinking his tea. It was all so absurd, so hateful; so unbelievable, yet so real. Again he had to fight to quell a deep loathing of everything and all things as irrational fury welled up inside him. And to top it all, Annabel refused to see him. Sheila, her sister, with whom he had always had a reasonable if not close relationship, had been patient and understanding but bewildered. She did not know what to do, and felt unable to force Annabel to seek medical assistance. Sheila had the same message for Milner each time he rang: Annabel was not going to go to Washington.

He could understand that, but not her outright refusal to see him.

As for himself, how could he go? How could he abandon a badly wounded son and a wife suffering from some form of breakdown? Which was why, that very morning, before driving down to the cottage, he had written formally to notify Trafford Leigh that he would not now be taking up his post. Everyone would understand. No one would criticize.

He heard a car pull up on the gravel outside but did not stir himself to find out who it was. His minders were there for that. He heard voices, then a firm knock on the door. In came a lean, fair-haired man, in his mid- to late thirties.

'Yes . . . ?' began Milner, getting to his feet.

'MacKenzie, sir. Inspector Andrew MacKenzie, Special Branch. Assigned to Diplomatic Protection Group. Assigned to you, sir.'

'What d'you mean?' Milner already guessed.

'Your personal protection officer, sir. From now on, sir. Here and in the States . . .'

'I'm not going to the States, er . . . Mr MacKenzie. I could not . . .'

'Right, sir.' The young man looked disappointed. 'That's why I volunteered, sir. But . . . if that's your decision, they didn't tell me.'

'That's because I hadn't told them . . . until today, Mr MacKenzie,' Milner said slowly.

At about four o'clock that afternoon he was dozing uneasily in his chair in front of an open fire he had somehow summoned the energy to light, when the call came from Number Ten. The Prime Minister, Michael Wilson, wanted to see him. They offered to send a car for him. He reminded them about his new bodyguard and the official car he had been provided with.

MacKenzie drove fast and in virtual silence, and they reached Downing Street at precisely six o'clock. The bodyguard had radioed ahead and the heavy gates swung open almost immediately to let them up the short drive to the famous door. Sir Martin

Milner was already set into the routine the policeman had insisted on from the start. MacKenzie got out first, looked around, though it was the most heavily guarded precinct in London, and only then was he himself allowed to get out. The uniformed policeman on duty tapped lightly at the knocker and the door opened silently inwards. Inside Milner could see the Private Secretary and the Press Secretary to the Prime Minister, hovering in the hallway waiting for him. Behind him, he was aware of the flashes of the cameras and the shouts from behind the press barrier, as he was recognized by the duty media pool on the other side of Downing Street. 'Ambassador! Ambassador!' 'Can we have a word, please?' 'How is your son, sir?' 'Can we have a statement?' 'May we know, Sir Martin . . . ?' The Downing Street press pack were, as always, waiting there, poised to shoot the wounded. It was a first-rate human tragedy and political interest story for the weekend's editions. It was Milner's first exposure to unwanted fame.

He did not have to wait but was shown straight upstairs to the Prime Minister's study. The Private Secretary tailed behind. 'I'm so sorry,' the man began.

'Please . . . Leave it, would you? I've had more condolences than I can take. What does he want me for?' Milner asked.

'I think . . .' The Private Secretary was panting slightly as he climbed the stairs behind him. 'He'd better explain that himself. Trafford Leigh is with him.'

At the top of the stairs a door opened and there stood Michael Wilson. The two men had met before, but only on the most formal of occasions.

'Do come in, Sir Martin. I'm so dreadfully sorry.'

'Thank you, Prime Minister.' They shook hands briefly.

'Come in,' repeated the Prime Minister over-solicitously, pulling up a chair. 'Do have a seat. I can't say how sorry . . .'

'Thank you, Prime Minister. I'd rather leave that. I've written . . .'

'That's why we've asked you here, Sir Martin. Trafford and I know how you must feel. Particularly with the sad news about your wife as well. How is she, by the way?'

'I don't know. I haven't seen her. She doesn't want to see me. She blames me.'

'And your son?'

'The worst is over, I'm told. His lungs will be OK. But what else lies beneath the bandages, I dread to know. He's still not conscious.'

Martin Milner sat erect in the chair he had been offered. He took in little of the famous surroundings; the pictures of past Prime Ministers hanging on the walls were an irrelevance. He felt immune, inoculated by his grief into showing no emotion. The two politicians were impressed by his superficial *sang-froid*; what they could only guess at was the deep numbness of despair that had settled upon him. He had given no thought to a future beyond Washington. Now that was not to be, he still was not prepared to think about where his life would take him from here on. He waited to be addressed. He guessed why they had asked him to come in, these two great men.

'We know how you must feel, Sir Martin,' repeated the Prime Minister, 'but I've asked you to come to see us to get you to reconsider. We would . . . Her Majesty's Government would very much like you, would urge you, to take up your appointment. Whatever lies behind the dreadful events of the last few days, and we still have no inkling about that, they must have been directed at trying to stop you going to Washington.' He half-smiled as he spoke, choosing his words with care.

'Relations with the United States are at a critical juncture,' added Trafford Leigh unnecessarily.

'Having to substitute somebody else for you at this late stage would compound the difficulties,' Michael Wilson continued. 'Your appointment has been widely welcomed in the British and American press. Now everybody expects you to pull out. My simple request is – don't.'

Beneath the controlled levels of his despair, Milner was impressed by such a high-level request. It echoed the telephone call he had had earlier from his friend Mark Ivor, who had argued that no one, least of all his family, would gain from his refusal to go ahead with the posting. He was flattered but far from convinced. He wanted to escape, get away from everything. He needed time on his own, to recapture his personal resolve.

'I . . . thank you, Prime Minister.' Milner paused, 'What about Mr Vincent? I gather you had him in mind before you got round to me.'

'Vincent's out. Not a good idea,' said the Prime Minister with a dismissive shrug of his shoulders.

'There are lots of other people,' volunteered Sir Martin. 'Radley in Paris, for instance. He'd make a first-class ambassador to Washington.'

'We're not going to be rocked off course by an assassination attempt, Sir Martin. That's no way for the British Government to behave. I repeat: I ask you to think again.'

'You must understand my position, Prime Minister. My wife appears to have had some sort of breakdown. My son is critically ill in hospital, having been shot by someone who, without a shadow of a doubt, intended to shoot me. How can anyone ask me to go to Washington at this stage?'

'What would you do instead, Martin?' interrupted Trafford Leigh briskly, deliberately calling him by his first name. 'Sit and mope?'

'Bit harsh, Trafford,' said the Prime Minister in conciliatory mode. 'Trafford didn't mean it like that, Sir Martin.'

'I recognize what the Secretary of State meant. He's right. That's probably what I would do. What else d'you expect?'

'Once again, Sir Martin. I am asking you to withdraw your letter. You can take as much time as you want here before you go. A couple of months if you like. Everyone will understand. You are the very best man for the job.'

'I'm grateful to you for saying so, Prime Minister. I will let you know by tomorrow, if I may. But there's one thing I have to know, and soon.' Milner bowed his head wearily.

'Which is?'

'Who my enemies are.'

'We're doing our absolute best, Sir Martin . . .' responded the

Prime Minister with a not entirely convincing show of firmness.
'. . . but I can promise nothing.'

Extract from an editorial in the *Daily Telegraph* dated Monday 28 April

In the aftermath of the shocking circumstances in which the son of Sir Martin Milner, the newly-appointed British Ambassador to Washington, was shot in a clear case of mistaken identity with his father, and the subsequent breakdown to which Lady Milner has now succumbed, it is deeply reassuring to hear the news that Sir Martin himself is determined to take up this most crucial post. There is need of a man of his character, who exhibits all the best traditions of the British Diplomatic Service, to fulfil this role at a time when everything in Anglo–US relations that could go wrong has gone wrong. Perhaps one glimpse of hope is the warm personal message of sympathy from the American President to Sir Martin which was coupled with a wish that Washington would be able to welcome the new ambassador and his family at some early date.

What must be a continuing cause of the deepest unease, however, is the total inability of the Intelligence Establishment to find any reason whatsoever for the attack. No group has yet claimed responsibility. In years gone by it would have been easy to blame the IRA. Now we tend to accuse the various Middle Eastern terrorist groups that are currently plaguing us. But Sir Martin, who has never served there, is far from being an obvious target for them. So who is to blame? Unconfirmed reports suggest that Sir Martin received anonymous warnings that something might happen to him. We ask again, why are Michael Wilson's government, and the Intelligence Services, not

*working harder to get to the bottom of this most
infamous act? Huge amounts of public monies have
been spent on MI5 and MI6 over the last few years,
not least on their glamorous headquarters that face
each other across the Thames in central London.
Surely it is not too much to ask that these desk-bound
warriors produce rapid results . . .*

*In the meantime, we wish Sir Martin a successful
tour of duty in Washington in the belief that he is
the man to return Anglo–American ties, if not back
to the level of the Special Relationship of bygone
ages, at least to a position of near normality.*

*Foreign and Commonwealth Office Telegram
to Washington*
Number 9916 of Wednesday 30 April.
Secret
Immediate for Chargé d'Affaires.

1. Ambassador Designate now leaving by British Airways flight number BA217, arriving Washington at
1625 hours on 2 May. Sir Martin will be accompanied by personal security guard, Inspector Andrew
MacKenzie. MacKenzie is to be accommodated at
the Washington residence in rooms as close as possible to the ambassador's suite. His duties will be to
liaise with embassy security personnel, CIA, FBI and
other diplomatic protection agencies. MacKenzie
must be accorded all possible assistance.
2. Secret and personal telegram on other aspects
of security is contained in my immediate following
telegram, Personal for Chargé d'Affaires' Eyes
Only.

A drip-feed hung suspended over the heavily bandaged figure lying on the bed. On a hard chair beside it sat Sir Martin Milner, head buried in his hands. He had been there for what seemed like hours when suddenly he was aware that the patient was showing signs of life. Milner sat forward in his chair and tried to smile.

'Hello, David. It's me.'

'Hi, Dad,' the faint voice whispered back. 'A bit groggy . . .'

'You'll soon be right as rain.'

'You know that's not true, Dad. I heard the nurses talking; they thought I was asleep.' David's voice scarcely rose above a whisper.

'I'm sorry . . .'

'Why are you sorry, Dad?'

'Because I must be to blame in some way . . .' Milner bent close over his son's recumbent body.

'Not you. Your position. Different thing.'

'David . . . I'm leaving for Washington tomorrow. I have to go. I'll be back soon.'

'Sure you have to go. Where's Mum?'

'She'll be here to see you soon.'

'Is she OK?'

'Fine, just fine. A bit upset, that's all.'

'That's good, Dad. Have a great . . .' David's words petered out, his eyes closed and he was asleep again.

Sir Martin Milner felt a deep sense of betrayal as he stood up and tiptoed silently from the ward. Once again, alien emotions welled up to confront the carefully planned pattern of his life.

Shortly before he left for the United States he telephoned an old and trusted contact, the Metropolitan Police Commissioner, who was someone he had known from years before when they had both been junior members of the same syndicate at a Civil Service College Top Management Course.

'You've allotted me a personal protection officer, Charlie. Thought I'd check him out with you, if you don't mind. We'll be thrown together a great deal and I wanted to know a bit . . .'

'The very best. An outstanding officer, Andrew MacKenzie.'

'Certainly got a first-class write-up from the head of SB.'

'Right. As he was rather too senior for the job, it came up to me for my personal authorization.'

'So why, Charlie, do I deserve . . . ?'

'The best? Until we know who's after you. In any case, MacKenzie was dead keen to go. You'll discover he knows a lot about America and the Americans.'

'No personal hang-ups?'

'None we know of. Pushed himself forward when we started looking . . . Just broken up with a long-term girlfriend, so he's doubly keen to leave London.'

'What's this American thing?'

'A first in American history.'

'So why . . . ?' Milner began, then checked himself.

'So why is he just a copper, was that what you were going to say? We do have some very bright . . .'

'I didn't mean . . .'

'Of course you didn't.' The Police Commissioner laughed agreeably. 'Let me tell you two things about Inspector MacKenzie,' he went on. 'Just to keep you thinking, Martin. First: he got to the finals of "Mastermind" two years ago. If you were a tele-addict you'd remember. Specialized subject: American politics since 1990. Second, and something to sharpen up your attitude: he killed a man while on active duty. So you see, Martin, even though he's a copper, he's no slouch . . .'

Telegram from Washington
to Foreign and Commonwealth Office

Number 7862 of Friday 2 May.

Restricted, Immediate.

Repeated for Information, Priority, New York, Bonn, Paris, etc.

I have arrived and assumed charge.

Milner.

3

Long ago he had mastered his body clock and so it was not jet-lag that woke him at six o'clock in the morning. He came to and took a moment or so to adjust to where he was. Then he recognized the heavy Laura Ashley drapes, the gilded splendour that was the ambassador's bedroom in the Lutyens mansion on Massachusetts Avenue, Washington DC. He had arrived *en poste*, the very pinnacle of his diplomatic career.

The British Ambassador's residence has more in keeping with a small palace than with a mere house. It was, and is, perhaps the most glamorous official residence of any British Ambassador anywhere in the world and, in turn, is one of the grandest and most ornate buildings in all Washington. Many of the rooms leave those of the White House itself looking remarkably dreary, for successive British governments of all political persuasions have allowed the building to be decorated and maintained in the best and highest style. Pictures of kings, queens and princes in heavy gold frames adorn the walls of great hallways, all lit by heavy chandeliers. The public rooms are furnished with rich carpets and ornate brocade. In the private suites, the best of modern British designers have left their mark. While many foreign embassies in Washington have to work hard to get the great and the good of American society to come to them, this has never been the case with the British Embassy. Invitations from there are eagerly sought and actively accepted. Guests are ushered in under cover of a portico, and led up a sweeping red-carpeted stair to the reception rooms on the floor above. The drawing room with its white grand piano, the beautifully panelled and pillared room which is the ambassador's book-lined study, the opulent dining room, the intimacy of some of the guest suites that have, over the years, provided accommodation for princes and prime ministers without number, each furnished with the best of British design. Living in the British Embassy in Washington, an ambassador can go mad with power unless he is careful to guard his own privacy in the quietness of the rooms that comprise his own personal suite. For embassy life is one of constant luncheons, dinners and receptions for visiting dignitaries. A huge agenda of social and political activity takes place there, only constrained by the dictates of the British Treasury. Yet while all the formality has to be blended with a certain degree of informality to cope with American practice, the grandeur, the feeling of the upstairs–downstairs living of a past age existing in the last years of the twentieth century, makes it a house like few others. Up to fifteen thousand people may be entertained there by the ambassador in the course of a single year. Now he, Martin Milner, was master of it all.

It should have been the summit of his career. He should have been overwhelmed by the splendour of his position at the top of his chosen profession. But, like a leaden weight, the memory of his son lay heavily upon him. He knew that to stay in bed, even for a few moments longer, would deepen his depression, so he leapt up, showered and, not even bothering to shave, slipped on a pair of light trousers and a shirt and ran quickly down the long circular staircase and outside into the early-morning light.

Washington on that late-spring morning was at its very best. The air sparkled with a freshness that would soon become saturated by the damp, stultifying heat of high summer in the capital. He resolved to go for a long mind-clearing walk. As he let himself out of the main door under the covered archway, a security guard's head appeared at the balcony above.

'You're all right, sir?' asked the man sleepily.

'Fine, thank you. Just going for a quick stroll. Get my bearings again.' Milner was brisk.

'You're going out of the embassy compound, sir? If so, I'd better get your protection . . . Inspector MacKenzie . . .'

'Don't. Jet-lag . . . He needs his sleep. I'll be good.'

'But, sir . . .'

Milner closed the door behind him. He was not going to start his mission by being cosseted by security men. Climbing the steps beside the residence he skirted around the back of the main embassy building – how he hated the fifties, office-block architecture of it – then turned left on the road that ran up past the New Zealand Embassy. Beyond that he walked rapidly along Observatory Lane, which followed the high boundary fence of the US Naval Observatory, the official residence of the Vice-President of the United States of America.

He had not been in Washington for many years but he remembered a path that ran through the woods, across Rock Creek, between the beautiful Dumbarton Oaks and Montrose Parks which led eventually to his once familiar stamping ground of Georgetown. It would, he guessed, take him fifteen to twenty minutes at most to get there. He would walk around for a while, get his bearings, clear his head and come back in time for a shave, breakfast and the early-morning briefing he had arranged for eight o'clock. With comfortable brown walking shoes on his feet he walked swiftly, yet, even at that early hour, he was regularly passed by joggers, a phenomenon as much part of the Washington landscape as the White House itself.

He wished he could be glad to be back. He *was* glad to be back, but the tragedies that he had left behind geographically, had travelled with him in every other way. He knew how easy it would be for a heavy cloud of doom, the 'black dog' that Churchill had always talked about, to settle on his shoulders. One thing he had learned at an early age was how to shut most unpleasant thoughts up in his mind – not for ever, but stored there, waiting until he was in the right frame of mind to face up to them and solve them. Most problems in his past had been soluble. He had seen life not as a series of conflicts and setbacks, but of achievements, of crests to reach and goals to achieve. He had been good at that, which was why, he supposed, he was now in Washington. How often had he seen great men and women brought low by domestic tragedy or misfortune such as he now faced. He had once seen a famous general cry over the death of a child. He had witnessed a key politician rigid with fear over a scandalous headline about him in a morning's tabloid. He had been spared all that until now. He had thought himself prepared and immune. In one way he was: he knew that no amount of emotional turmoil would advance by one jot his son's return to health. Then there was Annabel. In the old days he would have missed her, relying upon her to help him face the challenges of each new post to which they were sent. She had been calm and confident. Then had come her growing sense of her own lack of achievement, that she was only an appendage to him and his career, and all that, inevitably, had led to bitterness and worse.

And now? Had the old Annabel gone for ever? Hysterical, remorseful and vindictive, right up to the final moment of his departure, she had sought to blame him for what had happened to David. But she had gone beyond even that: he had sensed that she was unbalanced. He had gone to see her at her sister, Sheila's, on that last day before flying out of Heathrow. He had hoped for some slight sign that together they might try and resurrect something out of their shared tragedy. He was nervous and unsure of himself. It was absurd. He was the attentive husband visiting a wife who had had a mental breakdown. He was in charge: of course he was.

She had kept him waiting, like a child, for a full half hour before she emerged. He knew her too well, her, his own wife. He did not believe Sheila's fragile attempt to cover up the dire fact that she was actually refusing to see him. He simply did not believe that Annabel had a splitting headache and was asleep. Annabel was his wife. He demanded to see her.

It had been worse than he ever believed it could be. She emerged, unkempt and distraught, Sheila flapping helplessly in the background. 'Don't you understand, Martin? Don't you ever understand?' she shrieked. 'I want you to go away to fucking Washington and leave me in peace. Leave *us* in peace after the damage you have done to David and to me.'

'What I have done . . .' He was aghast at her appearance.

'You and your accursed, selfish, career. That's all you ever think about. And now this . . . that you have brought upon us.'

'I have no idea . . .' Milner tried to reason with her.

'You *must* have an idea. You nearly killed my son.'

'How can you talk such rubbish, Annabel? David is my son too.' He turned to Sheila as he spoke, looking in vain for some support and understanding. Then he lowered his voice. 'Look, my dear. You need professional help. I'll arrange to delay my . . .'

It was then that she had rushed forward and attacked him, scratching at his body and face like a woman demented, drawing blood from a wound made by her nails which ran down the whole length of his left cheek.

At the sight of the blood, her sister physically forced her back to her room. After that he waited in the kitchen, well out of the way, until a doctor arrived and gave Annabel some calming injection. Then he left and returned to the peace of London. What else, he asked himself, could he have done in the circumstances?

As he passed Dumbarton Oaks and the old cemetery at Oak Hill where, by some ironic trick of his mind, he recalled that the man who had composed the song 'Home Sweet Home' lay buried, he saw before him the neat, familiar houses of Georgetown. He was not usually one for memories, but they came flooding back unasked; happy memories, of a time spent as a First Secretary dealing with NATO, East–West relations, and the 'Evil Empire' that had been the Soviet Union. Things had been different then. He had the ambition; he had an alert body and an active mind; he had a happy family and stimulating social life. Had he been less formal, less rigorous, less intimidating then? People had seemed genuinely to like him; he liked most of them. He was a success. How he would have enjoyed, then, knowing what he had become now. Or would he? What *had* he become now? What was the old exclamatory phrase? 'Oh to be what I was when I wanted to be what I am now!' Had so much been lost and destroyed by those bullet wounds? Or had it all gone long before?

He forced such thoughts from his mind as he turned down 29th Street, then along Q Street towards Wisconsin Avenue. Before he reached it he turned left and left again and saw ahead of him the red-brick house with the green shutters where they had once lived. For a peculiar moment, as he walked by, he saw an image of a young child – his son, David, perhaps – standing at the top step, bicycle beside him waiting for his father to carry it down the flight of steps to the street. But there was no child there. He did however see that, in reality, the curtains were drawn back on the ground floor and there, clearly visible, was the silhouette of a woman. She was standing with her back to the window, in front of an easel, painting, benefiting from the clear early light. He resisted the urge to climb the steps, knock on the door and explain himself. But it was still barely quarter to seven in the morning. He was crazy. He hurried on.

He walked back up the hill towards the cemetery, through the park and back over to Massachusetts Avenue. At the junction with Observatory Lane he paused and looked down past the bland façade of the Chancery building towards the statue of Churchill that waved his perpetual victory sign to the early-morning traffic. Turning past security control at the embassy gate, he was greeted by his minder, MacKenzie. The inspector was furious.

'Where the hell have you . . . ? Sorry, sir. Where *have* you been, sir?'

'For a walk, of course.' Milner was deliberately offhand.

'But, sir.'

'Don't "But, sir" me, Mr MacKenzie. I went for a stroll. That's all. I am the British Ambassador. I wanted to get my bearings once again. I've a heavy day coming up.' Milner turned away to go towards the Residence.

MacKenzie faced up to him squarely. He had been about to explode with anger but was now under control.

'Sir, if you'll bear with me, sir, I have to say this . . . It's not you that would have been sacked if anything had gone wrong. Either we play by the rules, sir, or you can work with someone else.'

Milner stared back at him, a reciprocal flush of anger welling inside him at the policeman's impertinence. Then he checked himself. Of course the man was right. 'OK. Sorry,' he said briskly. 'It won't happen again, Mr MacKenzie. Goodbye liberty.'

'It doesn't help to be melodramatic, sir. Just common sense.'

'I said I was sorry, Mr MacKenzie. I don't need the lecture.' Then Milner turned on his heel and walked swiftly towards the residence, MacKenzie tailing lamely behind him. As he climbed upstairs to his suite for another shower and a shave, again he didn't feel particularly proud of himself. It was getting to be a habit. And most of the day was still ahead.

Action replaced emotion. The British Ambassador in Washington has the luxury of two offices: one a workaday room in the Chancery building with its outer office full of private secretaries and personal assistants; then he has the grand wood-panelled study in the residence itself. To make it immediately different from the routine Chancery meetings he would hold most weekday mornings from then on, he opted for the study. He wanted to be seen to be setting a new agenda.

A handful of his most senior staff were gathered to meet him when he arrived promptly at eight. He knew several of them from before. The most senior was his deputy, David Velcor, whose smile of greeting camouflaged the inner disappointments of a man passed over for top office. He and Velcor were of an age; they had served together in the Foreign Office and their paths had crossed in Bucharest and other foreign postings.

'Good to see you again, David,' he said, shaking him warmly by the hand. Their eyes met for a moment. The smiles were there for all to see but the eyes carried little warmth on either side. Milner moved on quickly to greet the other people in the room. There was the bright and breezy Head of Chancery, responsible for all the day-to-day workings of the embassy, from the political reporting through to overseeing the administration staff. He was the man who held the whole embassy together, a good choice, warm, friendly, and with a wife he had already met, who matched his style and had a certain motherliness thrown in – all key attributes when it came to looking after the many problems of the families of the diplomats who staffed the British Embassy in Washington. Without the turmoil and tension that Annabel normally brought with her, that would, Milner guessed, be one side of embassy life that was in safe hands.

'Ladies and gentlemen, do sit down. Glad to meet you all. We'll get some coffee in here in a moment,' he said, looking around the room as they settled on chairs and couches around his desk. To his left was Paul Fawcett, his hyper-intelligent private secretary, a keen, if rather overweight, young diplomat who had entered on the fast stream, a man on his way up, for whom a great career was out there waiting to be grabbed. Next to him was an army general, a traditional military attaché figure, with, beside him, the Economic and Trade Ministers, flanked on the other side by Terry somebody ... the Press Counsellor. Three or four others were ranged opposite him, including the only woman, Janice Yates, the Political First Secretary, who, though rather junior to be at the meeting, was a crucial figure who spent most of her time on the Hill monitoring and reporting on American internal politics. On his immediate right sat his formidable personal secretary, Victoria Dobbs, notepad and pencil at the ready, prepared to take a record as required. It was only when he had worked his way around the room greeting everyone that he realized he in turn had failed to identify one person to his new colleagues. His bodyguard, MacKenzie, was sitting quietly on a chair by the door. While still somewhat irritated by what had happened earlier that morning, Milner felt he had been discourteous.

'Sorry ... ! Can I introduce my ... er ... shadow, Inspector Andrew MacKenzie.' Milner smiled and swivelled in his chair to gesture towards his bodyguard. 'Part of the furniture ... sorry if that sounds patronizing ... but he is a key figure in my life and will continue to be until they find ...' His voice tailed off. The other diplomats nodded their welcomes, warmly or distantly, according to temperament. MacKenzie, looking distinctly uncomfortable, forced a bleak smile in return.

The residence steward, in a white, high-buttoned jacket, came in with a silver salver of coffee and Danish pastries.

'Please everybody, help yourselves, then let's get down to business.' When everyone had settled again, he began: 'I'll cut the formalities but let me say I'm glad to be here. You know I've been here before, a dozen years ago, in a rather different role and with a different rank, so I'm not totally unfamiliar with procedures.' He spoke crisply, almost brusquely as if to camouflage his feelings.

When he paused for a moment the Minister, David Velcor, took the opportunity and broke in 'May I say, Ambassador, how glad we all are to have you here. Welcome.'

'Thank you, David.'

'We all wanted to say . . .' Velcor hesitated, '. . . said I would, on behalf of us all, say how sorry we are about the . . .'

Milner interrupted him. 'Thank you very much. May we take that as read.' He knew that he was being sharp to the point of rudeness. Some of those in the room stared at him, others looked down in partial embarrassment.

Velcor coloured slightly. 'Yes, of course. I won't say any more.'

'Sorry if I was abrupt, ladies and gentlemen. I do appreciate it, David, but can we leave that for now. There is a security implication to it, as you all know. I'll be dealing with that separately with those concerned.'

At that moment the door of the study opened and in came a tall, gaunt man with very bushy eyebrows.

'Charles Nairn, sir. Sorry to be late. Slight crisis. I can explain . . .'

'Now if you wish.' Milner stood and shook hands formally with the head of the MI6 station at the embassy.

'Later, sir, if you don't mind.'

'Well,' said Milner, resuming his seat. 'I called you together for a first informal chat to get to know you. We'll have the main meeting at eleven o'clock this morning in Chancery. I think that's what Paul Fawcett has fixed up. I've read volumes of the background papers you've all prepared for me. Thank you, General, for that extensive military briefing which I devoured with interest back in London.'

The general nodded appreciatively.

'We've got a mile-high pile of problems on our plates on the Anglo–American front. I don't need to rehearse them. I'm here to try, with your assistance, to sort some of them out. The circumstances of my arriving here, when I thought I was bound for a rather lazier time in Canada,' Milner allowed himself a slight smile, 'must not be allowed to prejudice matters. Recent press coverage about my appointment hasn't done anything to better the situation, but we'll have to live with that. Just as I have to live with additional personal security ... Our task,' he paused and looked round the room to gauge reactions as he spoke, '... isn't helped by the political situation back in London, where the government has such a tiny majority and a leadership that is far from respected by its own backbenchers. In Washington we're face to face with a similarly low-quality American administration.' Milner again paused. 'No apologies for the lecture. You'd better hear me out first before I listen to you. Weak governments are dangerous. They do stupid things for quick advantage; particularly for good headlines in tomorrow's papers. Poor politicians push too much on to the shoulders of people like us: the crucial frontier between ministers and officials gets frayed. An article in a magazine the other week called me a player in the "Secret Garden of the Crown". I took them to mean that I was a manipulator behind the scenes. Well ... we diplomats all are secret manipulators. We try to keep things out of the headlines. There's a lot to be said for secrecy, even in this age of so-called open government. Take away the veils and everyone has to harden up on their attitudes. That's no way to conduct diplomacy. It also means that there's no awe left for the Establishment. The hinge, to change the metaphor, between the executive and the legislator is pretty squeaky at the moment and this spills over as Charles Nairn will understand only too well.' Milner nodded in the direction of the newly-arrived MI6 station chief. 'In the popular mind, our Intelligence system doesn't appear to be as effectively controlled by ministers as it should have been. We officials have to run things more smoothly, sort things out without appearing to be taking the reins away from the politicians. It's a risky course.

This is a time for rebuilding: rebuilding confidence in the system, rebuilding confidence in Anglo–American relations, rebuilding confidence, on the part of the British and American governments, in the secure and safe workings of this embassy. That is what my mission as ambassador is all about. I expect you to back me up all the way. This may be an early hour for such a homily. But that's my agenda, in the short term and in the long term. I used to study economics when economics was a subject to study, and I remember John Maynard Keynes said something to the effect that even though there are storms on the surface of the sea – he was talking about economic storms – a few feet down the water is still and quiet. Down below the public crises, we have got to get on with our work equally quietly. Thank you.'

Milner stopped abruptly, looked round and caught the despairing glance which the Political First Secretary, Janice Yates, threw at his assistant, Paul Fawcett. Was there a touch of a smile on her face? Was that a glimpse of irony in Fawcett's eyes? Would he blame them if he were their age? They were thinking: what the hell have we got here? Philosopher instead of ambassador? A man bruised by personal experience, now going all whimsically theoretical? Thought replacing action? Yes, that is how he too would have reacted in his youth.

One small incident stood out when, later in the meeting, Milner asked Janice Yates a specific question. 'I sat beside someone on the flight out who turned out to be the Junior Senator for Indiana. Nice man. Intelligent. I've forgotten his name. What is . . . ?' He turned inquiringly towards the woman diplomat.

'Sorry . . . For the moment I forget too, sir. I'll look him up straight after this. I'll have a file on him,' Janice Yates said, more than a little embarrassed at being caught out first time by her new boss. A glance round the room indicated to Milner that no one else was able to come up with the answer. Then behind him he heard a discreet cough.

'Senator Todd Werfel, sir. Republican, forty-nine, quite right-wing. Voted against the Healthcare Bill . . . Sorry, sir.' MacKenzie's voice tailed off as everyone else in the room turned to stare at the policeman. 'Sorry for interrupting, sir,' he repeated.

'Not at all, Inspector. Thanks very much,' said Milner before rapidly turning to other business. Nothing more was said, but the Special Branch man had made his mark very clearly indeed.

Milner knew that they would all be talking about him after they left. He had given them plenty of ammunition. None of the conversation between Janice Yates and Paul Fawcett would have surprised him in the least as the two walked together back towards the Chancery. From the window of his study the ambassador could have watched them, might even have been able to overhear them, had he so wished.

'I'm going to need danger money,' said Fawcett with a mirthless laugh. He was a bright, over-plump and over-confident young man, who redeemed his bumptiousness with a veneer of charm.

'He's hellish dry, I agree,' echoed Janice Yates. 'Mark you, after all he's been through . . .' She, in turn, was one of those women diplomats who felt that the only way to get on in her career was to become a male clone in the way she lived, spoke and dressed, disguising a not unattractive femininity in heavy spectacles, contour-hiding pinstripe suits, and an atrociously unbecoming hairstyle.

'He's going to get my loyalty,' said Fawcett firmly.

'And mine. At least until he doesn't deserve it any more.'

'He caused a security scare first thing this morning. Went runabout over to Georgetown. Poor man. No opportunity to do that any more.'

'Escaping from that heavy he's brought with him . . . ?' Janice Yates joked.

'Just because he showed you up in a big way, Janice,' Fawcett responded a little unpleasantly. 'Fancy him knowing the name of an obscure Junior Senator . . .' He stopped, aware that his female colleague was feeling more than a little bruised.

'There's one thing more dangerous than a person who isn't up to a job, and that's someone who's too good,' she said tartly.

'What d'you mean?' asked Fawcett.

'Too clever and not enough to do makes for trouble,' she went on bitterly.

'Mr MacKenzie *has* got under your skin, hasn't he?' Fawcett continued to prod her.

'No way. But I smell danger.'

Fawcett changed the subject. 'I can't believe MacKenzie's people haven't turned up clues on who tried to blow him away.'

'Some extreme Irish splinter group . . . ?' Janice Yates turned enquiringly to look at him.

'Out of the question. They've nothing to gain by exterminating an ambassador to the US. Not now. Bad PR. It's not their style, never has been.' Fawcett was adamant.

'Whoever it was, failed. How much the son looks like his father! I saw a press photograph.'

'Bastards. MI6 should be on to it.'

'Maybe why Charles Nairn stayed behind, why he was late arriving . . .' she speculated.

'Cold fish, Nairn.'

'I don't know. He's got a glad eye. Had to fight him off at the Christmas party, remember?' said Janice Yates, her good humour returning slightly.

'Sex and power go hand in hand. D'you find our new, dry-as-a-bone, workaholic ambassador attractive?' Fawcett turned to study his colleague's reaction.

'If I did, Paul Fawcett, I'd not tell you.' She laughed. They stopped talking as they reached the door of the Chancery building.

'The lean, cadaverous look. Sensuous lips . . . Hidden depths. Passion and all that. I bet he's into sadomasochism.'

'Keep your fantasies to yourself.' Janice Yates showed her pass to the guard at the door, then deliberately turned her back on Fawcett as he made his way up to his office.

Back at the residence, Sir Martin Milner stood talking quietly with Charles Nairn. MacKenzie stood discreetly out of earshot.

'Sorry I was late, sir.'

'The problem?'

'Strange GCHQ telephone intercept. They've been brooding about it for days. Only just shared the information with us. We think it's a conversation about the shooting, sir.'

'Who's speaking to whom?' asked Milner.

'Transcript is fragmented. A man and a woman talking about a bungle. The woman's very upset that the wrong person was hurt. The man tells her to shut up.'

'Irish accents?'

'No, sir. One Cockney English. The woman could be foreign. We're having the accent analysed.' Nairn's bushy eyebrows met in the middle together as he frowned.

The conversation punctured Milner's normal composure and he exploded. 'I cannot believe that the entire resources of the British Intelligence community can't come up with at least *some* suggestion of who was behind it. You know all about my career. I've no enemies, at least none I know about, who would go to these extremes. It has to be an impersonal thing. An attack on me as ambassador rather than an attack on me the person.'

'That's what we still presume, sir,' said Nairn slowly. 'And as to your past . . . There was . . . I suppose . . . only the Norway business.'

'Norway?' Milner felt a stab of almost physical pain at a long and deeply buried memory.

'It may have been thirty years ago, but some things have a habit of coming to the surface.'

'How much d'you know?' Milner asked, subdued.

'Didn't they tell you in London that we were looking that far back?'

'Nothing was mentioned but I'm not surprised. The PM and the Foreign Secretary were so bloody keen to get me over here, I guess they didn't want anything to rock the boat.'

'The PM and the Secretary of State don't know anything about it. It's history. No need for them to know – yet . . .'

'Then what are you on about? You can't think that the Norway incident . . .' A mixture of present anger and ancient fears welled up within him. 'Look . . . You're not doing this off your own bat, are you?' he asked. 'You're asking on instructions? I was working for you lot at MI6 at the time, remember?'

'I'll be absolutely frank with you, sir . . .'

'When somebody from Six says that to me, I start counting the spoons.' Milner was just managing to control his feelings.

'Right, sir. I've been asked to raise it with you.'

'What d'you know?'

'We know everything. We think we do,' said Nairn slowly and precisely. 'This is the story . . . Almost thirty years ago. We were closing in on the number two in our embassy in Oslo, Terence Malone. You remember him of course. He was very senior and very important. He was also a friend of yours. He'd been selling Britain for years. We were on to him. You knew he was in some sort of trouble, though probably not the extent of it, and you probably tipped him off, advertently or inadvertently. He disappeared. Went East, and we had to do a cover-up to avoid more accusations of service incompetence of the Burgess and Maclean variety. Fortunately secrecy suited the Russians too, so the story never leaked. Your name came up at the time. We guessed what had happened but didn't have enough to go on. You played the innocent. Life goes on.' Nairn paused to see what reaction his words had caused. He noted none, so he continued. 'Just recently, some KGB papers surfaced in Moscow. We've done a lot of file swapping with the Russians. We saw your name. One or two people got badly hurt by your friend, Terence Malone, when he spilled the beans in Moscow. The Norwegians were furious . . .'

'So after all this time,' said Milner defensively, 'I'm accused of tipping off a friend who was a spy, letting him escape to the embrace of the KGB? And yet you allowed me to pursue a successful diplomatic career, ending up by becoming British Ambassador to Washington? What the hell's this to do with the attack on David?'

'Agreed. It was a very long time ago. A long time sleeping. If we eventually have to tell the Prime Minister, it'll be in order that he can give you full immunity . . .'

'Immunity, for Christ's sake,' Milner exploded again. 'Why are you digging all this up?'

'Wanted you to know that we know. Just in case that's got anything to do with it.'

'You're putting me on trial. Are you asking me to confess to something?' Milner was cold and now back in full control of himself.

'Not even that. Don't want you to have to tell the truth . . . or to lie.'

'Then what? I assure you, Charles, never since that time have I had any inkling of anything coming out of the woodwork on that front. It can't have anything to do with it.' He spoke with finality.

'Agreed, sir. Unless someone somewhere has uncovered new evidence and still feels badly hurt . . .' Nairn paused then continued. 'Now, if you don't mind, I'll just take you through the questions I have to ask.'

The British Ambassador in Washington not only has two offices, he also has a plethora of secretaries. As well as his diplomatic secretary, Paul Fawcett, and his PA, Victoria Dobbs, Sir Martin Milner had a social secretary who worked at the residence. She dealt with his many invitations, his dinner parties, his other entertaining, his housekeeping. Her name was Lucinda Forbes-Manning and she was as upper-class as her name. A bit of a girl, a bit of a Sloane, frightfully well-bred, but, according to Charles Nairn who had also warned the ambassador about her sensational love life, she had a razor-sharp mind. With a head of dazzling natural blonde hair and a figure that spilled enticingly out of anything she wore, she dressed to kill. It was therefore something of a temptation for Milner, after a hard day of meetings with staff and a variety of briefings from various heads of departments, to arrive back at the residence at around seven in the evening to find that single-minded lady waiting for him. She bore down on him with a pile of invitations to dinner parties and cocktail receptions, and the other social trivia which goes with an ambassador's life anywhere in the world. He collapsed into a deep armchair in his study as she hovered over him, her shapely legs disappearing fetchingly under her short dress at about the level of his eyes.

'Sorry to bother you with all this, sir, but there are a number of important decisions. I know protocol is a bit of a bore but . . . if you haven't the energy now I could come back at crack of dawn.'

'No, let's get it over with,' he said wearily. 'But can you get someone to fix me a drink first?'

'Whisky?'

'Please. Fifty–fifty; water and ice.' He studied her closely as she went to a side table and poured the measures herself. The drink and the company helped relax him. He listened and responded. As efficient as her reputation, she rattled impressively through her list of queries.

'I've kept your lunches and evenings as free as possible for the first week or two, sir, apart from the most essential diary dates. Turned down most routine invites out of hand. Hope you don't mind. You've got the Defence Secretary coming to stay in ten days' time. He's the first VIP. After that, the Princess is coming for the Royal Opera House event. That'll take up one whole evening. Then, I'm afraid, you have to host a couple of dinners and glad-hand a parliamentary delegation. At last count there are seventeen invitations for you to speak; you've probably heard about most of those from Paul Fawcett. The only ones I wanted to highlight are, first, the Pilgrims' Dinner in New York. That's an absolute must for a new ambassador.'

'In my diary already, I think. Confirm with Paul, will you?'

'The English Speaking Union also want you. And the Washington Press Club. The last is the big one.'

'I'm not sure it's right to agree to any until I've paid my official calls on the Secretary of State and the President. Any news on those?'

'Paul Fawcett's baby, sir. He'd have told you . . .'

'OK. I forgot. I'm tired.' Milner knocked back the whisky he had been given and held his glass out towards her. 'Just this once I'll have another.'

'Would you like dinner in your room or shall I get you . . .'

'Sandwiches, unless it'll send chef up the wall.'

'I've already told him I thought you'd want something simple,' she responded efficiently.

'Good girl. How long have you been here, Lucinda?' Milner cautiously studied her swirl of blonde hair that would have graced any shampoo advertisement, her stunning cleavage, that little black dress hitched just a touch high, and those long legs that seemed to go on and on in each direction. She was having the effect on him that she intended to have.

'Too long, sir. Three ambassadors. You're the fourth.' It sounded like a list of her trophies. Perhaps it was.

'Never married?' He wondered how many of his predecessors had been similarly beguiled.

'You've seen my file.' She looked down knowingly at him. Milner checked himself. He remembered past indiscretions of other ambassadors around the globe. There had been one, a giant of a Deputy Secretary in the Foreign Office, when he had first joined the diplomatic service. That one had been posted to Moscow as ambassador and, late one night, had fallen for the wiles of a beautiful Russian maid at the residence. He had had to resign instantaneously. Then there was his distinguished predecessor in Washington who had got himself involved with the family nanny . . .

He did not want to be left alone. He was hyped up and he needed her company. 'Help yourself to a drink, Lucinda.'

'Thanks. I'll get myself a gin and tonic.' She disappeared briefly in search of some lemon.

'Caution,' said Milner to himself. 'This is when it gets dangerous. This is when I get tempted. Lonely equals vulnerable.'

He looked directly at her as she came back into the room. Her body language said it all: she would be an easy lay.

'Do sit down.'

'I can leave the rest till tomorrow if you'd like, sir.' She looked across expectantly.

'Cheers,' he said, raising his glass. 'Sorry keeping you so late. I imagine you've got other things to do.'

'I left tonight totally clear,' she said softly. It was as good an invitation as he could wish for. 'You're tired?'

'You're right. We'll leave it tonight.' He stood up quickly. 'I'll take this up to my room. Could you have the sandwiches sent up?'

Lucinda stood with him, not totally surprised but obviously disappointed. 'Yes, sir,' she said.

He turned and looked at her. 'Thanks for being so patient.'

He could so easily have reached out and touched her, and if he did, he knew she would respond. But no. This was only day one; there was a long time to go. He had too many problems to add one more to the list. It might be pleasurable; a night of passion would be followed by the next day. Tonight he might be a man, but tomorrow he would have to be ambassador once again.

4

'He's in a hell of a mood.' Paul Fawcett was speaking urgently into his telephone.

'Of course I'm in a hell of a mood,' said Sir Martin Milner coming in unexpectedly behind him. Fawcett slammed the phone down.

'Terribly sorry, sir. I was just . . .' Fawcett stood up, a flush rising in his chubby cheeks. He wasn't feeling too good himself: he seemed to have a perpetual hangover these days.

'And if I'm in a bad mood, haven't I reason to be? What the hell's happened to my call on the Secretary of State? And on the President? I've looked back through the files. You've given me figures. In the past British ambassadors have always been seen much more quickly than this. There are not even possible dates in the diary.'

'Antonio Delgadi has just arrived back from the Middle East, sir. You know all that. He'll be in touch soon. And the President, well, he's busy campaigning in the mid-west.'

'Excuses, excuses. Don't tell me who's busy. This telegram from the Foreign Office,' Milner waved a page of typescript furiously. 'Look at it. It more or less accuses me of not being active enough because I haven't yet had my call. I've got to raise the four or five key issues we have at the top of the heap. Put a call through. Now, please. To the Secretary of State himself.'

'Sir. Right away, sir.'

A short three minutes later, the British Ambassador was put through to the American Secretary of State. The voice at the other end could not have been more friendly and welcoming. It defused everything.

57

'We're really sorry to have kept you waiting, Mr Ambassador. The President himself is sure looking forward to meeting you. You've arrived at a really bad time. Oh ... and can I say how sorry we all are at the State Department about your family ... I tell you, Mr Ambassador,' he paused. 'To hell with the formalities. Come see me straightway. Like now?'

'To suit you, Secretary of State. Three o'clock?' asked Martin Milner slowly. In the background he saw Paul Fawcett watching with astonishment. As he put the phone down, he turned to him and said, 'Now, what's going on? Suddenly so very friendly.'

The British Ambassador's Rolls-Royce is bullet-proofed. It has been so ever since the days of the IRA terrorists. The doors open and close like tank doors. The tires wear out after a few thousand miles because of the heaviness of the bodywork. With MacKenzie beside him in the front, the ambassador's driver, a resilient man who had been working for the embassy for many years, was more worried about the car's hubcaps.

'With all the weight, they keep bumping off on the potholes, sir,' he explained. In the back, Sir Martin Milner, with Fawcett by his side, seemed remarkably relaxed and cheerful as they drove down Massachusetts Avenue, along Rock Creek Parkway, past the notorious Watergate building, then through the network of roads that led to the State Department which is sited between Foggy Bottom and the Lincoln Memorial. Foggy Bottom, Washington's early industrial centre, was where all the smoke and fumes from those days had been replaced by the contemporary fumes of political intrigue and international conspiracy. There was nothing foggy about the area; it was neat and tidy, and if the State Department was one of the most boring buildings in all of Washington, it too had its hidden treasures.

As a new ambassador, Milner was shown to the State Rooms to wait until the Secretary of State was ready to see him. A cheerful Chief of Protocol, a lady in her mid-fifties, bounced around him explaining all the artefacts as they walked through the reception rooms on the eighth floor. Sumptuous with furnishings, paintings and sculpture donated to the US Government largely in place of tax, they looked venerable and aged; in fact they were constructed in the 1960s in the style of some splendid old American stately home. The Chief of Protocol escorted him into the John Quincy Adams' State Drawing Room and left him alone with Fawcett. In this most secure of buildings, Mackenzie had been left behind and would wait for them by the main doors.

Portraits of Adams himself, of Jefferson, of Benjamin Franklin, of George Washington hung on the walls. 'You know about that desk?' Milner asked his assistant.

'No, sir.' Fawcett was still far from relaxed in his dealings with his ambassador. He never knew what his reaction was going to be to things. Sometimes he was distant, almost scholarly in his assessment of issues, at others, he was brusque to the point of rudeness.

'On that, the Treaty of Paris ending the War of Independence was signed.'

'Yes, sir,' said Fawcett rapidly.

'Not impressed, eh?'

'Other things on my mind, sir.'

'Not as many as I have,' said Milner softly.

As a further mark of reconciliation the Secretary of State himself, shadowed by a small phalanx of officials, suddenly appeared in the State Drawing Room to show Milner to his own offices.

'Many apologies, Mr Ambassador. Most discourteous of us. You know all the things that have been going on. Don't want you to think this delay has anything to do with the small blips in our relationship. Believe me: it's not the case.'

Milner cautiously scrutinised the diminutive Italian-American who had, only a year earlier, rocketed from nowhere into the position of the second most important man in the United States of America. Antonio Delgadi was a party man through and through, and his selection by the President, well after the new administration had come into office, had surprised everyone. The media thought he would fail. They combed through his New York Italian background to see whether there were any Mafia connections. But even the Senate Foreign Relations Committee and the myriad of other pressure groups and committees who scrutinized his nomination, failed to turn up anything suspect. Mr Delgadi, as Secretary of State, had, to everyone's surprise, proved to be a considerable success. He was popular, bouncy, and if some people thought he was a little lightweight, he certainly made up for it in the energy he put into his task. Today he was also in good humour. Martin Milner took to him at once.

'What d'you think, Ambassador? Good idea if we talked one-on-one? Four eyes only, as we say? I'm sure neither your Mr Fawcett here, nor my guys will mind leaving us alone . . . Gentlemen.' He made a gesture in the direction of the door of his office and the others left the two men alone.

'Now, Mr Ambassador . . . Can I call you Martin . . . ? Sit down. Like a drink?'

'Three-thirty in the afternoon is a little early for a drink. Maybe some mineral water?'

The Secretary of State went to a side-cabinet, poured his guest a glass of sparkling mineral water and handed it to him. He settled opposite Milner in a deep armchair by a big picture-window that looked out over the Washington skyline. In the distance they could see the Washington Memorial and the roofs and spires of the Capitol itself. After a few minutes of pleasantries, the Secretary of State began.

'You've arrived at a bad time, Martin.'

'I'm well aware of that.'

'Never was much of a believer in the Special Relationship. But . . . don't quite know how things have got to this pass. We had plenty of problems in the past: Suez, Northern Ireland, Bosnia and so on. Now everything seems to have heated up. I want to take you through our thinking on this.'

'You have my full attention, Secretary of State.' Milner sat back, weighing the other man up in his habitually meticulous way. He always found that by leaving silences in conversations, the other person usually felt obliged to talk on, revealing themselves to him as they did so.

'You Europeans may think that the American Government is like a bus driving along a pre-determined road. Trouble is that there are millions of passengers sitting in the back, each one with a pistol, each one wanting to go their way. Anarchy all dressed up to look like democracy.' Delgadi laughed. 'You need a strong president, a strong administration to cope with all the pressures you're put under the whole time. You, in Britain, for your own good reasons, have gone European. This has inevitably led to a diminution in the level of Anglo–American relations. No bad thing. It suits you when the going is good. But . . . here comes the bad news . . . every time you guys get a problem, a threat, as with the civil wars currently peppering Eastern Europe, you come running to us for cover. We've got plenty of other things to do, plenty other areas of the world demanding our attention: South America, the Caribbean, the Pacific Rim for example. OK, we need to keep in good line with the Russians because they've still got some nasty weapons out there, along with the Ukrainians. Otherwise, as far as we are concerned, you guys can keep policing the fighting in your own backyards. Leave us in peace.' The Secretary of State got quite flushed and excited as he spoke.

'That isn't serious American policy, is it, sir?' Milner, by contrast, was deliberately cool.

'Not quite. But that's the thinking behind a lot of our actions recently. You guys cry that we're going isolationist. It's nothing to do with that. We have enough problems of our own. We have to balance our domestic and foreign policies. So we get all angry and tight when you Brits start lecturing us on our global responsibilities. All that crap . . .'

'You won't hear me saying that, Secretary of State.'

'OK. So you're oiled up and polished shiny, like all professional diplomats, Martin. Any unpleasantness brushed under the carpet. All correct and *protocolaire*.' He flashed a quick smile at his visitor.

'We try to avoid shooting from the hip until all else has failed.'

'I can promise you, Martin, we're not going to go to war with you, but we don't like the way your government's been talking down to us recently. Remarks about us having an absentee president and abrogating our responsibilities in Europe are not the sort of remarks we expect to see made by the Prime Minister of a friendly country.' Delgadi had slowed down and spoke with a sudden strength of feeling.

'My Prime Minister was speaking to a very specialised audience.'

'Don't try to soft-soap me. He was speaking to your Institute of International Affairs. That's precisely the sort of audience that's listened to over here. We don't like it. And then we had your Foreign Secretary whining on about the White House's perspective of the outside world as being a host of faraway countries of which the President knows nothing. You know that's a loada bullshit.'

'Sir, I do.' Milner felt that personal honesty was best at this juncture.

'What's your excuse then? We also get accused of being bereft of conviction.'

'You have your priorities,' he responded cautiously.

'There you go again. Diplomato-speak. We have a priority list, of course we do. OK. We fudge and fiddle a bit. Like you do. And you sure aren't led by a Mrs Thatcher these days. But eventually we have to move. Certain things are more important to us than others. Bosnia, for one. It should've been Europe's war. Yet you kept on squealing and trying to drag us into it. Now we're getting stick for pulling out.'

'With due respect, Secretary of State, your American public opinion dragged you into it. It now wants you out.'

'Let's start this relationship well, Mr Ambassador – Martin. I'm not going to take lectures. Not from you, not from nobody, no time.' The little man bounced up and down with something approaching indignation. Then suddenly he flashed another of his quick smiles to defuse the situation once again.

'You won't hear me talking about the Special Relationship either, Secretary of State.' Milner came back at him. 'That's all in the past. But when it comes to things like the complete breakdown of the rule of law in Eastern Europe, particularly in Russia, the Atlantic partnership has to hang together. Or, as your

Ben Franklin said, "most assuredly we'll hang separately".'

'Sure, sure. We'll do just that . . . On American terms.' The Secretary of State paused, thought for a moment, then continued. 'And there's your press. Your piss-awful media.'

'Don't ask me to defend the inadequacies of the British press.' Milner feigned mock horror.

'I'm not throwing the blame around. But boy, have they really gone ape. They seem to *want* to create America as an enemy. If they want that, well . . . they can have it.'

'Tell me honestly, Secretary of State . . .' Milner hesitated.

'I'll always speak honestly, Martin . . .'

'What I mean is – the perception we have . . . not just the media . . . is that the President himself has his own particular agenda. That agenda seems unfriendly to the United Kingdom.'

'He has his likes and dislikes.'

'What drives his dislike of Britain?'

'The media tells you, they tell me, that it was because he was snubbed by your government when he went over as a young Senator. I don't know the truth of that. Ask him when you see him. I never have.'

'Have you any news about my formal call at the White House?'

'We'll get back to you.'

'That sounds ominous.'

'The President has his priorities, Martin. You don't happen to be one of them at the moment.' The Secretary of State stood up suddenly, smiled warmly, and stretched out his hand. 'So very good to meet you, Martin. Welcome to Washington. I mean that. I really do.' The meeting was at an end.

Top Secret and Personal Memorandum
For Addressee's Eyes Only
TO: *The Secretary to the Cabinet*
FROM: *Head of MI6*
Date: *23 May*
File No. *MM913/97*

1. As you know, the PM has spoken directly to the Director General of MI5, to the Metropolitan Police Commissioner, the Head of Special Branch and to myself, expressing his displeasure that we have as yet not come up with the information about those responsible for the attack which seriously injured the son of the British Ambassador to Washington.

2. It is misguided to suggest that we have not carried out the most intensive investigations. We have worked very closely with MI5 and Special Branch, consulting various European police authorities, including the Garda, as necessary. We are convinced that the perpetrators were not Irish-connected. All other regular sources disclaim any responsibility. We are fully inclined to believe them. In particular, key Middle-East contacts who would tend to know of any terrorist threat, have come up with nil results. Monitoring the relics of the Red Brigade and other revolutionary groups in Germany, France, and Italy has equally drawn a blank. In any event, we can see no reason why Sir Martin would be a likely target for any of them. This is the first occasion in our collective experience that no one, repeat no one, has claimed responsibility for an assassination attempt of this nature.

3. I request that the following should not, repeat not, be passed on to the Prime Minister at this stage since it is our view (and MI5 share this) that it would undermine the government's belief in and support for the British Ambassador at this crucial time. We also are worried about leaks through political channels. It is our current assessment that the attack must have been directed at Sir Martin for some personal reason. All evidence points to this, though the perpetrators were obviously professional hit-men. Yet he has, in various interviews and discussions,

revealed no known enemies and we have, as you know, spent a considerable amount of time going through his past to make sure that no stones were left unturned. He is, as you are aware, a difficult subject to interrogate. He is very self-assured, and set in his own opinions on this, and everything else. His autocratic attitude certainly does not lead to a build-up of understanding, but we believe he is answering questions truthfully. We have, with the exception of the thirty-year old Bergen affair (see report MM910/97), come up with nothing, repeat nothing, that might generate such antagonism. The only clue in this direction is the fragmented GCHQ intercept (MM903/97) between a man and a woman who may, repeat may, have been discussing the attack. Professional voice analysis suggests that the woman could be Scandinavian. We have, incidentally, rejected the idea that it might be something of an entirely domestic nature such as a jealous husband. Here too, any evidence of indiscretion is nil and the professionalism with which the attack was launched suggests this was no amateur attempt. We are continuing our investigations on Sir Martin and his past with maximum urgency.

'Glad you've had better news about your son, sir,' Charles Nairn showed his concern. He stood looking down at the ambassador who sat behind his desk in the Chancery building.

'Thank God. I'm flying back to see David at the weekend. Now . . . much more worried about my wife . . .'

'Anything I can do . . . ?'

'Thanks, Charles, I don't think so . . . You wanted to see me?'

'Still pursuing the shooting business, sir. Sorry to bother you about it again, but Head Office have asked me to take you through some of it one more time.' Nairn spoke cautiously.

'I've told you everything I can possibly think of.'

'The personal side, sir. Something directed at you personally rather than at you as ambassador.'

'Load of balls. I've told you. That's fantasy world.' Milner was totally dismissive.

'Anything you tell me, sir, will be treated in the strictest confidence. It will not be passed on to anyone outside the Service.' Nairn found it particularly difficult to interrogate this stiff intellectual figure who was, after all, his nominal boss.

'Charles . . . Don't strain my patience . . . There's nothing, no one, no incident, nothing.'

'So I leave it there, sir?'

'You leave it there.'

'I'll pass that on.'

'Glad if you did. Now . . . We've work to do. The real key to the bad state of Anglo–American relations is . . . ?' The ambassador paused and looked up at Nairn.

'You mean, sir?'

'It comes down to personalities.'

'The President?'

'Exactly. I got the bluntest of messages from Antonio Delgadi: the President is going to keep me waiting a long time. It's only a protocol call, but it's also a whopping big symbol. This never happened to any of my predecessors. Problems or no problems, we've always conducted bilateral relations in a civilized fashion. If that's out the door, I want to know why.'

'The snubs story?' Nairn volunteered.

'May be part of it. They used to say that about Rupert Murdoch, remember, that he hated the British establishment because they had once snubbed him. I don't know the truth of that; Delgadi claimed not to know the truth about it either. I've asked David Velcor and Paul Fawcett to pull together a paper listing every public or private occasion on which the President had made anti-British statements. I want you to use your network to get at the inner man.'

'The inner man.' Charles Nairn laughed emptily. 'Often there isn't an inner man . . . I'll see what I can find.'

'It often comes down to human personalities, individual backgrounds,' Milner said, looking down at the papers on his desk.

'Which was what I was saying when I came in, sir,' said Charles Nairn quietly, then he turned and left the room.

Two days later Milner's Norwegian colleague came to call. He thought nothing of it. Anders Berg was, after all, a very old colleague, a big bluff guy, ex-Olympic skier, who had made a name for himself as a broadcaster and sports commentator. He had spent some time in politics before joining the diplomatic service, and later, being chosen to be Oslo's man in Washington. Everybody liked Anders; they also undervalued him. They thought he was just what he seemed to be, yet he was much deeper, much more thoughtful. Martin Milner knew that: they had served together in Brussels and were friends as much as two foreigners can be in the diplomatic service. Drinks in hand, the two ambassadors walked side by side through the rose garden at the front of the residence, partly because it was a pleasant, early summer's evening, partly because they both knew from experience that it was better to keep away from listening walls when important matters were being discussed.

'Your problems are our problems.'

'Reassuring, Anders.'

'I am not being cynical. It is a fact. You and the Americans may no longer have a special relationship. Norway and the UK do.' Berg liked his colleague, but, like other acquaintances of Milner's, he felt he did not know him. What he did respect, however, was the other man's intellectual grasp of international affairs, and, having seen him operate in the Machiavellian world of multilateral diplomacy, he understood why the British Ambassador was at the zenith of his profession.

'You don't get the brush-off the way we do,' Milner responded.

'We are being tarred by the European brush as well. It is a bad phase. It will go away.'

'Will it? Do you really believe that, Anders?'

'To be quite blunt: no. But it is my line for outsiders,' said Berg.

'I'm no outsider. Tell me your analysis of the problem.'

'All the old stuff. With the end of the Cold War, the glue that held Europe and the United States together has dried up. We do not need to bond with each other as much. So, as is often the way with friends that fall out, we start slanging each other off. That is all.'

'There's more to it than that. The President?'

'Aah. The President.' Berg was silent for a moment.

'Well?'

'I have met him only once or twice. Otherwise . . . I read the stories. I hear the rumours.' Berg paused and bent down to admire a rosebush.

'And? You've been here a long time, Anders. You ought to have got to the bottom of it.' Milner waited while the other man looked about him.

'What a splendid garden you have,' Berg said, then he went on. 'I'm not sure I have. There's probably some truth about him being slighted when he went to Britain years ago. Ambitious men carry small rebuffs in their hearts like wounds.'

'Picturesque. But my predecessor didn't have problems at the beginning, even with the President.'

'Because the man was still finding his feet. Now, with that sharp Secretary of State behind him, he's liking putting the Europeans in their place.'

'We used to have a strong British lobby in Washington,' Milner said wistfully.

'It seems to have gone to sleep.'

'I'm not getting to grips with this, Anders. All the reports on my personal file say that my colleagues think I'm great at grasping problems, getting at core issues – identifying, isolating and solving.'

'You always did have a good career record. Maybe this has been sent to try you . . .' Anders Berg paused. 'May I ask . . . Have they got to the bottom of the shooting?'

'No they haven't. I don't want to talk about it.'

'Strange, isn't it . . . ?' He paused and looked around thoughtfully. 'You really do have a beautiful rose garden.'

'Don't change the subject, Anders.'

'I'm not. When you joined the diplomatic service, they never – how do you British say it – promised you a rose garden, Martin.'

'Nor problems like this. David . . .'

'I'm very sad about him. How is he?'

'Got some of the bandages off. The chest and lung are going OK. Groin's a question mark and there's a great scar on his cheek. I've spoken to him on the telephone. He sounds a bit more cheerful.' Milner in turn paused and bent down, pulling a weed idly out from among the rose bushes.

'Gardener manqué.' Anders Berg grunted.

Milner did not respond, but threw the weed onto a nearby pile of garden refuse. Brushing his hands together to shake off the earth, he straightened up. 'So, Anders, advise me.'

'Two things: get to the President; get to his mind. Then you'll solve your problem at a stroke. He's not as bad as he's painted. I'm still not sure he knows who I am, and I don't have the sharpness of intellect needed to get through to him, but . . . maybe you can. If you do that . . .'

'The second thing?'

'You're not going to achieve anything realistic here until you've solved your own problems, Martin. You'd see that a million miles away if you were one of your own staff. Go home. Sort out your life. Sort out your wife and your son, then come back.'

'I'm flying back to visit . . .'

'No flying visit. You need to stay a while.'

'I can't. I have a job to do.'

'You can. You have a job to do.'

The two men stared hard at each other, Anders Berg hesitated as if about to say something else, then suddenly reached across and slapped the other's back. 'Come on now. Let's go and charge up my glass. We Norwegians like more than one small drink, Martin.' The two men smiled at each other, turned, and walked together back up towards the Residence.

5

It was his first big set-piece speech a bare five weeks after his arrival. The Washington Press Club dinner was one of the ways any new ambassador made, or failed to make, his mark. The evening was agreeable enough and he was introduced around by his hosts to some of the key players in the media scene whose life's work was to make or break American politicians and other public figures. These were the men and women who set the nation's agendas, and of whom presidents and senators were, if not afraid, always at pains to oil, placate or appease.

As usual when he was to make a speech, he drank no alcohol, merely sipped a glass of mineral water throughout the meal. Then the moment came. The host for the evening stood and introduced him in glowing terms, only briefly mentioning the recent calamities in his life. Showing no nerves, he stood to polite but restrained applause, the mark of an audience that knew all was not well in Anglo–American relations. He was on trial. He, Britain's mouthpiece, was being assessed. As he stood up he noticed, out of the corner of his eye, that his private secretary, Paul Fawcett, had suddenly appeared at the far end of the room. That was odd: Fawcett had specifically excused himself from the evening, pleading another engagement. As he began to speak, he was aware of Fawcett making his way across the room to one of the corner tables where his deputy, David Velcor, was sitting with a group of senior American journalists. MacKenzie, who normally waited by the door on occasions like this, walked with him. He thought no more about it: he had his speech to deliver.

He began in formal mode, saying how honoured he was to be posted to the United States at such a critical time in

Anglo–American relations. He quickly reached the substance of his speech, knowing he had a hard-nosed and cynical audience that would be turned off by banal platitudes. He had worked on the text with great care over the preceding weeks, clearing the final version with the Foreign Office in London. They had watered down some of his more trenchant remarks since they did not want him to inflame an already tense situation. But in the end he pulled few punches and gave them his views with uncharacteristic direct-ness. These were not people who wanted sweetly-coated or coded messages.

Ladies and gentlemen, since the end of the Second World War, the United States has given every encour-agement to the unification of Europe. You supported the formation of the EEC and, later, the modern European Community. In the aftermath of the col-lapse of communism, you encouraged ever closer pol-itical and economic integration. You have, on the other hand, been wary of the dangers of Fortress Europe. We still need you when we have problems; you prefer to have our backing when you are faced with yours.

Yet sometimes, by creating this strong Europe, you feel excluded. You like our support but you do not like us asserting our independent views. You were extremely concerned recently when you discovered that certain NATO partners were considering meet-ing without an American presence at the table. That is natural. You have your own interests to safeguard. But you also have to see it from our side of the herring pond. We see a United States of America, a proud and distinguished and at the moment fairly prosperous country, which is more and more concerned with the events in its own hemisphere. It is more focused on developments in South and Central America. It follows closely the exciting economic and political changes that are taking place around the Pacific Rim. But, most of all, America is concerned with itself. That has always been and always should be the central motivation of American foreign policy. But because it is the driving mechanism, it cannot always sit easily with European aims. That should be no surprise to anyone here in this room tonight. That is why it is so important that we Europeans watch and study what you are doing, how you are doing it, what your leaders say and think.

Let me just briefly quote what your former President Richard Nixon once said. He made a speech announcing an offensive into Cambodia in April 1970. He said then, "If, when the chips are down, the world's most powerful nation acts like a pitiful, helpless giant, the forces of totalitarianism and anarchy will threaten free nations and free institution throughout the world." Ladies and gentlemen, I do not wish anyone here to think that I believe you are acting like a helpless giant. You are demonstrably not doing that. But at the same time you must realise the effect your every move has on events throughout the civilized and the developing world. If your leaders appear to lack inner conviction and self-confidence which is the mark of natural leadership; if your statesmen adopt a combative style that is merely seen as bombastic; if your politicians do not appear to have a broad geo-political grasp of world events, then transatlantic relationships are indeed in danger. I believe, ladies and gentlemen, that in this post-communist world, with all the dangerous wars and disorders in Eastern Europe, the apparent numbness which some western observers find observable in the White House and in the State Department cannot be ignored. I, for one, do not believe that numbness exists. I believe, as I said earlier, that America is merely pursuing its own natural self interests. But there are warning signs to be read. America cannot be totally inward-looking. It must maintain its role in the wider world, particularly with the dangerous instability in Eastern Europe. That is my simple and sole message tonight.'

After a few concluding remarks and one Anglo–American joke, the ambassador sat down to restrained applause. He knew that he would have inspired as many critics as allies in his audience, but he had never believed in mincing his public words. He was only partially prepared for what was to come.

There were two elements to that. The first was a huge political storm, partly anticipated, that was blown up by a headline-seeking media. The next morning's press went to town in highlighting the ambassador's far from veiled attack on the administration's policies as being too inward-looking. He was praised in the British press for his bluntness; in the American press, by contrast, he was marked down heavily by State Department and White House spokesmen. That fall-out would continue in the days and weeks ahead. That part, the public issue, he was ready to cope with.

What he could not have foreseen was what was awaiting him as he left the top table and made his way to the door. He was aware that Paul Fawcett and David Velcor, both white-faced and strained, were moving towards him. MacKenzie was one close step behind. At once he knew that something serious had happened. He walked rapidly towards them, leaving his American host trailing far behind.

'What is it?'

'Sir, perhaps could you come through to this side room,' said David Velcor quietly. Gone was his normal reticence. His deputy was not one for drama. What you saw with him was what you got. Bitter he might be about his promotion prospects, but he was totally honest, without guile, and kind and considerate when it came to dealing with other people's problems. And now he looked deeply troubled. Behind him, Milner was aware that Paul Fawcett

73

was whispering urgently in his American host's ear as Velcor led him through to the side room and shut the door.

'Ambassador. I'm sorry. I have very bad news. We got a phone call from London just as the dinner began.'

'David . . . ?' he whispered, the blood draining from his face.

'No, sir. It's your wife, sir. I have to say . . . I'm very sorry indeed to have to tell you that Annabel is dead. She appears to have taken an overdose sometime earlier today.'

Extract from the *Daily Telegraph* front page report. Wednesday 11th June. From our Washington Correspondent.

It would be difficult to imagine a greater number of personal and political problems falling on the head of the British Ambassador to Washington, Sir Martin Milner. Not only has he created an international outcry, particularly in an over-sensitive American media, over remarks that seem to be directly criticizing the White House and the State Department, but Sir Martin has also had to face a second appalling personal tragedy in the apparent suicide of Lady Milner. Her body was found yesterday morning at her sister's London home. A note, the contents of which have not been disclosed, was found beside her. It is understood that Sir Martin Milner is flying home to London today. The assumption in informed political circles is that, given this personal and political conflux of tragedies, he will be offering his resignation to the Foreign Secretary on his arrival.

Friends close to Sir Martin Milner have expressed their personal shock and horror at the events that led to the death of Lady Milner so shortly after the unexplained shooting which left their son, David, in intensive care. They expressed privately last night how deeply saddened they were at this combination of events but disclaimed any suggestion that personal factors would have had any bearing whatsoever on the tone of Sir Martin's speech to the Washington Press Club yesterday. Foreign Office sources confirmed that the ambassador had cleared his entire text with the Foreign Secretary before its delivery. It is therefore very evident that this was not some personal statement by Sir Martin, but the declared position by Her Majesty's Government expressing its deep disquiet over the present state of Anglo–American relations.

Our political correspondent, Marty Randle, comments: "It is essential that, in the aftershock of these dire events, both personal and political, the British Embassy in Washington does not remain without an ambassador for long. It will be incumbent on the Prime Minister and the Secretary of State to find an able and capable figure to replace Sir Martin Milner as soon as possible. Anglo–American relations abhor a vacuum; Whitehall sources confirmed last night the need to have a new man in place at the earliest moment. The name of Mr. Vincent has again been mentioned . . .

(continued p. 7)

The thick, bomb-proof curtains that draped the long windows overlooking St James's Park added a dullness to the famous room. Trafford Leigh, the Secretary of State, sat wedged behind his huge desk flanked by his private secretaries and officials from the American and European departments.

'Things can't get worse,' volunteered one of the under-secretaries.

'Things can get a great deal worse,' said the Foreign Secretary icily.

'We should have looked at his speech more carefully,' a private secretary muttered.

'So much has hit the poor man over the last twenty-four hours that he can carry the can on his own speech as well. It will be a fairly small additional burden for him and it lets us off the hook,' suggested another diplomat cynically.

'I approved the text of that speech. I carry the can,' Leigh barked angrily.

'Of course you do, Secretary of State. I was just suggesting . . .' whined the diplomat.

'I know what you were suggesting. I don't like it.'

'Secretary of State, all we are trying to do . . .' said Alexander, the Head of the American Department in a placatory tone, 'is to get ourselves out of this particular hole. We're very sorry for Sir Martin. We all know him personally. The point is that a breakdown in Anglo–American relations will long outlast one man's personal tragedies. We all – that is we officials – all agree, sir, that with the departure of Sir Martin, for reasons that the media and out other critics will fully understand, we could try to turn over a new leaf. Appoint somebody with strong political antennae, someone moderate, like Vincent, who is known to be ardently pro-American. He'll butter them up. We simply can't go on warring with them the way we've been doing in recent months.'

'I will not be party to using Sir Martin Milner's misfortunes as a scapegoat for policies that I and the British Cabinet authorised.' Trafford Leigh was about to lose his temper with what he considered a bunch of craven, disloyal officials.

'Very well, sir. What do you intend? Who are you going to choose for Washington?' asked Alexander weakly.

'I have one man and one man only in mind,' said Trafford Leigh with a menacing finality in his voice.

A small delegation was there to meet Sir Martin Milner as he stepped off the British Airways flight and they ushered him straight to a car which was waiting for him on the tarmac. That way they avoided the press photographers. He travelled back into London with the Chief Clerk, the title carried by the Head of Administration at the Foreign Office, and with Dr Mark Ivor, who had personally asked to come to the airport to meet him. MacKenzie, who had flown back with him, followed in a police back-up car.

At first the drive took place in silence; neither of the London-based men wished to impose their thoughts until Milner was ready to talk. Watching and waiting, Ivor wondered again, as he had done many times since he had heard the news about Annabel Milner, about the make-up of his friend. This was no single man: several conflicting personalities had always struggled within him for pride of place. At one level there was the thoughtful, capable, intelligent, charming friend; against that, there was the dark side, the unknown. Not that Ivor could blame him for being thrown in on himself in the present tragic circumstances. How could it be otherwise?

'My wife's sister, Sheila, won't speak to me,' were the first words Milner uttered. 'Annabel refused to. Now Sheila too blames me for what's happened.'

'Grossly unfair,' ventured the Chief Clerk.

'Very,' echoed Ivor.

'Unfair or not, that's the way it is. She shouted at me down the line that I'd abandoned my family . . .' He checked himself, then asked. 'How is David? Who's with him? Does he know?'

'There's a hospital social worker whom he's been getting on well with. Woman in her mid-forties. She's with him the whole time. She had to tell him in case he was alert enough to pick it up . . . he's started listening to the radio. She reports that David's taken it all rather better than might be expected. Of course, he's still under heavy sedation. The real reaction will come later.' Ivor saw no point in telling Milner that right to the end, Annabel had refused, as an old friend, to see him as well.

Milner picked up one of a bundle of newspapers that was lying in the back seat of the car. *The Times*' headline read: *'British Ambassador: Public Triumph and Private Tragedy'*.

'They're all like that I'm afraid,' ventured the Chief Clerk. 'You get a highly sympathetic press. The editorials are one hundred percent supportive.'

'Even the British press don't kick a man when he's down as far as I am,' said Milner softly.

'The *Financial Times* suggests that your speech has led to an overnight strengthening of sterling against the dollar,' said the Chief Clerk.

'I suppose it may benefit someone,' Milner shrugged.

'It's probably more to do with the Federal Reserve Bank's interest rates,' said Ivor wryly. 'The market's extremely sensitive at the moment, so anything that comes along to disturb things sends the rates fluctuating wildly.'

'I only wish I didn't have so much power this morning . . . Where are we going first?' asked Milner. 'I can't think straight at the moment.'

'We thought you'd want to go to the hospital to see David. We've set up a small task force to help you arrange other matters,' Ivor explained. 'Your lawyer knows of course; he's coming to the meeting, which we've arranged for five o'clock. News Department are refusing to comment further.'

'We thought you wouldn't want to go home. You've got a room at the Horse Guard's Hotel,' the Chief Clerk added helpfully.

'Perhaps that's best.' Milner looked as low and dispirited as he felt.

'If you're up to it, the Foreign Secretary would like to see you. Any time this evening will do. He has to be at the House of Commons.'

'He'll want to know what you intend to do . . .' Mark Ivor began. 'But I'm sure . . .'

Milner's voice dropped to a whisper and the other two had to strain to catch his words. 'Thanks. Tell him I'll be there,' he said.

6

As with many of life's relationships, he did not miss her until she had gone. She had always been there, a habit, a demanding and difficult partner, but the other half of his life. Never close, seldom intimate, she had been a mainstay, a buttress to his hectic public life, despite her increasing complaints about being a mere appendage, sidelined into insignificance. He had always denied it: it had none the less been largely true. Now he was left with a mix of emptiness, regret, guilt and shame. It was all so final. Why had she done it? Why, after all these happy as well as difficult years, could she not have talked to him? All so final: no way to argue, to explain, to promise that it would all be better in the future. She had always got on so well with David, living for him, while regretting – and this was largely his fault – that he was their only child. Above all, why had Annabel deserted her son in his hour of misfortune? What had triggered this final, horrific act? The suicide note was almost unintelligible: all it really said was – goodbye.

Later he came to agree with friends and with her doctors. The reason was all too simple: her mind had snapped. He must not blame himself, they consoled him. But he knew, as they knew and as Annabel probably did when she took her life, that for him the guilt would remain, would fester and would grow. He would realize that he was guilty of her death, by abandoning her and David for that empty gesture of a nation's good.

The ever-present person in his life in the days after his return to London was someone whom, up until then, Milner had largely tolerated or ignored. There had been a few surprising exceptions, as when MacKenzie had come up with the name of the Senator at his first staff meeting, but otherwise, he had merely been there all the time, a never-resting presence, his protector and shadow. MacKenzie, by contrast, had come to know a great deal about the ambassador, this able, intelligent man whom he had campaigned so vigorously to be assigned to protect. Sir Martin Milner was, to his staff, difficult, remote, high-minded, a strain to get through to. MacKenzie, who was a far from simple copper as his superiors all recognized, did not rush to develop the relationship. Whatever his private feelings, he was single-minded in his present task: to make sure that no harm befell his protégé. MacKenzie's appointment, personally approved by the Commissioner of the Metropolitan Police, was made because he was known to be resilient in a crisis, had consistently passed out top in self-defence and small-arms competitions, but, above all, because he was so keen to go. He was in line for a good Deputy Chief Constable post in the Midlands, but had lobbied hard for the Washington assignment and had been awarded it through grit, determination, and because he knew so much about modern America. In the few weeks since he had taken up the position he had been constantly questioned by his superiors about whether the ambassador had let slip any additional clue that might lead them to finding out why he had been an assassination target. So far MacKenzie had discovered nothing. Deep down, he, like Mark Ivor, realized that there was a hidden side to his ward which he had yet to fathom. In other men it might be a vice – homosexuality, an affair – but MacKenzie had not let him out of his sight for long enough for anything untoward to happen. MacKenzie's own assumption, a view increasingly shared by his superiors, was that the key had to be somewhere deep in Sir Martin's past. Yet if that was so, surely MI6 and MI5 would have come up with it by now, from evidence somewhere in their records or in his personal file at the Foreign and Commonwealth Office.

A partial breakthrough in the highly formal relationship between the two men, when it came, was in a form which MacKenzie found difficult to handle. One day early on, the ambassador asked him outright if he could rely on him not to pass on to

Special Branch every thought and idea that he might overhear or that came to be exchanged between them.

'To be blunt, MacKenzie,' Milner explained, 'can I talk openly in front of you if I'm with colleagues, or do I have to watch my every word? You're used to being a bodyguard. I'm certainly not used to having one. Tell me the ground rules.'

This thrust MacKenzie into an immediate conflict: loyalty to the man he was protecting against loyalty to his superiors in London.

'There are no rules, sir. It's all a matter of trust . . .'

'Exactly. Which is why I'm asking.'

'Unless you do something illegal or stupid, sir,' said MacKenzie slowly, 'my loyalty and discretion are assured.' His words were carefully chosen. In the end he found a middle way which suited his conscience, though, on reflection, it might not have pleased either Sir Martin or the head of Special Branch.

Looking back at it, the relationship, almost a bonding, built up out of Milner's increasing need to confide in someone else, and who better than the man who was his constant, enforced companion. Increasingly isolated, Milner was delighted to find a remarkably well-informed travelling partner with no axe to grind. This high-flying ambassador, valued by the government as a key agent of influence in so much of the behind-the-scenes diplomacy of the last decade, a man who had negotiated treaties and formed the thinking of successive foreign secretaries of all political persuasions, in his turn, gradually allowed himself to be influenced and advised by a mere bodyguard, a diplomatic protection officer of inspector rank.

'Salt of the earth, man-in-the-street reactions, that's what I need,' he thought to himself when he started opening up to MacKenzie. It became very much more than that as he discovered, in his turn, the depth of character and the judgement of his personal protection officer.

This mutual confidence increased almost without either of them noticing, during long periods of travelling together by plane and car. Milner began by discussing routine matters, then moved on to explaining issues and anxieties which, in the past, he would have talked about only to his wife or to one of his few long-standing friends. Only gradually did MacKenzie too realize what was happening: he was being willingly dragged into a very different role. While it suited his intellect and his wide knowledge of contemporary American history and politics, he would have to watch carefully how he played his hand as far as outside observers were concerned.

This new relationship flowered in the black days when they returned together to London after Lady Milner's suicide. Before then Milner had shown little curiosity about MacKenzie's background. From a cursory glance at his personnel file, he knew the man was not married, but not whether he ever had been, whether he had children, what his aims and ambitions were. Much of it was easily told. Andrew MacKenzie had emerged from a lower-middle-class Glasgow background, had gone to a tough but good city-centre school, had later studied American history at Edinburgh, obtaining a good first-class degree, and then, to his widowed mother's chagrin, had joined the police as an ordinary constable. But he had soon been singled out for his sharp intelligence and dogged determination and was cross-posted to Special Branch. There, after training, he had undertaken a number of routine duties, usually as protection officer to various VIPs, and, for a brief time, he was seconded to Buckingham Palace as bodyguard to one of the younger princes. He had been about to be posted in the Midlands when he had heard about the opening as Sir Martin Milner's personal minder. His American knowledge would be an asset at the embassy. That he had few personal ties also meant, he had argued, that he could leave for Washington immediately.

MacKenzie had few friends – in this he was not unlike the ambassador. A difficult Glasgow childhood – his father had deserted his mother when he was young – had made him wary of most of his colleagues; it took a long time for anyone to break down his defences. He was his own man, dogged and determined, with – his main failing – an inability to put up with stupidity and a habit of questioning authority which did not always read well in his personal file. If he felt that a superior was on the wrong track he was inclined to say so without using the degree of tact necessary for a character who is going to make it to the top. An example was his brusque facing up to the ambassador on that first morning in Washington.

MacKenzie and his boss were sitting in the back of an official car taking them to the London hospital for one of his visits to David when the barriers really started to fall.

'Why all this? Why me?' Milner murmured, almost under his breath.

'Sir?' asked MacKenzie, judging whether a response was expected.

'I don't expect you to know the answer any more than anyone else does, MacKenzie. Thinking aloud, that's all.' Milner paused and looked at the other man, as if for the first time. 'You don't say much, do you?'

'No, sir,' said MacKenzie in his normal, clipped voice.

'You're thinking nevertheless. D'you know you're the only person who hasn't offered me any gushing condolences?'

'I watched how you reacted to getting them, sir. I didn't think it was my job. You can have them if you like, sir. I'd mean them,' MacKenzie volunteered.

'I appreciate that. Tell me. How do you cope with this sort of thing, MacKenzie?' Milner asked.

'What, sir?' MacKenzie was not sure what the ambassador was driving at.

'Having to live somebody else's life the whole time. Waiting up till I feel like going to bed, getting up when I feel like getting up, moving with me almost everywhere except when I go to the bathroom. Even then lurking outside the door.'

'Got used to it, sir. Done it for a long time now.' The reply was matter-of-fact.

'Don't you want to live your own life?' Milner was increasingly curious.

'I do get time off, sir. You know that.'

'I don't mean that. How long can you live like this?'

83

'It's a job that pays, sir.' MacKenzie shrugged. 'It's got its interesting moments. I meet some special people. I've always been interested in the United States but, apart from a couple of short visits when I was a student, I never got a chance to really live here.'

'I remember now. You got as far as the "Mastermind" finals . . . Not bad . . .'

'For a copper?' MacKenzie flashed a sudden half-smile.

'I didn't say that. But why, MacKenzie . . . ?'

'I see a lot of things. I hear a lot of things. As I said, I meet a lot of interesting people. Not many people have met princes and kings and secretaries of state and presidents. I've met a lot of them. Some of them even shake my hand; get to know my name. I prefer being called Andrew, by the way, sir.'

'Rude of me – Andrew. Old habits . . . Unthinking . . . So it's all reflected glory?'

'Call it that if you will. I'm thirty-eight. I've got a long time ahead of me. It pays well. I don't have any ties. Sure, it gets boring from time to time but I have my interests.'

'Interests?' Milner disguised what he realized was an absurd surprise.

'Policemen can have interests too, sir. Apart from American history . . . it's poetry, if you must know.'

'Poetry . . . I'll ask you more some time if we get a chance to know each other better.'

'There'll be time, sir. You don't know a thing about me. I know an awful lot about you.'

'I suppose you do.' Milner was taken aback at that all-too-obvious revelation. He suddenly realized how aloof he had been, that Andrew MacKenzie was in a position to understand a huge amount of what he had been doing and saying. Only the most confidential political or intelligence meetings at the embassy took place without his being present. There was very little he said or did without the other man observing it. MacKenzie was a shadow in all senses.

'Are you religious?' Milner suddenly asked.

'If you'd grown up in Glasgow, you'd know you have to be religious – one way or another, sir. Prod or Papist, it didn't much matter. You followed Rangers or you followed Celtic. Even the Paki shopkeepers had to side with one or the other.' MacKenzie laughed. 'It was all a bit primitive to me so, later, I stopped bothering. It was all part of my upbringing, I suppose. My father was in the HLI – the Highland Light Infantry . . . Met my mother after the war . . . left her . . . came back after several years away . . . married her . . . they had one child – me – then he left her again. Died several years ago. Saw him only once or twice. He ended up in an old people's home – Alzheimer's. Sad case. He hadn't a clue who I was by the end . . . A broken home makes you take things as they come. No, I'm not religious. I have my beliefs, but they aren't to do with the supernatural.'

'I suppose you've been interrogated by your superiors about the assassination attempt and what might lie behind it?'

'Sir.' This was more dangerous ground.

'Your theory?' asked Milner.

'I don't have theories, sir. I just report facts.'

'I don't think I believe you, Andrew.'

'Your prerogative.' MacKenzie shrugged.

'You're a difficult man to get to know.'

'That's what they say about you, sir, if you don't mind me saying so.' The statement was delivered in a matter-of-fact way.

'Defence mechanism?'

'Defence mechanism, sir.' MacKenzie nodded his agreement.

'Apart from "Mastermind", your CV told me one other thing: you've killed a man?'

'The job . . . sadly.'

'Are you going to tell me about it?'

'I don't usually, but the CV's got it wrong. I've actually killed twice. It's a terrible responsibility being judge and executioner. One . . . a drug dealer in Manchester . . . years ago. The other . . . sad, really. Deranged. Holding a woman and her kid hostage. We had to stop him. I was the chosen marksman.'

'You lost sleep?'

'If you take someone's life, you don't rest easily . . . at least for a while.'

They were approaching the hospital. Milner gave a slight shiver, then turned and looked straight at MacKenzie for the first time.

'That must be true,' he said quietly, then went on: 'I'm sorry I've ignored you, embarrassed that I know so little about you.'

'You've had other things on your mind.'

'Maybe . . . maybe we should talk more? Between ourselves, Andrew. I'd value that. But . . . if we did, I hope it wouldn't all go straight back to your superiors. Would you find that difficult?'

There was a long pause before MacKenzie answered. 'You asked me something like that early on, didn't you? I suppose I should say it would depend on the circumstances, sir. But if you ask me, then, yes, I will. I may be making a wrong decision but . . .' he hesitated '. . . you can rely on me.'

'Good,' said Milner, settling back in his seat. There was a silence, then a deep sigh. 'And now . . . David . . . Poor, poor boy. What have I done to my family?'

MacKenzie turned to look at his ambassador. Some emotional valve had suddenly been released. Tears were welling up and running down the hard but tired face of his superior. He reached out and put a comforting hand on the other man's shoulder. It was the natural thing to do.

MacKenzie positioned himself beside the young uniformed policeman who was on guard outside the door of the private ward. Sir Martin Milner went in alone to see his son. David, looking pale and drawn with his fair hair hanging in an unruly frond across his brow, was partly sitting up in bed, eyes closed, earphones on, listening to the radio. Sensing someone was there, he suddenly opened his eyes and saw his father.

'Oh, Dad . . .' he burst out, '. . . what has happened to us all?'

Milner came across to the bed and kissed his son lightly on the cheek.

'I'm so sorry for being the cause. You and now your poor mother.'

'You mustn't blame yourself, Dad.' David was crying. They were both crying.

'How can I help it? If it wasn't for me, none of this would have happened.'

'You don't know that. You know what Mum was like. Even I remember her flaring up and suggesting that life wasn't worth living.'

'That was a bad patch many years ago. You remember that still?'

'Of course I remember it. How could a child forget his mother saying something like that? And now it's happened.'

Milner pulled up a chair and sat close by his son's bed. They had never been a demonstrative family but now he took and held David's hand. They had had no physical contact for years but this was something they both needed now. 'How are you feeling? I've talked to your doctors. They are optimistic.'

'I've been lucky, I suppose. Lung is fine. They've drained it and it's going to be OK. My groin . . . well, the good news is that it probably won't affect the Milner dynasty. Reproductive bits will eventually get back into fine fettle . . . In fact, did you see that pretty, dark-haired nurse as you came in . . . ?' David smiled weakly, then closed his eyes. 'Still tired though . . . She'll have to wait,' he added.

Martin Milner smiled back and also waited.

'Then there's this.' David, eyes still shut, pointed to the large bandage covering the left side of his face. 'An almighty scar on my cheek . . . though I don't need a skin graft. Really spoilt my looks . . .'

'You'll be jumping around in no time.'

'I can't wait. The only thing is . . .' His son opened his eyes again and turned and looked at his father.

'What is it?'

'It's the fear. It's the fear of not knowing why . . . why it all happened. Maybe that's what drove Mum . . . That someone might try again . . . Does nobody . . . do you really not know?' David was almost pleading with his father.

'I really do not know.' Milner was firm.

'They let me see the newspapers now. I got some of the back ones that covered the shooting. I've read the editorials. Not one terrorist organization has claimed responsibility . . . The *Telegraph* said this was most unusual. They quoted security sources as saying they were totally baffled. Could it have been a random madman or was it a professional . . . ? Dad, tell me. Is there anything . . . anything? I need to know.'

Milner looked away for a moment. 'I promise, David, it's still a total mystery to me too. I keep coming back to whether it could have been some awful mistake, but the man called my name. Then . . .' Milner hesitated. 'Then there was the warning telephone call. Anonymous. I've thought that through a thousand times and it still doesn't add up.'

'What exactly was said?'

Milner recalled, with the greatest precision, the words that had been used.

'*Sir Martin Milner?*'

'*Who's speaking?*'

'*It's not necessary you should know.*'

'*I don't accept anonymous calls. I'm going to ring off.*'

'*You will listen when I tell you – this is a warning. I . . . we now know about you. We may hate you for it . . . But they . . . they are people who like to cut the strings. All the strings.*'

'Weird. A nutcase?'

'No. Not a nutcase.'

'Are you sure there's nobody you've offended in your past?'

'David . . . No . . .' Milner stared into the distance as he spoke, as if, for that moment, unwilling to catch his son's eye.

'There's something I want to tell you, Dad.' David was suddenly more alert.

'What?'

'The other day . . . I was doped to the gills. The pain had been bad again and they'd given me something to kill it. I was only half awake listening to some music on these headphones. Something made me open my eyes. There, standing beside the bed, was a young woman . . . about the same age as I am.'

'Nurse? Social worker?'

'I'm certain neither of those. I have my own social worker who keeps on telling me how to cope with life's problems, how everything's going to be all right. She's a nice soul, warm, comforting, motherly. And the nurses. Well, this woman wasn't in uniform or anything . . .'

'Somebody came into the wrong room, that's all.'

'That's not how it was. She was standing there looking at me. Half with it though I was, I have an image of a good-looking woman, fair-haired, dressed in a smart, dark coat.'

'I don't see . . .'

'The thing was, Dad, she was standing there . . . and she was crying. Tears were running down her face. She was crying so much. Then she said something.'

Milner waited in silence, watching David as, with an effort, he turned in his bed to look at him. He felt a sudden unease.

'She spoke through her tears. She said: "So sorry. I am so sorry." Then, without even wiping the tears that were drenching her face – I noticed some of them had fallen on her coat – she turned and left the room.'

'Stray visitor? Somebody upset by finding you lying here so badly injured.'

'You can see as well as I can, Dad. Above the blankets, apart from the bandage on my cheek, I look fine. There's nothing for a stranger to cry about, Dad. She couldn't see how badly I'd been hurt. She knew. There's no doubt . . .'

As they left the hospital, Milner shared this new information with MacKenzie.

His reaction was traditional. 'Bad security,' he muttered. 'There's meant to be a policeman outside the door all the time.'

'What are you going to do?' Milner asked, genuinely curious.

'Think about it, sir . . . Always do before acting. How's your son?'

'Waiting further tests.'

'You, sir. What are *you* going to do?' It was the first time MacKenzie had asked him a direct question.

'Seeing the Foreign Secretary this afternoon. Handing in my resignation. I can't go on. Not like this. It's not good for me, for David, for Britain.'

MacKenzie sat in silence until Milner felt himself forced to continue.

'I didn't have a reaction from you,' he said.

'Sir. You didn't ask for one.'

'I'm asking for one. You must be personally disappointed.'

'You'll guess what I think, sir. It's not for me to . . .'

'I want to know.'

'Then I'll have to break a habit and talk about myself first, sir. If you don't mind . . .'

'Go on,' Milner prompted.

'My father – I told you he was in the army – was posted overseas a lot. My mother brought me up on her own. She was OK but we didn't really get on.'

'Brothers and sisters . . . ?'

'No . . . not exactly, sir. But the point of this is that when I fell in love, it was something very special in my life. For the first time I felt part of someone. That I belonged . . .'

Milner waited in silence. It was not the reaction he had expected. He wondered where it was all leading.

'We married . . . She was called Veronica . . . We were . . .' MacKenzie paused. 'I'm only telling you this so that you'll understand that I understand . . . Married for seven months. She was pregnant. Then . . . a car crash late at night, on the A9 coming back from seeing friends in Inverness. I'd had a drink or three, so she drove. We overturned. I walked out without a scratch. She was killed instantly. She was driving but . . . but, in a way, I killed her. It was my fault.'

'How long ago?'

'Ten . . . almost eleven years.'

'You can't blame yourself, Andrew. It wasn't . . .' Milner paused, suddenly realizing what he was saying. Then he nodded gently. It was a sad, clever lesson.

A little later, MacKenzie broke the silence. 'So . . . sir: you asked me a straight question, so I'll answer it. You're not going to do anybody any good if you give up.'

'That's what David said. That's what Mark Ivor said.'

'I look forward to meeting your David,' volunteered MacKenzie.

'You might just get on,' responded Milner thoughtfully.

Their conversation had continued in the back of the chauffeur-driven car on their way to the Foreign Office, where he was to wait until the time of his meeting with the Secretary of State.

When he arrived, a secretary greeted him. 'Urgent . . . From Number Ten. The Prime Minister wants to talk to you.'

'Right now?'

'I've to get them on the line.'

Milner shut himself into the office he'd been allocated. MacKenzie waited on a chair outside.

The internal phone rang almost immediately and the Prime Minister's Private Secretary was talking. 'If you could hold for a moment, Sir Martin, the Prime Minister will be with you.'

'Thank you.'

There was a delay of about a minute, then the familiar voice came on.

'Martin, once again . . . how deeply sorry I am about all . . .'

'Thank you, Prime Minister,' said Milner. 'If you don't mind, can we keep this very formal? I might just break . . .'

'Of course . . .' There was a brief pause. 'I've been talking to Trafford Leigh and my other colleagues. We'll quite understand now if you wish to resign. It's all been a hideous shock. Maybe we were wrong to have persuaded you to go to Washington so soon after the shooting. We blame ourselves.'

'No need to do that, Prime Minister.'

'As I say, Martin, you must feel yourself free.' Michael Wilson showed unusual reticence, as he waited for the diplomat's response.

It came with a surprising degree of determination. 'If you don't mind, Prime Minister, I very much want to go back. I have a job to do.'

7

Flying back to Washington that following Sunday, he read the anonymous half-page profile of himself in the *Sunday Times*. He guessed that Mark Ivor might be the generous source of some of the quotes. It was his style. It began along predictable lines and then went on:

> *What drives a man like Sir Martin Milner? After all the personal tragedies that have been heaped on him over recent months, plus the continuing uncertainty and suspicions over the reasons for the attack on his son, he has insisted on going back to resume his duties as British Ambassador to Washington. While people can sympathize with his personal predicament the question has to be faced whether he is still the right man for the job at this critical time. It must not be forgotten, in the welter of speculation that has surrounded his private life, that there was considerable annoyance in American governmental circles over his speech to the Press Club. Does Britain need someone who seems, for whatever reason, accident-prone, representing our interests with the American administration? The answer, according to his close colleagues and senior government sources, is a resounding yes. Sir Martin Milner is widely perceived to be the very best possible candidate for the job. The suggestion that Mr Vincent, the former Party Chairman, might be a better replacement, politician talking to politician, has found little favour: a highly*

professional diplomat, with all the skills and expert-
ise of his calling, is required. It is also recognized in
Whitehall that the American Administration would
prefer to continue to deal with Sir Martin Milner, if
only to avoid any suggestion that it was using his
personal tragedies as a reason to be rid of him. Senior
government sources also suggest that the President
of the United States said as much in a short telephone
conversation with the Prime Minister in the middle
of last week . . .

Milner laid the *Sunday Times* article to one side. The rest of it continued in a similar vein. He could not complain, as it ended up fully supportive of his decision to return, noting, in passing, that David had expressed his intention of joining him at the earliest possible moment. Similarly favourable comments were reflected in the other Sunday papers, though the *Mail on Sunday* questioned, in a lead editorial full of sporting metaphors, whether someone with so many personal handicaps could possibly keep his eye on the ball on such a tricky wicket. The *News of the World* had a ridiculous 'exclusive', quoting a woman who claimed she had once known him, under a headline which read: 'My Sex Frolics with Our Man in Washington'. The accompanying photograph showed an ageing lady whom he failed to recognize. Then he saw the name. Twenty years ago . . . one night . . . somewhere in Eastern Europe. Not much of a story. He tossed the paper aside.

At the bottom of the pile was *Private Eye*. Somebody in Heads of Mission Section had flagged up an item that ran under the 'Street of Shame' section. It suggested that the *Telegraph* had been about to run a story about him being interrogated by MI6, and that the paper had suppressed it because of pressure from the government. The item – it was only a few lines long – ended up with the question: 'If there really is nothing to hide, why was the government so keen to suppress the *Telegraph* article?'

94

They were flailing around; in his jumbled thoughts, he was acting no better than they were. He shut his eyes, resting his head on the back of the airline seat. He would sleep for a while. As his mind began to drift into something approaching peace he again went over the uneasy interview he had had a few days earlier with the head of MI6 at their palatial headquarters at the south end of Vauxhall Bridge. It had not surprised him in the least to see a totally unembarrassed Charles Nairn, his Washington Head of Station, leaving the Chief's room as he was shown in. Members of that service always did their own thing and were certainly not fully responsible to mere ambassadors.

The two met alone. He had come across the man who was still, in this age of open government, known as 'C' once or twice in the past and had respect for him. For the first few moments the spy chief waltzed round the subject, then he homed in. 'The first time in my professional career I've drawn a total blank, Martin.' He stared at his visitor across a highly polished desk that was free of any papers whatsoever.

'We all have our frustrations.'

'We've got to get to the bottom of this. The Prime Minister will not have an unexplained attack on his most senior ambassador. That or my head on the block.'

'That is your problem,' said Milner quietly. 'I cannot help further.'

'Your problem, too.' 'C' began to show a glint of steel.

'I recognize . . .'

'You were the target. Yet no terrorist organization has claimed responsibility. They always do. That's in the nature of terrorism.'

'It has to be mistaken identity,' Milner said, for the hundredth time.

'You know that's nonsense. They called your name. Something, somewhere in your past must have triggered this action. You have given us – you say – a list of anyone who might, at any time for any reason, no matter how trivial, have felt aggrieved by your activities, within or without the service. We have been through every inch of your career. None of these suggests anything of any significance. You agree?'

'For the umpteenth time, yes. I agree,' said Milner wearily. 'Why do you keep going on?'

'That is in the nature of our business. We go on and on and on. If we let go, we lose. There has to be a reason,' 'C' repeated.

'Then it has to have been some madman.'

'That neither of us believes. I'm going to talk you through it all again slowly and carefully.'

'At least spare me the apologies,' said Milner curtly. 'Get on with it.'

'So ... What if the key lies in your Norway posting? Thirty years ago ...'

As he began to drift towards sleep, soothed by the silence of the flight, Milner again questioned whether, like someone who has been abused as a child, he had put some part of that incident into the deepest recesses of his mind. How could he unwittingly have caused such a deep-seated hatred? Yes, the Norway business had been unpleasant at the time, but it was far, far too long ago. If someone felt hurt, it would have surfaced decades ago. He had, more recently, been involved in many tricky diplomatic negotiations in the Middle East, in southern Africa, in Bosnia. There were countless, anonymous people out there somewhere who might, if they were to know what he had done, have felt that he could have acted more expeditiously or efficiently in bringing some crisis or conflict to an end. A few hundred, a few thousand people might, had he behaved otherwise, have lived when they had died. But he was a cog in all that. He could not be held personally responsible. He had been a mere adviser to ministers, to the peace-makers in Washington, Pretoria, Tel Aviv, or as an observer at Dayton, Ohio when they had eventually propelled the Serbs, Bosnians and Croats towards an unwilling peace. One task of many; there were dozens of others stretching back to his first posting ... The head of MI6 had concentrated on that.

Yes, he remembered Oslo. His posting, in January 1966, was

to that snowbound capital, to a warm little house on the hillside overlooking the fjord. He had been surprised at being sent to Norway. He had, somehow, expected something more exotic: Singapore, Bangkok or some sweat hole in South America, or, perhaps, to be posted to learn Arabic, Chinese or Japanese. Oslo had been pleasant enough, comfortable, friendly, unexciting. As he drifted half in and half out of sleep, he thought of all it had meant to him. He had told them again and again. Beyond what they knew already, there was nothing more. What they already knew ... What they had always known ... That last thought drifted out of his mind as he fell into dreamless sleep. He awoke only when the plane began its descent into Dulles Airport.

Shortly after arriving back at the residence, MacKenzie marched into his study unannounced.

'What is it?' asked Milner.

'My US Secret Service contacts tell me – I don't know if you've realized, but they've been keeping an eye on us – that somebody else may have been trying to tail you. It could have a fairly innocent explanation. As soon as they tried to approach the car in question it made off and they lost it.'

'I'm still at risk? Without knowing why? Is that what you're telling me?'

'Just a possibility, sir.'

Top Secret and Personal Memorandum
TO: *The Secretary to the Cabinet*
FROM: *Chief of MI6*

1. Personal interrogation of ambassador produced no results. He is either a very good actor or genuinely knows nothing. MacKenzie (personal protection officer, inspector rank) was tasked to see if he could extract anything further but he too has drawn a blank. We have to watch that particular source, given the traditional bonding that tends to build between

principals and their minders. It is not that we don't trust MacKenzie; we have to watch he doesn't go 'native'.

2. The CIA/FBI report from Washington of possible third-party surveillance of the ambassador is worrying. On the other hand, it may offer the chance we've been waiting for.

3. Item of communications intelligence: a chance telephone intercept from an unknown speaker in Oslo to another in London may, repeat may, have some significance. We are still analysing the exchange with the help of a Norwegian linguist. Will report urgently on this since it could reinforce one earlier course of enquiries.

The message inviting the ambassador to pay his formal call on the President of the United States of America arrived by special messenger the next morning. It was couched in formal language, but an informal telephone call from the Deputy Chief of Staff at the White House said that the ambassador would be seen as soon as practicable. Follow-up messages between the White House secretariat and Paul Fawcett eventually fixed the meeting for the following Thursday.

When the ambassador arrived in the huge stretch limousine sent by the White House, as was the practice on such occasions, the White House's press corps moved out in force to greet him. He recognized some of the British contingent but had agreed with the President's Press Secretary not to react to any of the many questions called out to him from the press stand as he entered the White House itself.

At the main door under the portico, the Deputy Chief of Staff to the President and a smartly uniformed military attaché were waiting to greet the ambassador, who was accompanied only by David Velcor, the military attaché, and Paul Fawcett. Both sides had agreed to keep protocol to a minimum instead of going through the normal practice whereby a new ambassador presents his credentials and the letters of recall of his predecessor, accompanied by a much larger retinue of members of embassy staff. This was not an occasion for many diplomatic niceties.

Milner had been to the White House many years ago in a much more junior capacity. Arriving again that day he marvelled at the bustling atmosphere but remembered what a modest building it was, compared even with his own residence. He recalled too, that far from being venerable, it had been almost totally rebuilt in Truman's time in the late fifties. That day he was led, not to any of the major state rooms through which the tourists perpetually thronged, but along a portrait-hung corridor to the west wing where the Oval Office is tucked out of sight from public view behind a barrier of sniper-defying trees.

The Secretary of State met him at the door of the Oval Office.

'Good to see you again, Mr Ambassador . . . Martin . . . We're all very sorry . . . Please accept, on behalf of us all at the State Department, our deepest condolences.' Antonio Delgadi's normally cheerful face was creased with concern.

'Thank you very much, Secretary of State. I . . .'

'We should go straight in.' Delgadi interrupted him. That little formality of regret was past and there was work to do. 'He's on a heavy schedule. The White House press corps are waiting to take some pictures. I hope you were expecting that.'

'Yes, Secretary of State. Thank you.' As Milner walked in to the famous room to be greeted by the President, the latter stood up from behind his desk, came across and shook his hand warmly. For the first few minutes of the call, the two men posed together in front of the Oval Office fireplace while twenty or thirty British and American press and camera teams jostled for position. Given the circumstances the smiles were few, but the warm handshakes were repeated for the media's benefit. Such a meeting not only had to take place, it had to be seen to take place. Eventually the two men sat down. The Secretary of State sat to one side of the President; the ambassador sat opposite. A press secretary shepherded the media from the room and the President and his handful of staffers were left alone with the ambassador and his colleagues.

'You come at a difficult time, Mr Ambassador. Difficult time,' the President repeated.

'Indeed, Mr President. I'm here to help improve them in any way I can. I had a very constructive talk with Mr Delgadi the other day . . .'

'I heard . . .' The President's voice was clipped and he looked distracted. Milner could hardly blame him. A protocol call by a new British Ambassador was hardly a key event in the life of a man who had to govern the United States of America.

'We have a number of tricky items on the agenda, Mr President. The question of the continuing deployment of US troops in the former Yugoslavia . . .'

'. . . will again have to be a matter for the Europeans in future,' interrupted the President dryly. He was obviously bored by the way the conversation was going and the ambassador noticed him glancing down surreptitiously at his watch. He guessed he'd be allowed twenty minutes maximum.

'Her Majesty's Government is most appreciative of the support you've been giving the British and Irish governments over your continued economic support in cementing the Northern Ireland solution.' Milner was working his way through the mental list of topics he hoped to raise.

'Glad we could be of help there. The Irish-American lobby is, by and large and excepting one or two extremists, going along all the way with us. One unhappy chapter out of the way at last . . .' The President allowed himself a brief smile.

'Most grateful . . .'

'Let's get down to the wire, Sir Martin.' The tone of his voice had hardened appreciably. 'I was particularly unimpressed by your speech the other week. I know you personally have been dealing with a lot of strain, but to me it looked like a . . . challenge?'

'It was meant to be a statement of the current situation, Mr President,' said Milner firmly.

'Not the way our press took it. And it definitely fuelled up your yellow press, who are becoming more and more anti-American by the day. The reports I get from the US Embassy in London . . .'

'You know too well, Mr President, that the British Government are not responsible for the eccentricities of the British media,' Milner dared to break in.

'I know that as well as the next man. But you have ways of putting on pressure. Newspaper owners are interested in your historic system of honours?' There was almost a sneer in the President's voice.

The exchange between the two men, with the others listening and taking notes, continued in like fashion for several more minutes. Most of the expected ground was covered. Then the President turned to the Secretary of State and said: 'Say you guys, I want to add something strictly off-the-record to this . . . Why don't you leave Sir Martin and me alone? We should have a few minutes heart-to-heart.' The Secretary of State looked apprehensively at the President then shrugged and stood up. He, David Velcor and the others quickly left the room and the two men sat in silence on each side of the fireplace, until they were on their own.

'An honour having this opportunity to talk to you directly, Mr President.' Milner opted for a formal opening.

'No bullshit, Martin . . . I'll cut the "sir", if you don't object . . . I hear good things about you. You've had a pretty horrific time. I'm very sorry. But we've both got a job to do. I have to tell you: Britain comes a long way down on my list of priorities right now. Like I said, I don't like the way things are going. And I didn't like the tone of your speech. We don't like being lectured to. And to top it off, I hear that you've been moseying around asking everyone, including Antonio, why the hell I'm so anti-British. Well, there're a pack of reasons for that and you might as well hear them straight from me so you don't need to speculate anymore. I find you guys pretentious, living in the past, riddled with class distinction and, above all, thinking you know more about the big wide world than the rest of us. That may have been the case . . . once. It sure isn't now. People say I'm anti-Brit. I'm not anti-Brit, I'm just anti the British attitude to international affairs. Dean Acheson, our former Secretary of State, once said that you were a damned toothless bulldog: you'd lost an empire and had yet to find a role. In my book that's still the case, Martin.'

'May I . . . ?' Milner dared to interrupt.

'What is it?'

'May I ask, Mr President, what triggered it off?'

'It needs something to trigger something off?'

'Gut feeling . . . yes, Mr President. Something somewhere in the make-up of each one of us sets us on a path with attitudes about a whole raft of different things in this life. I wondered what it was with you.'

This conversation was either going places or he was about to be thrown out on his ear.

'Blunt question, Martin.'

'I felt I must . . .'

'Now that you ask me . . . I'm not sure. I've read reports that I'd been snubbed when I was a Junior Senator when I went to London. Well, if I was, I've forgotten all about that.' The President gave a short bark of laughter. 'There're lots of other things. My Mom – though, as the media will have told you, I don't have much time for her either – was once messed around by some upper-class twit. That set me thinking.'

'One man's bad behaviour doesn't mark down a nation,' Milner interjected.

'Depending on how we get on maybe one day I'll think it through, talk to my shrink and tell you.' The President smiled mirthlessly, and they turned to talk of other matters for a while. Then, at the end of the visit, the President suddenly stood up and said: 'For the meantime, let me spell it out: I don't like current British attitudes; you're not big enough in my book. But if you behave, we can live together quietly enough. Is that crystal-clear, Martin?' The President did not even look at him as Milner silently nodded his head.

*　　*　　*

Outside, on the White House lawn, His Excellency Sir Martin Milner was accosted by a group of mainly British journalists. His Press Counsellor from the embassy was there too to make sure things did not get out of hand.

'How was it with the President?' shouted one correspondent above the general noise.

'Did you get to grips with the President's anti-British feeling, Sir Martin?' asked another.

'Mr Ambassador, may we have an interview?' requested the man from the BBC.

'What did the President say about the US troop withdrawals . . . ? On the riots in Moscow; did . . .' There was another shout as cameras flashed in the background.

'Mr Ambassador, did the subject of your . . . your son's shooting come up?'

Milner waved the group to silence, then read from a carefully prepared statement he had worked on earlier with his Press Counsellor. It was deliberately empty and downbeat. Today, boredom would rule.

> 'I was happy to have the opportunity to meet with the President today to discuss subjects of common interest. The meeting passed in the most constructive and useful way. We covered many of the difficulties as well as the solutions we see to existing Anglo-American problems. I am delighted to be here in Washington and am glad to have established such a good working relationship both with the President and with the Secretary of State. Thank you very much indeed, ladies and gentlemen. That is all.'

'Shit, Ambassador, didn't you even . . . ?' yelled one American journalist.

'But, Ambassador . . . hey Sir Martin . . . don't give us that crap,' shouted another.

Leaving the Press Counsellor to fend off the mob, Milner turned and walked towards the Rolls-Royce with the pressmen calling angrily after him. He knew he would have to butter them up with an off-the-record chat and a drink later. As he walked away, he saw the ITN correspondent, Clive Crick, turning to the camera with his prepared comments. He could have written them himself.

'Britain's new Ambassador, Sir Martin Milner, freshly returned from attending the funeral of his wife in London, paid his first courtesy call on the President of the United States at the White House today, Thursday. After the meeting both he and the White House press spokesman made anodyne statements about the nature of Anglo–American relations. But nobody is deceived. Everyone knows that the tensions under the surface are considerable and in some quarters vast. No amount of papering over the cracks by Sir Martin and his officials, nor indeed by the White House Press Office, can disguise this fact. Things have come to a very sorry pass. And the fact that this British Ambassador has returned to Washington with a whole host of terrible personal problems hanging over him, can hardly bode well for the future. This is Clive Crick at the White House, Washington, returning you to the studios of ITN in London.'

Top Secret and Personal Telegram
TO: The Secretary of State for Foreign and Commonwealth Affairs
FROM: British Ambassador, Washington
For Your Eyes Only.
Immediate. *Desks by 0800 hours GMT.*

1. I had my first meeting with the President this afternoon. It started off in friendly mode: we went over the familiar ground. He was in good humour. After some time, to their surprise, he asked the Secretary

of State and his and my staff to withdraw and we had a one-on-one meeting in the Oval Office for some twenty-five minutes. I was unable to take notes. He gave me his line on his anti-British stance. It was compelling stuff but I am not convinced. The real reasons are yet to emerge.

2. He questioned me very closely about the attack on David, and wondered whether it was some group opposed to my representing the UK in the United States. I assured him that no one, repeat no one believed this. He has arranged with his nominated CIA representative and members of the National Security Council to meet with whomever you deem it right to send here, to discuss ongoing security arrangements for my continued presence in Washington.

3. I must make it clear to you and to the PM that I do not wish security considerations to overshadow the many other problems that exist in Anglo–American relations. Grateful however if the President's wishes could be met.

4. The President said he was much looking forward to the Prime Minister's visit to Washington next month. You and the Prime Minister must be under no illusions that this will be an extremely difficult visit. No amount of window-dressing is going to disguise the undertone of distrust. It is for consideration whether the meeting itself should not be postponed until a more opportune moment . . .

The reply from London was sharp and swift. The Prime Minister's planned visit to Washington was to go ahead on the agreed dates.

Diplomacy is not a one-way business. For every British Embassy abroad there is a foreign embassy in London, their ambassadors accredited, under ancient tradition, to the Court of St James's, their diplomats reporting on bilateral relations in a way, with a style, and with a priority that can match badly with the elegant and well-considered telegrams from British missions overseas. Thus are international affairs tempered by the eye of the beholder.

One of the other less known British traditions is that certain of the oldest and most distinguished London men's clubs discreetly offer honorary membership to some resident ambassadors. Some of them, the Athenaeum, the Travellers, the Reform, have a great history of political influence and intrigue; the Garrick does not, being for members of more rakish persuasion, from the arts, letters and the law. The Garrick is truly exclusive, with a genuine waiting list: it takes up to nine years to reach the top. Which is why the cream of British and foreign diplomats meet and mingle there. No papers or discussion of business is allowed at the Garrick; the rule is strictly enforced. This is why a huge amount of business and diplomacy is done there in the best way – where nothing is seen.

While a grand old actor held court at the members' central table there were many eyes which recorded the fact that Dr Mark Ivor and His Excellency, the Honourable Hiram K. Suskind, American Ambassador to the Court of St James's, dined at a side table in the coffee room one Wednesday evening. Ivor was there to measure the abilities and tap the influence of the ambassador. Mr Suskind was there, as he said, to dipstick Dr Ivor's position in British political life, and to cull what he could from the evening's gossip.

It was an amusing dinner. The two men hit it off. Both admitted the failings and weaknesses of their respective governments in matching the challenges of East European anarchy. Both marked the other's card over the realities of Anglo–American relations. They agreed to meet again.

At the end of the dinner, over glasses of Garrick Club port, they concurred in the view that Mr Suskind had an easier task in London than Sir Martin Milner had in Washington.

'I saw the lunchtime ITN report. Crazy and unfair . . . Nobody's shot me up. Nobody's maimed my child,' said the American Ambassador almost angrily. He was not making light of his remark.

'Martin Milner is an old friend,' volunteered Ivor.

'I know. He told me. In fact my guess is . . . no, don't confirm or deny . . . that you pushed for him to get the job in the first place. He's a dry stick, Milner . . . not a bunch of laughs . . . but we had an agreeable lunch, before he went out . . .'

'He can't read your President,' cued Ivor.

'So what's new . . . ? I can't read my President. What's Milner's problem? He may have a hard task. What about me? Do my reports, if they even begin to say nice things about the British Government, get a sympathetic hearing in the White House? No pennies for your answer.'

'Martin's worried about his reporting not matching yours.'

'Tell him not to. I'm on the end of the line any time he wants to ring and confer. If he or I report different from the other, the President isn't going to give me a Congressional Medal for honesty.'

'Can I help?'

'Yeah. Just feed Martin Milner what I said, will you. I guess you would have anyway.' Hiram Suskind stared hard at the spin doctor to make sure he had got the message.

A few hours later, His Excellency, Sir Martin Milner, KCMG, Her Britannic Majesty's Ambassador at Washington, gave in to temptation. Who could blame him after all that had happened? He needed comfort. He needed reassurance. He needed the soft, gentle embrace that Lucinda Forbes-Manning, discreet, well-bred, able and all too willing, at last could offer him. It happened as it had nearly happened on their first working evening together. They had again worked late in the ambassador's study, dealing with the mound of invitations and social engagements that had piled up waiting for him while he had been away. On top of all the tragedies, he found it unusually difficult these days to cope with the minor details of diplomatic life, though the major problems of state still had his fullest attention. That was where Lucinda came in, knowing she had to make him buckle down to get the protocol elements in hand as well.

They had finished talking about the arrangements for a visiting parliamentary select committee delegation which was coming to review aspects of American agricultural policy. Milner had sighed at the news as any British diplomat anywhere in the world sighs when he hears about a delegation of British MPs coming out on any fact-finding mission. There is a special reaction in the British diplomatic system, a certain bleak realization that here come the second-rate, a free-loading bunch who demand drinks, hospitality and nannying and, in return, deliver well above a fair proportion of complaints.

This time there were six MPs representing the major parties. Milner remembered the leader of the delegation.

'Mycroft bores for Britain,' he said cynically.

'We had him out here once before, sir. I remember him. He fell asleep before the pudding was served.' Lucinda smiled sweetly.

'The others?' he asked, wondering what other horrors were in the gossip.

'I heard of only one of them. We'll manage to cope, sir. The Agricultural Attaché and the Economic Minister will take on most of the chores. All you'll have to do is throw one reception for them. Not too much of a burden, I hope.' Again Lucinda smiled a warm, reassuring smile. Everything would be well in her capable hands.

Later, when they had finished their work, she poured him his second generous whisky. It was about then that they looked at each other as, stifling a yawn, he muttered: 'I must be getting upstairs.'

'So you must. You look dead beat. Would you like me to run you a bath or something?' She smiled, this time more demurely. It fooled neither of them.

'What a good idea,' he said, his normal instincts of self-control and self-preservation for the moment abandoning him.

Who could blame him for what happened next? 'Yes,' he then said, he would welcome yet another drink brought up to his bedroom. Why not fix another one for herself as well? They could watch the late-night television news together while he relaxed.

From then on it was inevitable. He had already changed into a towelling dressing gown when she reappeared, a glass in each hand. 'I've taken you at your word. I have run you a bath.' She stood there, watching and waiting.

'Are we playing a dangerous game?' he asked.

'Dangerous?' she smiled again, then came slowly towards him. He moved to meet her and somehow his bathrobe undraped itself, she, still dressed, he, fully exposed in the dim light in the bedroom.

'Don't worry,' she whispered. 'I'll still call you sir in the morning. Now what you really need to do is to relax.'

8

As he dressed for the black-tie embassy reception he was hosting that late-September evening, he thought back over the events of the last few months since his return to Washington. Much of it stood in such sharp relief. Much had been eventful, even enjoyable; much was pure misery. Like the nightmare of his wife's funeral these four months ago. That hellish event had been over in half an hour. Sheila, his sister-in-law, and her family, had barely spoken to him. He had had to sit alone throughout the short service. David had been still too weak to attend. Dr Mark Ivor had sat with Andrew MacKenzie at the back. No one had wanted it to last a moment longer than it needed; when someone commits suicide it does not seem proper to have hymns and orations. The chaplain had done his best; his words had brought tears to most eyes in the small crematorium chapel. There had been no socializing afterwards. A number of his closer colleagues from the office and their wives, there out of uncomfortable duty, shook his hand sombrely. No one knew what to say to him about the end of a life that could have been otherwise.

Martin Milner selected a black bow tie from the rack in his wardrobe and tied it in front of a mirror. He could not have insisted on returning to Washington and then refuse to participate in the social entertaining that was part and parcel of it. He had opted for small dinner parties over the last months. This was one of his first big receptions, which was probably why he now thought of Annabel. She had been good at co-hosting such things. He hated them. Yet such entertaining was a key part of the business of diplomacy. It provided the grease; it was the fulcrum around which so much diplomatic activity revolved. It was not just about eating, drinking and getting fat. It was about meeting people in less formal surroundings. It was about thanking people who helped the embassy in its work, and it was about showing the flag. It was about picking up hot gossip. It was about making contacts. It gave his junior staff a chance to meet Washington's great and good, which they would not otherwise do outwith the doors of the residence. Even HM Treasury thought entertaining was worthwhile. Yes, he hated them.

In this as in many things he was greatly helped by Lucinda Forbes-Manning. After their first night of love-making it had happened only once or twice more before they reverted to their previous workmanlike relationship. Not that anything had gone wrong, nor that they had quarrelled; it was simply that neither of them had got enough out of the affair. Instead they reached a largely unspoken agreement that, rather than spoil their amicable working partnership, they would cool it on the physical front.

As host, he stood by the door, while the residence steward, assisted by Paul Fawcett, announced the guests. Lucinda hovered in the background, prompting them all by putting names to faces and sorting out who was who from her list of guests. He knew a few of them and had studied her list with care, but many of the men and most of the women were still unfamiliar. David Velcor, who stood beside him in the receiving line, was at his most useful, whispering odd pieces of information and gossip as the guests came up one by one to shake hands, exchange a few words, then file past him into the reception rooms. Senators, politicians of all hues, editors, journalists, lobbyists, all the good and the not so good of Anglo–American society. They tended to be warm and friendly. They offered words of encouragement as they greeted him and moved on into the ever more crowded rooms and the terrace beyond. He played the game well. He knew how to shake hands and move people on without being too dismissive, talking to those who were important to talk to, muttering a few platitudinous words to those who could be followed up later. In the background, Lucinda also supervised the residence staff, ensuring that drinks were being properly served, that no one was left alone and unattended. It was a good home team; he was proud of his embassy.

Preceded by a team of Secret Service men, the Vice-President, a well-bred, well-mannered, empty suit of a man, arrived with his wife. In Anglo–American relations, that was a positive sign. Then the Secretary of State, Antonio Delgadi, also arrived. Things were looking up. Milner knew that there was no need for these two important American figures to come to a routine embassy reception; it was pleasing to him and threw out a marker to those journalists present, that all was not downside in Anglo–American relations. Tonight the Administration was deliberately hoisting positive signals.

While these two important men were present, Milner had to give them his full attention, but after their departure he went back to pick up on some late arrivals. One couple in particular he had spotted standing by themselves at the long french windows by the terrace.

'Who're they?' he whispered to Lucinda.

'Sir?'

'Couple over there. Man with the beard and the woman with red hair.'

'Caught me out, sir, I'll find out.' Flustered, she disappeared for a few moments and then returned. 'That's Mark Van der Dring. Something to do with the Metropolitan Opera. One of the cultural attaché's names on your guest list. The woman's his partner. They live in Georgetown. I'll wheel them over . . .'

'Don't worry, I'll drift their way later.' Milner moved away, mind on other things, until, towards the end, when most of the guests had departed, he spotted Mark Van der Dring and his flame-haired partner also making to leave. As the woman turned towards him, he extended his hand.

'Hello. Martin Milner. Sorry to have missed you when you came in. I was stuck with the Secretary of State.' He smiled.

'Delighted to be here, Mr Ambassador,' said Van der Dring, introducing himself. 'Meet Flora Simons.'

Milner and the red-haired woman shook hands. 'I live in your house, Mr Ambassador,' she began, looking at him intently. The remark was as unexpected as it was inexplicable. 'You should come visit me.'

'I'm sorry . . .'

'The house you used to live in in Georgetown. I live there.'

She had surprised him. Now it was his turn. 'Then you're a painter.'

'God. How d'you know that?' She flashed a fresh, open look of mock astonishment.

'Through the window . . . I saw you painting. Early one morning, several months ago. When I first arrived. I remember the morning too well: I'd just escaped from my minder.' She unsettled him somehow and his words came in staccato form.

'You came past my house in Georgetown?'

'We were all very fond of that house. Especially my son, David. He's the one who . . . you've probably heard. He was still quite young and cried a lot when we left, because it was his home. That's the trouble with the diplomatic service. You can never throw down roots without getting hurt.' Why was he suddenly confessing so much?

'I can understand,' said Flora Simons. She spoke softly, sounding as if she meant it.

'It was one of the happiest times . . .' Milner was silent for a moment. It was true what he said.

'Your son's coming out to join you I hear . . .' she prompted.

Milner and Flora Simons were talking one to one. Mark Van der Dring had drifted away to talk to another guest.

'You must come round to visit . . . if you've time in your busy schedule.' It was no empty invitation.

'I'll find time,' he said, surprised by the determination in his own voice.

'I'd hate your job. A lovely residence, this.' She gestured with a hand free of rings. 'Lutyens . . . all this beautiful furniture . . . and the paintings . . . It must be a great privilege living here, I suppose, but, as you say, it's all so transitory . . .'

'I haven't had much time to think about it recently . . .' He looked at her, increasingly aware of what a handsome woman she was. Fine cheekbones with that soft complexion that goes with red hair. She stood tall, well dressed in a shade of green that showed her colouring to perfection. As he glanced down he again noticed her hands, strong, almost masculine hands, well cared for, unlike those of so many professional artists he had known, who seemed to think that personal care for clothes and body was beneath their artistic remit.

He spoke to her for a little too long, aware that Lucinda and Paul Fawcett were hovering in the background, urging him to bring the party to an end. His questions were angled at finding out more about her and what her relationship was with Mark Van der Dring, but the answers eluded him.

Lucinda Forbes-Manning coughed impatiently in the background.

'I'm sorry, I must go and say goodbyes to my other guests or I'll get into a terrible trouble.' He smiled. 'That's the inconvenience with this job. Protocol rules.'

He held out his hand and they shook hands again, holding on to each other a fraction longer and with a touch more feeling than would have been normal.

'Do come. I insist.' She smiled back at him.

'That I do promise,' he said decisively.

The next day he flew to New York for a long-delayed familiarization meeting with the Consul General and with the staff of the British Trade Development Office there, for both of whose offices and work he was ultimately responsible. He took the early-morning shuttle to La Guardia accompanied, as he was everywhere, by Fawcett and MacKenzie. He chose a window seat with Fawcett beside him, while MacKenzie sat in the row behind. In a way he would rather have sat with MacKenzie, since he found the Scot's dour conversational style and unexpected insights into American life stimulating, while Fawcett, quite correctly, constantly bombarded him with the minutiae of the programme that lay ahead of him. But even though he was the ambassador, such a small change in seating would have been impossible; Fawcett would have been deeply hurt by being relegated to a less important position. He knew too that he would have to watch his relationship with Andrew MacKenzie. He had seen it happen in the past: VIPs and their bodyguards bonding together for no more reason than that they spent so much time in each other's company. After a while he turned his face away from the young diplomat and pretended to sleep, but instead stared out of the window through half-closed eyes.

He had read Paul Fawcett's likely reactions better than he might have guessed. Fawcett, plump-jowled, intelligent, ambitious but deeply insecure, was increasingly irritated by the contact and access that the policeman, MacKenzie, had to his boss. Fawcett could put up with the female private secretaries, Victoria Dobbs, Lucinda Forbes-Manning and the others, but he saw MacKenzie increasingly as a barrier, not so much by what he said – and the policeman had been cautious never again to reveal the extent of his knowledge of things American to a wider audience – but because he was always there. He was constantly overhearing everything that Fawcett and others in the embassy felt should be confined to senior diplomats alone.

There was nothing tangible that Fawcett, David Velcor, or on increasing occasions Charles Nairn himself, could put their fingers on as to why MacKenzie unsettled them. They all recognized that the policeman had a different agenda from the rest of them. He was always courteous; he avoided gossip and small-talk; he socialized, but not too much. It was probably because he was always so alert and watchful, as if waiting for something unforeseen to happen, a sort of angel of death. Fawcett had joked unsatisfactorily about him on one occasion to his erstwhile friend, Janice Yates, the Embassy's Political First Secretary. She, in turn, while she had not quite forgiven MacKenzie for providing the ambassador with information about a Junior Senator that she herself had not known, had gradually managed to bury such feelings, not least because she found MacKenzie quite attractive. He had been more than passingly nice to her when she stood alone and something of a wallflower at an embassy party. Later, they had danced a little, much to Fawcett's malicious behind-the-hand amusement over a diplomat cavorting with somebody from 'below stairs'. Away from the embassy something indeed developed out of their meeting, though the social niceties and a great deal of caution on their parts ensured that this fact was not shared with the outside world and especially with Fawcett, who was known as the pre-eminent embassy gossip.

Meanwhile, Fawcett, ignored by his boss, whom he guessed was deliberately turning his back on him, brooded at the little injustices of his life, the fact that he had too much work, that he had a hangover once again, that he could do with more sex, that he would far rather stay on in Washington and pursue the rather dull but willing girl from the Spanish Embassy he had started dating, than twirl around after the ambassador to New York, a city whose strident intensity he greatly disliked.

It was a clear, cloudless day and below the wing of the aircraft Milner could see a whole swathe of the east coast of the United States stretching away from him out towards Chesapeake Bay and the Atlantic beyond. As they approached New York City itself and as the plane descended, he had a breathtaking view of the whole of Manhattan, crisscrossed with its regular streets and avenues, broken only by the great green rectangle of Central Park. From the distance it all looked so perfect, yet down there, there was no limit to the extremes of richness and poverty, of extravagance and squalor, of intellectual achievement and crassness, of tranquillity and violence which marked that amazing city. What an exciting place it was. He, unlike Fawcett, had always loved it, even its dirt and its vice, a city that truly never slept, where he too felt he needed less sleep. Would he, in his new high-profile position, still be able to sample and be entranced by its many extremes?

A huge stretch limousine was waiting for them at La Guardia Airport. The Consul General was there to meet him to explain what MacKenzie had already briefed him on, that the official Daimler could not be used for security reasons. They were to travel incognito in this vast dark-windowed automobile. The Consul General, a vain, busy little man, a good foot shorter than his ambassador, took over where Fawcett had left off, mapping out in the greatest detail every moment of the twenty-four hours he was to stay in New York City. Like many self-important men of small stature, he made up in pedantry and precision what he lacked in height. He rattled through the programme. Lunch with the British–American Chamber of Commerce, where Sir Martin was to make a speech. This was to be followed by briefing meetings at British Information Services, then at the Trade Development Office and the Consulate General, followed, late in the afternoon, by a courtesy call on an old colleague, Sir Hugo Smart, the British Ambassador to the United Nations. When most ordinary people would be finishing their day he was then expected to turn up as guest of honour at a reception for two hundred at the Consul General's residence followed by a small private dinner at the Twenty One Club for forty key British businessmen who lived and worked in New York. It was a long day ahead; he insisted that they planned into it a clear hour's break before the reception to give him time to relax and unwind in a long hot shower.

In the back of the limo, the Consul General continued to fuss his way through a sheaf of notes, briefings and guest lists, with descriptions of the most important people he was to meet. He was handed a folder with the text of his lunchtime speech – the bread-and-butter bits with all the facts and figures that the business community in New York expected of him. He would be required to add the introduction and the ending, the jokes, the delivery and the style. This was another crucial aspect of the business of diplomacy: how he communicated, how he said what he had to say. For the hundredth time in recent months, while the Consul General wittered on, Milner wondered why he subjected himself to all this on top of his other problems. Maybe he should have opted for the quiet life after the tragedies, the Mastership of his old college, for example, which he had tentatively been offered. On the surface he was like ice, efficient, inscrutable;

only Andrew MacKenzie, watching him from the jumpseat, realized something of the multiple tensions behind his boss's exterior calm.

'After the meeting with the Hanson people on Park Avenue tomorrow morning, Ambassador, you've got a fairly easy time. They've promised to give you the background to their latest takeover bid. You've not got to do anything other than listen. It is a huge chunk of American industry that British company has bought up over the years.'

'Tomorrow's briefing notes get read tomorrow,' said Milner brusquely.

'There's also that request for you to take part in that CBS talk-show. Watched by millions. Wonderful opportunity to get your points across.' The Consul General was oblivious to the effect he was creating.

'The host. What's he called?' Milner demanded.

'Neil McCoy. "The Neil McCoy Show". You must have seen it, sir.' The Consul General looked astonished.

'Goes out at the wrong time of day for me. No, I haven't.'

'What do I tell them?' asked the Consul General.

'The Press Counsellor thinks it'd be a good idea, sir,' chimed in Fawcett.

'Be specific.' Milner was having to contain his irritation.

'As I said, sir, it's a good opportunity to put . . . to set out HMG's policies on current issues . . . dealing with the East European mayhem, NATO and so on.' The Consul General waved a paper in his direction. 'It's all in the briefing notes,' he added plaintively.

'What audience am I trying to convince? My job is to make sure the President, the Secretary of State, the Senate and the other people on the Hill understand our policies. What value is to be gained in letting the great American people watch me? Can we control the range of questions I'm going to be asked?' Milner barked out his questions.

'No, sir. 'Fraid not. I'm sure you can cope,' muttered the Consul General lamely.

'I'm sure I can cope. That's not the point. I repeat: what's in it for us?' Milner stared out unseeing at the New York traffic, waiting for a response.

'I just thought . . .' The Consul General was uneasy, and like Fawcett, far from sure how to read the terseness of his new ambassador.

'Very well, I'll do it,' said Milner on an impulse. 'But I need a steer from you on his likely line of questioning. No questions whatsoever about my private life, my wife, my son, or anything else. Can you make that very clear to Mr McCoy?'

'Sir. I'll do my best.'

'Your best has to be good enough,' said Milner. The words came out nastier than he had intended, so he warmed it up by smiling briefly at the Consul General. It helped only a little.

The rest of the day passed uneventfully enough, ending with the planned dinner at the Twenty One Club. He had toured and glad-handed round his various offices; he had talked to his opposite number at the UN; that was the business environment socializing at which he was supremely adept. An alert Fawcett had acted with considerable commonsense, and all the people Milner met had been warned in advance not to raise the spectre of his personal problems. The ambassador wished to concentrate on public issues only. But behind all the formalities, Milner felt himself subject to a growing tension, imprisoned though it still was in the deepest recesses of his mind.

At the Twenty One Club dinner one man was included at the main table, much to the Consul General's disapproval. The ambassador had insisted that Andrew MacKenzie eat with them and that, in the Consul General's mind, was not protocolaire. Security guards should eat with the servants, somewhere below stairs. But an ambassador was an ambassador and what he wanted he got. At the end of the dinner, one of the businessmen who had been sitting beside MacKenzie came up to say goodbye to Milner and remarked: 'A bright fellow, your Mr MacKenzie. If he ever gets tired of doing what he's doing I'll give him a job.'

'I agree,' said Milner slowly. 'But I'd hate to lose him right at this moment.'

'It's easy to undervalue men in roles like that,' the businessman went on. 'I mean it. As sharp as a razor. Knows American history better, I guess, than anyone else in the room, *and* reads and writes poetry . . . Can you believe it? Plus . . .' the businessman laughed '. . . ten times fitter than anyone else in the room.'

'It's reassuring to realize that when I get up each morning,' said Milner thoughtfully. The other man was right. He still took Andrew MacKenzie too much for granted. He would make even more of an effort in future.

Two other things happened later that evening. Milner was taken by a couple of the more relaxed of the businessmen, together with the ever-present Andrew MacKenzie and Paul Fawcett – fortunately the tiresome Consul General made his excuses and left – to the piano bar at the Carlyle Hotel for a nightcap. As they entered, the black pianist was singing the theme tune from *Casablanca*. The words of 'As Time Goes By' spilled out.

> It's still the same old story
> A fight for love and glory
> A case of do or die . . .

'It could be my theme tune,' mused Milner to himself, bringing back far from happy memories of long ago. He had been foolish then and there had been more than a few tears.

For most of the time at the piano bar, Fawcett sat in moody silence, annoyed at being ignored by the businessmen at the expense of all the attention MacKenzie seemed to be getting. As a result, he drank rather too much, downing two or three night-caps to the others' one, before they all called it a day. One way or another, it was very late when the ambassador got back to his hotel bedroom. He undressed, took his wallet and his small notepad from his jacket pocket and went to put them in his briefcase which he had left lying on a side table by the bed. He wheeled the security combination lock and opened up the top to glance through his briefing papers for the next morning's meetings. It was then, even though he himself had been drinking, that he noticed. As an old trick he had learned in the dim and distant past when he was involved in Intelligence work, he had placed his pens at a very precise angle across the top of the files. Then he had linked one particular page of his notes in and out among the others. They were now out of place. Yet the case had been locked. There was no doubt about it. Someone professional had been through the contents of his briefcase. He thought of ringing MacKenzie in his adjoining hotel bedroom but then decided that the damage had been done. It would wait till morning.

Another event that evening of which the ambassador was totally unaware, was that, while they had been at the piano bar at the Carlyle Hotel, in a distant corner watching them intently sat a tall, fair-haired man, a rather pretty girl beside him. They were both in their late twenties or early thirties. They looked like any fashionable New York couple. But there was something about the man, a distant hardness in the eye, that suggested that here was someone uneasily different from the norm. When Milner, MacKenzie at his side, got up to leave with the businessmen, the young couple also stood. They had taken the precaution of already paying their bill so that they could move quickly. Outside in the darkened street they waited for the ambassador and his party to emerge. On an impulse, as the young man moved his hand slowly and deliberately towards a bulge below his shoulder, the girl held his arm. 'No,' she whispered urgently. 'Not now. There're too many people.'

The man angrily pulled his arm free but did what she said. He stood and watched in bitter and frustrated silence as the small group of diplomats climbed into the back of a long, dark limousine, its doors slammed shut and it sped away into the New York night.

'The Neil McCoy Show' went out live to a huge audience. McCoy himself, a self-indulgent, overgroomed anchorman with a smile full of polished, evenly capped teeth, was unctuous in the extreme. The questions started off harmlessly enough and Milner dealt with them with easy charm. He downplayed the accusations of difficult times in Anglo–American relations, speaking optimistically about the future. He highlighted the economic and social catastrophes which were causing the multiple conflicts all over Eastern Europe. He lightly deflected questions about recent sex scandals involving British government ministers, responding amusingly by referring to the difficulties in any democracy of choosing between efficient government and unblemished government. Some of the best and brightest political figures on both sides of the Atlantic were known to have strayed from the straight and narrow, he said. History was littered with examples of strong men and women with equally strong sexual drives – remember JFK, he added.

Thus far so good. He had, through the offices of the Consul General and the head of British Information Services, got a sort of guarantee from McCoy that he would not stray into personal matters. But, in the media world, ratings are everything; promises are broken with great ease. The inevitable came. When the cameras were off him, a researcher handed a piece of paper to McCoy. He glanced at it, then looked up, all charm and concern.

'One final question, Mr Ambassador, before we let you go. I've got a news report here . . .' He picked up the piece of paper and studied it thoughtfully. 'Just come on the wires from London. It's an accusation made in one of your tabloid newspapers last night, by your wife's sister, Sheila, that your posting here drove your wife to suicide and, I quote, ". . . that because of all your personal problems, you are temperamentally unsuited to remain British Ambassador in Washington". Would you like to comment? Will your private problems interfere with your public duties?'

Even the studio technicians were shocked. A frisson of terror tore through the Consul General's heart as he saw his career prospects disappearing in smoke. Milner felt a cold blade of fury inside him and, for an instant, thought of standing and pacing out of the studio pulling the wires of the microphone from his jacket as he went. But he knew that this would play into his antagonist's hands. So he turned, stared coldly at the suitably concerned-looking Neil McCoy, and spoke quietly and coolly.

'That, Mr McCoy, I believe, must be one of the most intrusive questions ever put by an American journalist. When I came on to this show I had your personal promise, and I want your audience out there to know this . . .' Milner waved his hand dramatically towards the cameras, 'I had your guarantee that you would not raise personal matters. You lied. You debase yourself, Mr McCoy. You debase this network. I think, I hope, that your audience, and the American people are renowned for their fair play, will think the same.' Milner in his fury noted with satisfaction that, through his make-up tan, his interlocutor had paled visibly.

'I will not avoid your question no matter how dishonestly you put it to me. I am assured that I have the full confidence of Her Majesty's Government in my appointment. The British Prime Minister has personally expressed his backing for me and has done so directly to the President of the United States of America. I have spoken directly to the President and to your Secretary of State, Antonio Delgadi, and I know their feelings as well, Mr McCoy. Your audience will have to judge whether they think that I am a fit and proper person to represent the United Kingdom in Washington.' Sir Martin Milner smiled a cold, dry smile, carefully folded his long, thin hands in front of him and stared back at the interviewer. 'And now, I'm sure you will agree, Mr McCoy, that this interview is at an end.'

Then, and only then, did Milner stand and, with the live cameras following his every move, pull the small button microphone from his jacket and stride slowly out of the studio. It made for great television.

At the door Fawcett bounced up to him like a puffy young spaniel. 'Sir, that was excellent! Really excellent!' he yelled. 'What a bastard, sir. By Jove, you showed him.'

'I'm terribly sorry . . .' began the Consul General meekly. He too looked like a dog but one that had just been soundly whipped.

'Get me out of here,' snarled Milner directly to MacKenzie, walking past both Fawcett and the Consul General. MacKenzie read the signs and, pushing aside an apologetic knot of producers and television executives, led his ambassador down and out to the waiting limousine. MacKenzie pushed Milner almost forcefully into the back of the car and, without waiting for Fawcett or the Consul General to catch up, yelled at the startled driver, 'Drive, man. Drive.'

MacKenzie had read the signs well. He saw, as no one else was to see, how Milner's hands were trembling, how his whole body was shaking, how tears of anger and frustration were pouring down his cheeks.

For the second time, MacKenzie put a comforting arm on the other man's shoulder. 'You'll be OK in a while,' said MacKenzie quietly. 'Then, maybe, we'll go back and pick up the others.'

Paul Fawcett was less fazed by the whole television interview and less insulted and upset by his boss rushing off without waiting for him than he might have been, because, despite his sometimes equivocal attitude to women and his current dalliance with the Spanish girl, something rather special had happened to him just that morning. The previous evening in the piano bar at the Carlyle, while in sulky, anti-MacKenzie mode, he had spotted, sitting in a corner, a very attractive girl accompanied by a tall, fair-haired man. Both seemed to spend a lot of time gazing at the ambassador and his party. Fawcett, in his turn, had spent an inordinate amount of time trying to regain his good humour both by recourse to his several nightcaps and by staring back at the girl. Then, as they had left the piano bar, she just happened to be standing at the hat-check by the doorway and had smiled at him. He was enchanted. More was to come. The next morning, on his way to meet the ambassador, by pure and wonderful coincidence he just happened to bump into her again outside the doors of his hotel. Not particularly well-favoured, he marvelled to himself that he had never found a pick-up easier in his life, and was consequently very pleased, since such things did not normally happen to him. She was blonde, she had short-cropped hair, she was pretty with a splendid figure and she seemed, remarkably, to have lost her male companion. She also appeared incredibly friendly and available, and to any man that is always the greatest aphrodisiac.

Secret and Personal Telegram
TO: *Chief of MI6*
FROM: *Charles Nairn, Head of MI6*
Station, British Embassy, Washington
SUBJECT: *Oscar Romeo*
DATE: *26 September*

1. MacKenzie is becoming increasingly difficult to debrief: the usual divided loyalties have emerged. He has however reported that the ambassador's briefcase was professionally tampered with while he was in New York. Additionally, and more importantly, MacKenzie is in no doubt that they are under some sort of surveillance. Despite their denials, all this may be official American activity. The FBI, understandably, have no wish to see the assassination of a friendly ambassador on their doorstep. I am sounding out my American contacts but do not wish to upset them, so this has to be handled carefully. Nor do I want to reveal to them that we have noticed their efforts.

2. After a private dinner at the residence yesterday, the ambassador was in forthcoming mood. Unusually, he had a second, then a third large whisky after the meal. We sat talking in his study. The other guests had gone. He made a remark about the Norway incident being the only black spot in his professional life, then refused to be drawn further. Suggest we again revisit those files.

3. He is proving increasingly successful with embassy staff. His personal problems are well

disguised, and he is handling the deepening political crisis with skill. On this and other matters, including the Ambassador/MacKenzie relationship, see my immediately following telegram.

A rather different view of events in Washington was interpreted to the PM, Michael Wilson, by Dr Mark Ivor at Downing Street, shortly after the two men had, together, watched the dramatic extracts from 'The Neil McCoy Show' that were screened halfway through the BBC 'Nine O'Clock News'. Communication is much more visual than the words used. The Prime Minister, a man who thought only what other people thought, who was in office rather than in power, who had grown zombie-like in the care of his advisers, believed he knew what he had seen. Ivor explained what had really happened and then it all became clear to Her Majesty's First Minister.

'All the good points that he was making will be totally lost. People will only remember the row,' said Ivor, philosophically. 'It's a pity. Still . . .'

'I'm worried, Mark. I have to tell you. Trafford and you bullied me into agreeing to sending Milner back. He's got so much personal baggage, it's bound to show . . .' The Prime Minister looked deeply concerned. It was an expression that he had practised in front of a mirror, one that he could put on in front of the cameras when there was a crisis looming.

Ivor was not fooled. 'He betrayed nothing on TV. He didn't let himself or Britain down, did he?'

'I admit . . .' the PM faltered.

'He's fine. He's going to do a great job in Washington.' Ivor stood up, bringing the meeting to a close.

'You're a friend. You would say that,' the PM ventured.

'I never let friendship interfere with my judgement. I'll be watching,' responded Ivor cautiously. 'If, at any time in the future, I don't think he's going to make it through, I'll be the first to warn you, Prime Minister.' He almost believed what he was saying.

9

By the beginning of October – and it had proved to be a long, hot summer – things were going better for Sir Martin Milner on the personal front. People stopped referring to his past tragedies, David had flown out to join him and was, with the help of orthopaedic experts at the Washington National Hospital, back on his feet once again and able to walk with the aid of only one stick. His arrival proved popular at the embassy; he gave his father an increasing amount of support in his social duties and was doubly welcome among the staff because he added a warmth his father notably lacked. Milner welcomed David's company and this, coupled with a greater ease and familiarity with his duties in Washington, led to him being a less formidable boss to those who worked for him.

MacKenzie was another matter. In mid-October, Special Branch tried to have him pulled back to London and replaced. Milner put his foot down. MacKenzie knew the embassy, his ambassador argued; he knew his ways of working; it was too early to withdraw him yet. Reluctantly, the head of Special Branch agreed that he could stay for a further three months. MacKenzie had become a critical component in Milner's life, accepted by even the most status-conscious members of the embassy as someone who could handle Sir Martin. A happy Head of Mission meant a happy embassy.

Some staff, like Fawcett, were far from convinced. As Private Secretary he continued to be jealous of the access which Mac-Kenzie had to their mutual boss and, particularly after he had had a drink or two, he would indiscreetly confide to colleagues that he thought the relationship was becoming too chummy to be healthy.

'HE doesn't do anything now without talking it through with that policeman,' he said, unwisely, to David Velcor late one evening.

The ambassador's deputy was sufficiently old-school to disapprove of such a show of disloyalty. 'MacKenzie's very sound,' he said softly. 'A safe pair of hands.' This was the highest accolade Velcor could offer.

'Far too bright for his own good.' Fawcett slurred his words. 'You know he writes poetry . . . a copper, writing poetry . . .' He burped, mockingly.

'I do. And I approve.' Velcor looked at the younger diplomat with something approaching distaste.

Fawcett failed to read the warning signs. 'Too big for his hob-nailed boots.' He giggled.

'He has a better knowledge of the roots of this country than most of us in Chancery. Told me all about the original Sherman Antitrust Legislation the other night . . .' Velcor mused distantly.

'Too clever by half. Reminds me of Dirk Bogarde in that old film *The Servant*. Taking over the master . . .' Fawcett smirked.

Velcor looked hard at Fawcett, then suddenly spoke very firmly. 'Two things, Paul . . . If I may advise you. One: keep that sort of remark to yourself in future, and two: don't drink so much.' Then the older diplomat turned and walked away.

Some days later Fawcett tried the same line on his Chancery colleague, Janice Yates, but here he was given even shorter shrift, largely because, unknown to him and to the rest of the embassy, a satisfyingly deep physical relationship was well under way between the Political First Secretary and the policeman. One of the more useful sidelines of MacKenzie's professional training was an ability to hide certain truths from others, and he and she together had managed to spend an increasingly passionate amount of time with each other without the wider world knowing. MacKenzie was sensitive to the needs of his new mate: there would be those who disapproved of her upstairs–downstairs relationship with him. He was big enough to be able to live with that. She, in turn, felt ashamed of being secretive about their liaison –

after all, what had either to hide, since both of them were single?

So when Fawcett came sidling up to her one day and told her that he thought MacKenzie was too big for his boots, adding more of the 'PC Plod'-type invective, she told him in no uncertain terms where to go, and not make a complete fool of himself.

Undaunted in his little vendetta, he took the opportunity of a journey with Charles Nairn to a conference in Chicago, further to release his spleen.

Nairn, on the surface, appeared a much more sympathetic audience. 'Tell me more about it, Paul,' the senior MI6 man prompted. His was a trade in secrets of all kinds.

'I don't know what his agenda is, but the ambassador does nothing now without having MacKenzie around.'

'That's what he's paid to do, isn't it?' Nairn was skilled in getting others to unburden their hang-ups. Knowledge of the weaknesses of others was always useful.

'In one way yes, but does he need to sit in every meeting at the embassy? Nobody's going to shoot the b . . . Nobody's going to shoot the ambassador in the Chancery, surely.'

'So what bugs you about him, Paul?' The Intelligence man continued to prod carefully.

'Nobody listens to me, but I think it's a bit beyond the pale. Sir Martin's arranged for him to read confidential, even secret, Chancery files on the President of the United States. Thought MacKenzie – can you believe it – might help His Excellency unravel the mystery of the President's attitude to us.' Fawcett barked an unpleasant laugh of disapproval.

'He did that, did he?' Nairn was genuinely surprised.

'Sure thing.'

'Odd. I wonder . . .'

Thereafter Fawcett got no further reaction from Charles Nairn, though the older man took the news seriously enough.

During October the swings of fortune tilted the other way and the political background worsened dramatically. The British Embassy picked up a lot of direct flak over the way NATO negotiations were handled in New York and Brussels. The US Administration were up in arms over European intransigence and again turned to blaming a weak British Government that sought to justify its decaying international position by constantly wheeling and turning in its attitudes to the United States. Sometimes London seemed to want them as a bulwark against the threats from the food riots, revolutions and major conflicts throughout Eastern Europe. When things got quieter, they squeaked that the Americans should stay right out of European affairs. 'You can't damn well have it both ways,' said the President to Sir Martin Milner tartly when they met by chance at an Irish diplomatic reception. The ambassador dutifully reported this exchange back to London, adding his own view that the Americans might just have a point. This annoyed the Prime Minister, who responded by injecting a phrase into one of his subsequent speeches, about the Americans trying to run British foreign policy. This in its turn was taken badly on the Hill and at the White House; Milner, as any ambassador often has to do, then had to come along behind with a brush and shovel to clean up, to soften, to explain. This time it was to little avail.

On top of everything else the Northern Ireland Unionists had at last got their act together in the United States. Working on the fundamentalist Protestant community in the southern states, they had built up an increasingly effective lobby to demonstrate over what they saw as the sell-out which the American Government had engineered with London, Dublin and the IRA. Gone were the headline-grabbing pro-IRA demonstrations of the past. The publicity given to the hunger-striker, Bobby Sands, decades earlier, and the media circus that had followed Gerry Adams around, had been replaced by reports of the antics of Protestant extremists protesting daily outside the British Embassy in Massachusetts Avenue. It was a small matter in the great scheme of things; it was not an issue that seriously divided the British and American governments. But it was an added issue with which the embassy staff had to deal.

In the American media, more or less openly briefed by the White House Press Office, the Brits were again seen as playing their

Perfidious Albion role, leading the European nations in a war-dance against America. As a result the ambassador was constantly being interviewed on television and being quoted by the newspapers, defending Her Majesty's Government's position. The American press had little against him personally: there were supportive profiles of him and his impossible task in both the *Washington Post* and the *New York Times*, though these, read and reported on in London, tended only to deepen the problems he himself had with his political masters in Whitehall. When he was the subject of that supreme accolade, a *Time* magazine cover, which described him as being an apologist for the Wilson Government, he was firmly instructed by the Foreign Office to cool it. It had always been so. There were many historical precedents where British Ambassadors to Washington and elsewhere around the globe had first been praised, then chided by HMG for having 'gone native', being perceived to be more supportive of the policies of the country to which they were accredited, than of their own.

To those who got to know him privately – there were few – one of the more surprising things that had happened was that Sir Martin Milner had suddenly taken up painting as a hobby. He had, he explained, painted landscapes in his youth, but had abandoned it because of lack of time and because, with his highly developed self-criticism, he felt he was not good enough. Now, as means of relaxation at the end of a troubled day or at a weekend, he would set himself time to paint. He bought brushes and oil paints, and took over a small north-facing room at the residence to practise when the opportunity allowed. MacKenzie was one of only a handful who recognized the true motivation: his growing involvement with the American portrait painter, Flora Simons.

It began innocently enough. After meeting her with her friend, Mark Van der Dring, at his own reception, their paths had not crossed for some time. He was busy settling himself in and readjusting to life with David. Flora, as he was to discover later, was occupied in getting Mark Van der Dring out of her life.

The second time that the ambassador and Flora Simons met was at the home of Mrs Martha Liniver, the imperious Washington hostess. They were both in an emotionally vulnerable, yet freer state of mind. By design or accident – later Milner was to discover that it was by design, since the alert hostess, noticing how well he and Flora had got on when they were reintroduced before dinner, quickly rearranged the seating and placed them together at the long and glittering table. They talked; they rapidly took to each other; they ignored their other neighbours rather too obviously. He learned that she had been brought up in a comfortable, academic New England home, had gone to a private school on the outskirts of Boston and then on to art school in that city. Only in the last few years had she migrated to Washington, where she was making a reasonable income catering to the pretensions of the rich and famous by painting their portraits – her words for what she did.

'You talk yourself down,' he volunteered.

'Perhaps a bit,' she said with an amused shrug. 'I enjoy my work but to pay my way I have to submit to the vanities of those who can afford me.'

'And what kind of person is that?' he asked, mischievously.

Flora Simons stared sideways at him, taking in, as a painter would, this gaunt man with the blue piercing eyes beneath their hooded lids, noticing the strength of his nose and chin, but above all, the fullness of his lips. As he spoke, there was something enticing about him, something visceral, something that told her that she would get to know him well. She boldly began the relationship by offering to paint his portrait.

The rest was inevitable. A few days later they spent their first night together at her Georgetown house in the forlorn belief that only the faithful MacKenzie would know. But, Washington, vast and important though it is, is also a small place, and such very private news travels fast. Because the British Ambassador is an important resident, the FBI ensured that Antonio Delgadi, the US Secretary of State, knew by the following weekend.

*　　*　　*

Extract from BBC World Service Report, 31 October. From James Tedding, Our Own Correspondent in Moscow

As winter arrives, rioting in the streets has continued unabated. The army and other law-enforcement authorities appear to be in total disarray. Gangs of looters, well armed from the arsenals of disaffected military units, roam the streets terrorizing everyone. Much of the normal life of the capital has come to a grinding halt, to be replaced by people struggling to find enough food to eat. The overthrow of the latest Russian President, Kaliakin, and his government, is but a surface sign of the deeper tragedy that is rapidly unfolding inside Mother Russia. Ukrainian forces are massing on the border. Their more disciplined military apparatus and the fact that their government looks more secure, suggest that the possibility of an invasion of Russia is now a distinct possibility. Total anarchy, last seen in the heady days of 1916, is the order of the day. Western businessmen and non-essential diplomats have mostly been evacuated to the safety of the West.

Meanwhile, as seen from here in Moscow, NATO wrings its hands in despair, totally incapable of taking any decisions, particularly given the isolationist attitude of an American Administration which clearly believes that if war is coming, Europe must handle it alone. The signs point the clock firmly back to the period immediately prior to the Second World War . . .

The BBC's diplomatic correspondent, Robert Forson, followed this with his report from Westminster:

As seen from London, the most dangerous consequence of the East European turmoil is the breakdown in relations between the United States and Western Europe and, in particular, between the British and Washington administrations. Each complains about the other's lack of action. In the long aftermath of the Cold War, both countries recognized that there was no longer one monolithic, threatening, Soviet Empire. The Americans, consequently, do not feel themselves directly challenged, and believe they can stand apart from the fray. What they do not realize is how rapidly this East European anarchy is spreading like a cancer; there are far too many nuclear warheads in the hands of highly unstable factions, too much enriched plutonium falling into the hands of unstable Middle East and Third World regimes. The Germans, in particular, recognize how critical it is to have a unified Western approach to what is becoming a global problem. Everything is happening on their own doorstep ... It is difficult to see what the outcome will be.

Against this troubled background, the British Prime Minister is about to visit Washington, but this move is seen as mere window-dressing, and too little, too late. Diplomatic efforts are continuing in Brussels, within the European Community, the Western European Union and at NATO. The pathetic wringing of hands at the United Nations in New York, as it is perceived in Whitehall, adds nothing but confusion to attempts to find a possible solution. HMG believes that this is a moment when the West should stand firm and united, but these wishes seem to be but a pipe dream. The British Foreign Secretary, Trafford Leigh, in an exclusive interview with the BBC last night, offered no speedy remedies. Platitudes have replaced action, hand-wringing has replaced resolve. Meanwhile, in Washington, the British Ambassador,

Sir Martin Milner, has been summoned urgently to the State Department . . .

The ambassador had indeed been summoned to the State Department, but that was an appointment for later in the day. At that precise moment, he was in danger of being in dereliction of duty, sitting motionless as he was in a high-backed leather chair, in the studio of Flora Simons in Georgetown. Behind him were shelves of books. She was hard at work at his portrait; he was pictured full-length, in a formal business suit. He was pleased with the way it had developed, flattered by the initial lines, the warmth she had sketched into his eyes and facial expression. In life he was seldom so relaxed; she had this effect on him. Early on they agreed that the portrait painting would make an excellent cover for their developing relationship. Though neither of them had any family ties, Milner knew that public awareness of an affair would look far from good so soon after his wife's suicide, and he was particularly keen to avoid David finding out about it. MacKenzie, by contrast, could hardly not have been aware of what was going on. He sat in an anteroom with a book of poetry and a pad and pencil, glad too of the opportunity to relax away from the formality of the embassy.

As he sat motionless, Milner, when his thoughts were not on Flora, pondered, yet again, at how the policeman could bear to do a job of such mind-boggling boredom – the protection of one man from his predators. Meanwhile, Flora herself worked vigorously, flashing her brush back and forward from palette to canvas with a dedicated rapidity he found appealing. He was meant to sit still, looking to one side, but when her eyes were off him he kept glancing surreptitiously at her, at her proud profile, her flowing hair, her full figure, disguised though it was under her billowing painter's smock. They had been to bed only twice so far: today he had tried in vain to persuade MacKenzie to leave them so that, if she wanted a break, he could entice her in that direction.

MacKenzie was not to be dislodged. 'I won't disturb you, sir. Forget that I'm here.'

'That I can hardly do, Andrew,' Milner responded with a resigned shrug of the shoulders. Both had smiled; they were getting to know each other very well indeed.

Flora Simons was a warm-hearted but complex person who lived for her painting and her emotions. She came from a long line of Scotch-Irish immigrants who had settled in the mid-west before their ambitions brought them towards the east coast of Boston and Harvard where her father had been Professor in the Department of Humanities. She was highly cultured, the offspring of a family which had wished her to pursue a purely academic career. However, her talents as an artist were soon all too apparent, and because she was, above all, an individualist, she felt more sympathetic to that profession, preferring to work on her own rather than with others. She soon admitted to Milner, by way of a warning to him that all would not be easy, that she had had a number of tempestuous affairs in her life, most recently with Van der Dring. It had, she admitted, been a huge emotional upheaval when that relationship ended.

From their first brief meeting she had been attracted by the British diplomat, impressed by his intellect, haunted by his looks, his eyes, his hands. Once in a television interview she had heard the former US Secretary of State, Henry Kissinger, argue that power was the greatest aphrodisiac. Was she, she asked herself, attracted by the power which Milner's status gave him in Washington? True or not, she had always found it tempting to be with significant people, though she generally mocked the type with which Washington was overstocked, who were there solely for the prestige of being there.

Her growing relation with Milner had an extra dimension to it which she found difficult at first, and then an added bonus. The ambassador came with his minder, Andrew MacKenzie. He, in a strange way, she found equally compelling. As everyone else who came into contact with him quickly gathered, here was no simple, flat-footed bodyguard. That he read, wrote and appreciated poetry, that he appeared to relish the opportunity of sitting talking to her on the occasions when both of them had to wait for the ambassador to emerge from some business function or other, added to his fascination.

To both men Flora Simons was impelled by emotions that were a mix of intellectual and physical. She felt attracted to Martin Milner's mind, but, equally, from the first taste, she hungered after his body in an overwhelming way, surprising even herself with her lust. It was not that she had ever felt inhibited by her Protestant Irish upbringing; now she revelled in the secret wickedness of her relationship with him, which she felt was on a new and elevated plane.

With his twin, as she teasingly called MacKenzie, it was otherwise. Here was a less complex person, yet who had decided ideas and a blunt attractiveness that was also appealing. Not that she would ever have admitted that she found him physically attractive too. He was too straightforward for her. But she enjoyed the intellectual opportunities she had to tempt him further and further out of his shell, getting him to reveal things that even Milner did not know, for example about his burgeoning relationship with Janice Yates which, in an indiscreet moment, he revealed to her. His secret, she assured him, was safe with her; she delighted in knowing something which Milner did not share. For her it was an innocent mix of divided loyalties: she found it quaintly amusing that the British diplomatic service should cling to their reputation for being class-ridden, by forcing a senior woman diplomat and a mere bodyguard to keep their liaison secret for fear of upsetting embassy etiquette. When, after she had got to know MacKenzie better, she said as much, he swiftly retorted that one of the great fictions of American society was that *it* was not class-ridden. He had, he made it clear, found it just as class- and status-conscious in terms of who might liaise or work with or make love to whom, as anything he had ever come across in the British Isles. Flora Simons had smiled, taken note, and held her peace, realizing that there was much truth in what MacKenzie had said.

With the door shut, Milner would also talk to Flora about MacKenzie.

'He seems to have a better grasp of the political scene here than a lot of my First Secretaries.'

'Poetry and politics . . . A powerful combination,' responded Flora with a smile.

'As I get to know him better, I begin to understand,' Milner continued.

'You have a strange relationship,' she challenged.

'To outsiders, yes . . .' Milner nodded.

'And I'm still an outsider?' Flora teased.

'I didn't mean . . .'

'What did you mean?' she asked, genuinely curious.

'He and I see huge amounts of each other. It's only natural. Think what it would be like if we *didn't* get on.' Milner laughed.

'I've got to know him quite well too, you know. There's a lot to find out. Perhaps it's the mind of a trained policeman: he retains an amazing amount of detail. He seems to know a huge amount about the President, for example.' Flora paused as she mixed oil colours on her palette. 'While you were tied up on that long conference call to London the other day, he told me the President was a Taurean, four years and five months older tha him . . .'

'I realize it: Andrew's special. It worries me. What's his agenda, his ambition, working at the level he does . . . ?' Milner reflected.

'Another day, while we were waiting for you . . . again . . . he asked me if I realized what a huge effect the development of barbed wire had had on the great American way of life.' Flora paused in her painting, looked towards Milner and laughed.

'I don't . . . ?'

'It's fascinating. When the vast cattle ranches started fencing with it, it spelled the end of the road for the cowboys. No more Wild West.'

'I hadn't realized that.' Milner shrugged.

'It's not that he's at all precocious with his knowledge. He's low-key, modest almost. It just comes out,' Flora continued.

'As does his advice,' added Milner thoughtfully. 'I thought I'd get man-of-the-people stuff. His judgement is sound.'

'And he likes you, which, come to think of it, makes two of us,' said Flora Simons.

Michael Wilson summoned Dr Mark Ivor to Downing Street the night before his much-heralded visit to Washington.

'Advice, Mark. You know the US Ambassador, Hiram Suskind. You know Martin Milner. Who's telling the truth?'

'Both are.'

'The Washington embassy telegrams tell me that the President is going to rub my nose into every conceivable piece of dirt. Suskind, who came to see me for a brief pre-visit protocol meeting yesterday, said the President was very much looking forward . . .' As usual, the PM, wet-finger leader that he was, was holding it up to the political wind to see which route he should follow.

'That's what he's paid to say,' explained Ivor in his usual confident manner. He talked as if to a child. '. . . All will be sweetness and light. As I said: both are right. On the outside, for the press and the great British and American public, it will be all smiles and kisses. Behind closed doors, I suspect it could all be very different.'

10

Some nine months earlier, on Monday 10 February, to be precise, the Under-Secretary at the Norwegian Foreign Ministry in Oslo, a skeletal, dignified figure in his late fifties, had paced slowly across to the long windows of his office and looked out and across towards the Royal Palace. Snow had fallen heavily the previous night, indicating that winter had still a long time to run. Just this side of the main road, under its blanket of white, a lively statue of the former King Haakon stood on its granite plinth. He had always admired that statue just as he had, as a child, admired the man who had been the nation's hero during and after the Second World War. The Under-Secretary paused, then turned to face his unwelcome visitor. 'You think it is so important what you've found, Petter?' he asked. 'It's a long time ago. Is it so essential for you to dig around in these old archives?'

Petter Hauge stared back at the Under-Secretary. He was a small, intense little man, dark and un-Nordic-looking. Always methodical and precise in his actions and his words, he had never been popular with his colleagues, but he had a reputation for letting nothing slip between his fingers. The Under-Secretary might not like him but had a forced respect for what he might have to say.

'A long time ago, maybe. But it is essential to set the record straight,' said Hauge. His voice was taut and forbidding.

'Why?' The word was equally cold and challenging.

'Too many sins of the past are forgotten and buried. It's always easier and less embarrassing that way. Too many people have got away with too many things.' Hauge stood his ground.

'It's a long fifty years since the end of the Second World War.'

The Under-Secretary sighed as he went and sat at his desk. He had more urgent matters to attend to.

'But a short three decades since the sixties: a time when we were all in this office together. All young, remember. This is about the death of our colleague. Olafsen was a hero. A man betrayed.' Hauge was implacable.

'All conjecture. Nobody ever found his body. It might have been an accident.' The Under-Secretary shuffled some papers in front of him.

'Might, might, might. That's what we always said. But now we know.' Hauge's voice was triumphant.

'What do we really know?'

'That's why I asked to come and see you. We now have hard evidence. We have the files. Out of Moscow. They prove he was being followed. They knew exactly what he was doing. They were waiting for the right moment to pounce. We've copies of the reports. We've had them translated. He completed his last mission; he got back safely; he boarded a ferry and there he was . . . and there they terminated him. The KGB really do use that James Bond-like phrase "Terminate with extreme prejudice".' Hauge came right up close to his superior's desk and stared down at the other man. He watched as the Under-Secretary picked up the file he had been given and flicked quickly through it. 'That's how it looks. I agree.' He too was cautious. 'Why stir things now? Why can't we leave things buried? His wife and daughter were well looked after by us.'

'His daughter is alive. She is young. She has a right to know the truth.'

'You're pursuing this for personal reasons, Petter? You knew the family?' The Under-Secretary looked up from his desk and stared at the other man, wondering at his motivations.

'I worked with her father. It's all on file.'

'Personal thing, is it?' The Under-Secretary continued to press his point.

'I'm trying to get at the real truth.' For a moment, Hauge looked uncomfortable, then he regained his composure and spoke with barely concealed anger. 'We know he was betrayed. It's on file,' he repeated. 'We know that whoever revealed what he was doing to the Soviets was a British diplomat. We believe we know who that diplomat was.'

'But the traitor died in Moscow in the early eighties.'

'Not the man who tipped him off, who warned him, who let him fly to the East to betray Olafsen and a hundred like him.' Hauge slapped his hand down on the desk to emphasize his point.

'Let sleeping dogs lie, Petter.'

'Too many sleeping dogs have been left to lie.' Hauge almost shouted his accusation. 'We Norwegians spend a huge amount of time raking over the skeletons of our own collaborators in the Second World War. We still remember the sons and daughters and families of notorious quislings and give them hell. Now here is a real post-war betrayal and somebody died. Yes, he was a friend of mine. Yes, I worked with him. Yes, I want the truth.'

'I can't give you *carte blanche* to go round making accusations against British diplomats, given the current state of our relations with the European Community.'

'All I ask: can I contact MI6 through our liaison staff to follow up on what we have? Find out who and where that man is now?' Hauge was shaking in his attempt to control his feelings.

'You know exactly who he is, Petter. One of their top men.'

'Precisely. Why should he have got to the top when Olafsen . . . ?'

'What really drives you, Petter?' asked the Under-Secretary. 'Revenge?'

Hauge looked down at the carpet and shrugged. 'Not revenge. It's just that . . . I don't believe in injustice. I may be old-fashioned but we owe it to history.'

The Under-Secretary was basically a weak man. He was also busy. 'I have no desire to get personally involved,' he said. 'Write me a memo. I will seek authorization. Only then can you speak to MI6. Through the usual channels please, not direct. Report back.'

'Thank you, sir. I'll do that. You can rely on me,' said Petter Hauge. Then he smiled a thin, bitter smile of contentment.

The British Ambassador stood talking to the US Secretary of State, Antonio Delgadi, as they waited for the RAF VIP flight to taxi to a stop. 'We're going to have to drive hard to make this visit a success, Mr Ambassador,' shouted the Secretary of State above the noise of the plane's engines.

'Agreed, sir,' Milner bellowed back.

'Whatever the turmoil behind the scenes, we've got to present a united front to the media. No parading of difficulties. Agreed?'

'At one on that. The Prime Minister is, however, looking forward to real progress being made.'

'Perception is everything,' said the Secretary of State, dropping his voice as the sound of the aircraft's engine died away. 'We have to get the headlines right, Martin. We tackle the difficult issues strictly in private.'

'Some of it will leak.' Milner shrugged imperceptibly.

'Sure, it will. But if we keep smiling broadly, shake hands warmly enough in front of the cameras, say nice things at the formal dinner, most of the heat gets taken away. Visual image . . . Think mediagenic. You know all about that.' Delgadi grinned unexpectedly.

'Sir. I agree.'

The two men, flanked by protocol people from the White House and a handful of embassy staff, walked along the red carpet that was being rolled out in front of them right up to the foot of the aircraft steps. Union Jacks and Stars and Stripes fluttered everywhere. Behind them, a US Airforce band was brought to attention as the door of the aircraft opened. First down the steps bounded a couple of Special Branch men, then the Prime Minister with his wife. Behind him, the ambassador could see Trafford Leigh, the Foreign Secretary, the Permanent Under-Secretary and a clutch of other Foreign Office officials – all of whom he knew well. For the benefit of the small press corps standing at the right of the aircraft steps, the Prime Minister gave a well-trained publicity wave to no one in particular, then steadily descended the steps. The US Secretary of State moved forward to greet him.

'Mr Prime Minister. I welcome you to the United States on behalf of the President and the American people.'

Courtesies exchanged and brief handshakes given all round, the Prime Minister was ushered by the Chief of Protocol across the tarmac to inspect the guard of honour. They waited by the podium while the Airforce band played the two national anthems. Milner watched dispassionately as the Prime Minister, a lacklustre figure in many ways but well enough trained in the disciplines of public performance, inspected the guard of honour, walking easily in step with the meticulously turned out guard captain. Then, as if from nowhere, a long black cortege of limousines, national standards fluttering from their bonnets, pulled up, everyone piled in, and they were whisked off and away.

The British Ambassador travelled in the car with his Prime Minister and Foreign Secretary. David Velcor had taken the PM's wife straight to the residence to rest. The US Secretary of State, duty done, had rapidly departed to his other duties. The three men sat in the back of the huge stretch limousine with the PM's Private Secretary. A Number Ten security man sat in front with the driver, while MacKenzie had been relegated to a back-up car. It was Milner's best chance to make his points directly to the Prime Minister.

'How easy is it going to be, Martin?' asked Trafford Leigh. Milner could see straight away that his assessment was correct: the Foreign Secretary rather than the PM was in charge of the agenda, no matter how it might seem to the outside world.

'I've just had Delgadi's renewed assurance. The public perception is going to be wonderfully warm.'

'No invitation to stay at the White House this time, though?' To the PM, the trappings were everything.

'That was a one-off in the past, Prime Minister. They have other ways of providing the apparent warmth without you staying there. In any case you'll be much freer at the residence. The state dinner at the White House tonight is the occasion for everything to be preened and paraded at its best.'

'Your reading of the President's likely attitude behind the scenes . . . ?' asked the PM a trifle apprehensively. 'I've got to make a success of this visit for a pile of domestic reasons.'

'Unchanged, sir. Still to get to the bottom of what really drives his distaste for us. But he won't show it to you. I've seen him a couple of times socially recently and he's been nearly all charm and smiles. I know it doesn't make things any warmer in private. There's still a complete lack of rapprochement on NATO and on Eastern Europe. The Americans still want it both ways. They want us Europeans to cope with the East European crisis on our own, yet they scream like hell if they're kept from meddling in that mess when they feel like it.'

The limousine, shadowed by the FBI back-up car, was gliding along the freeway towards the outskirts of Washington when the PM turned to look at the ambassador. 'And you, Martin? Your problems? How's your son?'

'David's fine, sir. Getting on famously. Been a great help to me. I'm glad to have him with me.' Milner showed he did not want to talk about it.

'I'm still deeply dissatisfied with the security services.' Michael Wilson contrived his most concerned look.

'I've tried to put it out of my mind, Prime Minister. MacKenzie, my bodyguard, can do the worrying.'

'OK . . . I'll leave that. Back to the President. Will he give me a hard time in private?'

'A bit, but he's past-master at window-dressing. You'll go back to London with ringing headlines. None of the Special Relationship stuff but lots of apparent friendship.'

'Why is it a long way from the reality?' asked Trafford Leigh. He knew that life was more than a warm smile and a carefully chosen tie.

'The reality . . . ? I've been kicking myself and my staff silly to get at what drives his agenda,' Milner responded carefully. 'He's his own boss in a way that few of his recent predecessors have been. A thinker. He makes policy. He's got able staffers at the White House and in the military but he is a leader who's truly in charge . . .'

'His ambition . . . ?' Leigh continued to press.

'To stay in office, to get good headlines, to come back for a second term. Nothing's going to get in the way of that. He smiles a lot for the cameras, but can play tough if he has to. He's pulled a lot of his domestic problems into better shape than his predecessors. His health and welfare reforms are pretty well up and running, employment is rising and he's even beginning to have some effect on the hellish crime problems in the black ghettos.'

'I *have* read the briefs, Martin. Again: why this anti-British thing?' The PM was almost petulant, like a spoilt child.

'I've reported every hint. We've talked to everyone we can get any sort of access to. The President personally dismissed the suggestion of being upset by being snubbed when he came to London as a Junior Senator. He told me it just wasn't true. The only other thing is the old story, you'll remember, which the press on both sides of the Atlantic went over with a microscope when he first started running for office, about his mother having run away with a British officer when he was a young boy. There were unsubstantiated reports of the President having once suggested that the man had maltreated both him and his mother, but I wouldn't have the gall to ask him about it directly. When his mother finally abandoned him, his grandparents brought him up . . . It may have left some sort of lingering personal scar.'

'You don't really believe that the President of the United States would . . .'

'Simple things, deep personal things wound people, sir. I'm not saying it's *the* reason, but it could be *a* reason. The story's been well documented. Everyone knows he was still bitter about his mother right to the end. He never spoke or saw her again, even when he became famous. She died a year or so ago. He's a hard man; he never forgave her. You probably recall that he seemed to relish it when she tried to make amends when he started running for President. He gave orders: "No contact. Nothing." She was filmed, she was photographed, she was interviewed. She pleaded; she said she had been misunderstood; she was in tears. He was resolute. He said nothing. The majority of the public sympathized with him. She became the pariah, the outcast, the woman who had deserted her family, her son, a future President.' Milner shrugged.

'The British officer?' asked the PM.

'For a while the press went wild looking for him. You remember that the Ministry of Defence was bombarded with queries. But no one ever traced him. The man had used a false name, so the President's mother said. There were no records. He disappeared. In any case he's not relevant; if anything, he was just the trigger.' Milner efficiently reviewed the main points of the story.

When he had finished, Trafford Leigh turned in his seat and looked long and hard at the ambassador. 'Guns have triggers, Martin. And guns are dangerous.'

The visit went well. At the state dinner at the White House the President and the Prime Minister said glowing things about each other. They glossed over the problems on Eastern Europe and most of the rest was smiles, handshakes and much friendly posing for the TV cameras. The two men went for a well-publicized walkabout together, from the White House to the Air and Space Museum, greeting well-wishers and tourists all the way. It was all media-orientated, all done for public consumption.

Even behind the scenes the talks themselves could have gone worse. There was much tense posturing at the beginning, but when they got down to the detail, helped by the ambassador's prearranged tactics with the State Department, most issues were tackled head-on. At the end of the visit when President and Prime Minister went out on to the White House lawn to face the press corps, both men kept smiling and handled the questions adroitly, as befitted two past masters of the art of appearing sincere.

Afterwards, as they drove out to the airport for the return flight, the Prime Minister turned to the ambassador. 'I'm satisfied, Martin. Well done.'

'Your doing, sir,' said Milner modestly.

'Don't give me that, Martin. I know how much work went on behind the scenes. But we still didn't get at what's biting him. There was one brief moment, when we were on our own, when I thought he was going to come clean. He started on the lines of ". . . There's something that always bugs me about you Brits . . ." Then he stopped. Started being polite again. The truth never came.'

'Exactly my experience.'

The Prime Minister looked across at Milner. 'You'll keep working on it, won't you, Martin?'

'My key task, Prime Minister,' he responded resolutely.

Along with all the positive news reports, a much less helpful story out of Washington hit the British media about then. It appeared first of all in the tabloids. One of the major problems facing British diplomats overseas is in fact that, not only are they reporting the affairs of the nation to which they are accredited back to London, but the newspapers are doing a similar job in rather more sensational and shorthand terms. Sadly it is often the media headline rather than the well-thought-out diplomatic report that grabs the attention even of the most astute political leader back in Britain. Despite this, most stories on the political and economic front are easy enough to cope with by the Foreign Office News Department. The British Embassy in Washington has a press office staffed to do just that as well.

But every now and again, particularly in the tabloid press, some human-interest story is played back to London which causes more than a little irritation. Thus when the *Sun* newspaper ran an 'exclusive' headline reading: 'The Man Behind Our Man in Washington' shortly after the successful visit of the Prime Minister to the United States, it caused a minor stir. While it did not merit hitting the newsstands back in Washington, the newspaper article itself was faxed to Sir Martin Milner via his Press Counsellor, much to a number of people's amusement and a few people's deep annoyance. The story from the *Sun*'s Washington correspondent – a freelance stringer by the name of Cripps – suggested that there was a Rasputin-type figure at work in the British Embassy, influencing all political decisions there because of his hold on the ambassador. That Rasputin was alleged to be none other than Andrew MacKenzie. While this caused some laughter in the embassy, and indeed became the subject of a musical number in the cabaret review which the embassy theatrical society was staging at the time – and everybody including the ambassador and MacKenzie laughed at it – it left an unpleasant aftertaste, if only because somebody had been talking to the press out of turn. Cripps had gone to ground and when the Press Counsellor eventually managed to track him down he, with some choice East End Cockney invective, refused to reveal his source. It was only much later, in a drunken conversation with her young colleague, that Janice Yates uncovered telling evidence that the source of the story had been none other than Fawcett. As a result of their secret liaison, this was reported to MacKenzie, who decided, after careful reflection, to keep his own counsel. But it did alert him to the fact that embassies are small places and that, in his relationship with his ambassador, he had to act with ever more caution. If Milner guessed at the source, he too gave no indication of it.

*

Renate Olafsen's life changed from the moment she met Petter Hauge. It was as if by accident, but later she realized it had all been very carefully stage-managed. As she sat motionless in her chair by the window of her apartment, looking out over the pines and the birch trees towards the distant waters of the Oslo fjord, she knew what she must do. Throughout her life, Renate had lived in the shadow of the memory of her father. He, in turn, had been a great admirer of the German statesman, Willy Brandt. The young Olafsen had been close to Brandt at the end of the Second World War, and was with him when the future Mayor of Berlin, who had fought the Nazis with the Norwegian Resistance, actually entered his future city dressed in Norwegian army uniform. Olafsen had not lived to see Willy Brandt reach the pinnacle of his career as German Chancellor. He was murdered long before then.

Later, much later, after her mother died, Renate herself travelled from Oslo to Germany, and, as a student, became heavily involved in the fresh, new environmental politics of Petra Kelly. Kelly, beautiful and highly charismatic, was leader of the German Green Party during the eighties. Renate, equally attractive and constantly having to fight off a host of would-be admirers, worked closely with her and, later, with Kelly's renegade ex-army lover, General Gerd Bastian. In those heady days when the Greens seemed poised to seize power from the established German parties, the Norwegian girl was a welcome additional activist in their environmental struggle. Then came the fall of the Berlin Wall and the breathtakingly speedy collapse of communism. Other issues such as reunification came to the fore in the German political agenda. As a foreigner, Renate Olafsen felt she had less of a role in those dramatic national events, and she was already considering returning to Oslo when, in 1992, came a second great personal tragedy for her: Petra Kelly and her partner, Bastian, were found shot dead in their beds. The triumphant days of the Green Party had been eclipsed and it was ironic that the body of this heroine of an age lay undiscovered for almost three weeks. The theory was that the general, jealous, had shot her, then killed himself. Whatever the truth, it led to Renate's bitter disillusionment, and her speedy return to her native Norway.

It was in her second month back in Oslo that Renate met Petter Hauge outside the Munch Museum. She vaguely remembered his name as having been an old colleague of her father's; he said he remembered her as a child.

'How are you?' asked Hauge, with a concerned smile.

'Not so bad.' She was cautious, not wishing to reveal too much to this stranger.

'What are you doing?'

'Back after several years studying in Germany. I'm not sure what I'm going to . . .'

'Looking for a job?' Hauge enquired. He had a disturbing, intense way of looking at her.

'Yes and no. Nothing seems to appeal.'

'I'm glad I met up with you.' Hauge appeared to hesitate.

'Why?' Renate stared hard at the man. She judged he must be in his mid to late sixties.

'Something I came across the other day. By chance. About your father. We used to work together at the Foreign Ministry.'

'I remember mother talking about you,' Renate lied.

'I worked with Willy Brandt too, you know,' Hauge boasted. 'He was much older, of course. A real European hero.'

Hauge invited her for a coffee and, hesitantly, she went with him into the museum, where they found a corner table in the cafeteria. Renate explained to Hauge a little of what she had been doing in Germany. Then: 'What have you found?' she asked, taking the bait he had proffered.

'You don't mind me talking about how your father died?'

'He was murdered, wasn't he? My mother knew but refused to tell.'

'Undoubtedly. Undoubtedly,' Hauge repeated. 'Communist agents, working in Norway. Body never discovered. We knew he had crossed the border far to the north, that he had come in from the cold. But he never reached home.'

Renate shrugged. 'It's so long ago. It doesn't matter so long as he's at peace.' She paused, then: 'What have you heard?' she asked curiously.

'How he died ... What led to it ... What made the Soviets believe ... believe he was worth killing.'

'What was he doing?' Her words hardly rose above a whisper.

'His language skills – he could speak with the Laplanders – he had been dropped into the northern Russian frontier area several times. His task ... as always ... to find out about the Russian nuclear industry ... their defence establishments that stretched right across the Arctic.'

'I remember some stories ... from my mother.'

'He was highly thought of, your father. A brave man. He was coming back to a desk job in the office. He was glad, for your sake and for your mother's. He'd done his bit. He'd done his duty. It was his last run.' Hauge paused as he sipped at his cup of coffee.

'What happened?'

'He was betrayed.'

'Betrayed?'

'We guessed, but never knew for sure. Now, at best it was foolish incompetence; at worst, it was *evil*.' His voice shook as he emphasized the final word.

'Tell me.'

'A young British Intelligence officer, working under diplomatic cover in Oslo. Ambitious. He thought he knew all the answers. He had a friend, a fellow diplomat, who turned out to have been working for the KGB for years. British Counter Intelligence were on to him, but before they got him, this young man tipped him off and he escaped East. With a lot of secrets, a lot of names.' Renate watched Hauge closely. He was looking away from her with a strange intensity in his eyes.

'With my father's name?' she asked quietly.

'Have another cup of coffee? Or hot chocolate, perhaps?' Petter Hauge turned and smiled unexpectedly. 'Then I'll tell you.'

Largely due to an upbringing of benign neglect – David had been sent away to boarding school from an early age – father and son had always got on reasonably well. But theirs had been a distant friendship until now. Since his arrival in Washington, however, as they got to know each other better, with that knowledge set against the terrible background of his mother's suicide, small tensions began to emerge between them. This was partly due to David's enforced inactivity and the insecurity engendered by his injuries: he was particularly sensitive to the ferocious scar that ran vividly across his cheek, but he was also deeply concerned, his father realized, about whether his groin injury might have affected his potency. He had recently had some good news, however, in that his City employers had agreed to keep his job open until he had completely recovered. In the meantime, Milner did his best to excuse his son's many mood swings and hang-ups.

Milner had many other public matters on his mind and he was

less than mentally prepared to arrive back at the residence one evening, to find his son in the deepest of depressions, about himself, about his physical state, and about what he saw as his futile existence. Milner excused himself briefly, rang Lucinda Forbes-Manning, and got her to telephone his last-minute apologies for pulling out of a dinner he was meant to attend that evening. He had learned many lessons of late and he would never again allow his public life to come first, particularly that evening, with David in the state he was in. So it was that father and son sat uneasily together over a hastily-prepared dinner, and eventually managed to talk through many of their problems. In the end there was a little laughter among the many tears; it did them both good.

Later that night, when David had gone up to bed, the ambassador went through to catch up on his official correspondence in his study. It was nearly eleven and so he was surprised when Lucinda suddenly appeared at the door.

He looked up from his desk. 'What are you still doing here . . . so late?'

'Been at an Embassy Dramatic Club rehearsal and thought I'd look in to see . . .' She paused a little uncertainly. 'I hope you don't mind, but I recognized the state David was in earlier and I thought I might be able to help.'

'Thanks. We talked through a lot of his . . . our . . . problems.' Milner stood up. 'Like a nightcap?' he cautiously volunteered.

'I've already had one or two,' she said, a trifle unsteadily. 'I don't want to disturb you. I'm not looking for anything more . . .' she added a trifle lamely.

'No, please. I was going to have one before turning in.' He wondered for a moment whether she was there to make herself available to him once again. If so, she was out of luck.

They poured themselves drinks and sat down opposite each other.

'You don't mind me saying . . . David's got a lot of problems,' Lucinda began tentatively. She looked as if she was regretting having come.

'Hardly surprising.'

'Thinks he's lost his attractiveness to women,' she continued. Her words were very slightly slurred.

'Is he right?'

'The reverse. That scar makes him look quite heroic.'

'Have you told him?' Milner asked with a smile.

'Not yet.'

'Maybe you should.'

'I didn't want to get too familiar . . . without your . . .' Lucinda paused, embarrassed by bringing up the past.

'You're both adults.' Milner shrugged.

'I'm a bit old for David, if that's what you're suggesting.' Lucinda giggled unexpectedly.

'Wasn't suggesting anything.' Milner smiled back kindly. 'You were, I suppose, a bit young for me . . . It's really up to you,' he went on. It was not a conversation he was enjoying.

'After the father I thought it might be a bit . . .' She dried up.

'You're a wicked girl, Lucinda.' He stood up.

'You've known that from the beginning.' Lucinda stood with him. 'Look, I think I've had a drink too many. I must go before I say anything more.' She paused in the doorway, then turned towards him. 'If anything happens between me and David, just consider it as a little bit of voluntary therapy on my part. That's all.' Then, embarrassed, she fled.

In the cold light of day Sir Martin Milner was more concerned about his own developing relationship with Flora Simons than any between Lucinda and David, but at that precise moment he was fully involved with trying to keep his eyes open. Sitting still in the big leather chair was tiring. He felt his lids drooping.

'You're beat,' Flora said.

'A little.'

'Want to give it a break?' As she spoke she continued to work furiously at the canvas. 'I can't quite get the mouth . . .' she continued.

'You want my mouth?'

154

'Fool! Your expression, I mean.' She laughed. 'It keeps changing. Sometimes I see a warm, compassionate man; sometimes I see . . .'

'A cold and angry man, that it? Or a tired old man?' He grinned back at her.

'Not far along from the last . . . Can you stand another five or ten minutes?' she begged.

'Course.'

'Before the light fades. I feel I'm getting somewhere with this damned thing, at long last . . .'

'I promise to keep my eyes open.'

'Talk to me. Tell me something,' she pleaded as she continued to work furiously at the canvas in front of her.

'About you?'

'No, for Christ's sake. About you!'

'OK. I'll talk.'

Milner started to talk. He thought he would soon dry up, that it would all sound contrived. He explained about how lonely he felt at the top, how he, as ambassador, could never delegate final responsibility. He talked about the pressures over keeping in with David. He talked about MacKenzie, and how he valued his judgement. 'There was a bit of truth in that unpleasant *Sun* story. He's got depth. And knowledge. To hell with the huge difference in status . . . What does that matter?'

Flora avoided interrupting his flow, and continued to paint as he moved on to explain to her how the pressures of the recent prime-ministerial visit had drained him. He had been widely praised. He was delighted it had gone so well. He was amazed by how excellent the headlines had been in both the British and American press. But it was all so empty. He talked hard and fast, first to keep his eyes open, then in a desperate attempt to make sure she understood him. Later, long after Flora's five or ten minutes more of painting were up, he started to talk of other pressures, pressures intruding from the past.

He was aware, as he changed to this new subject, that she had stopped painting and was watching him. He did not stop. 'It was a long time ago,' he said in a distant voice. 'I was very young, you know.'

'Would you like to tell me about it?' Flora asked quietly. At once she knew she should not have spoken. It interrupted his flow.

He pulled himself together and quickly shook his head. 'No, not now. Later perhaps.'

'There it goes again.' Flora sighed, picked up another brush, looked at the portrait, then at the sitter, then at the canvas once again. 'Every time I feel I have you, your mood shifts and I don't know whom I'm painting. I don't know what makes you feel, what makes you exist as you do. Sometimes there is this wonderful man I think I am deeply in love with, then there's this self-destructive coldness that sweeps through you, a remoteness, a self-centredness that in no way could I ever be part of. D'you know what I mean, Martin?' She turned towards him again and saw that his eyes had closed. He was asleep.

Two days later, David was sitting in a corner of the study watching the CBS evening news when his father returned from a briefing meeting with a visiting team of British exporters.

'Terrible,' his son said, looking up.

'What is?' he asked.

'The earthquake. San Francisco. Not too bad they don't think. God, how can they bear to live there?' David's voice was shaking. 'Look at those pictures. Those injuries . . .'

'I heard the newsflash. I'm waiting to hear how the consulate is.' Milner sounded equally concerned.

'It seems to have escaped major damage. There's a telegram waiting for you on your desk. Paul brought it over half an hour ago. Asked me to give it to you. He's available at home if you want to talk. The Consul General rang to say everyone was safe.'

'I'll put a call through to him.'

Milner went and stood behind his son's chair. David was sitting, stick by his side, one foot balanced uneasily on a footstool in front of him.

'How're you feeling?'

'All right. God, I couldn't live in an earthquake zone, so danger-ous.' He was not trying to be ironic. The flickering screen showed fire engines and ambulances screeching along fractured motor-ways. 'Thank God it happened on such a sunny day,' he con-tinued. 'Everybody seems to have been outside.' He was entranced by the images on the screen.

'The way Californians like to live. Danger. Live hard, play hard.'

'Many are leaving.'

'Just the superstars. California won't miss them. May be a better place without them.'

'Cynic,' said David.

'By the way . . .' Milner paused. 'Lucinda came to see me.'

'I know.' David turned suddenly cold.

'She asked for a few days off. Sadly the ones she asked for are out. Too much going on here. I suggested she go a week later.'

'I'm bloody furious. Why can't you let her off for a day or so . . . ?'

'She knows the ground rules.'

'Ground rules. For fuck's sake, Dad!'

'She *is* my social secretary, David. She can't just disappear when she feels like it . . .'

'Your bloody social . . . Jesus! What else has she been to you, I wonder . . .'

'David . . . please! I told her . . .' Milner was shocked by his son's sudden outburst.

'What did you tell her?'

'I told her when she could go. Otherwise it's none of my business. It's up to you both.'

'Thanks awfully. How very kind,' David sneered back at him.

'David, don't be like that,' Milner pleaded.

'I'm bloody furious.'

'Don't be hard on her. She's in a difficult position.' He tried to reason with him.

'I know she's your personal sec . . . for Christ's sake. But if we want to go off, she doesn't have to . . . Jesus!' David's voice screwed in irritation as he flicked the switch on the remote control of the television set and the picture went dead. He turned to look up at his father. 'Dad. It's difficult enough for me living here without being . . .' he hesitated.

'Without being what?' Milner prompted.

'Without being watched . . . pandered to by . . .'

'If you think Lucinda's the sort of person who's going to pander to you . . .' Milner interrupted, trying to control his irritation at what he saw as David's irrational reaction.

'I don't mean that. She's been sympathetic. I like her.'

'You realize she and I have to work very closely. She, like Andrew, knows more about what I'm doing than I know myself. Never out of each other's sight. She has to deal with my moods and hang-ups. It would be quite wrong, given her job, to go off on a jaunt with you without making me aware . . .'

'Your personal assistant and your injured son . . . Hand in hand,' David broke in with unnecessary bile.

'You're almost recovered. Don't be bloody stupid.' Milner was losing his patience.

'Don't quibble, Dad.'

His father turned away angrily. 'Look, if you're going to talk like that, David, I'd better go and change. I've got a dinner to go to.' He had had enough. Injury or no injury, he was not going to be spoken to like that.

'I'm sorry, Dad. I didn't mean . . .' David back-pedalled like mad.

'Do what you like. Don't involve me. Just do what you like. D'you understand?' his father burst out.

'I'm sorry,' David said lamely.

'And don't make it more difficult for Lucinda than it is already,' responded his father dismissively, before turning on his heel and walking up the long, winding staircase to his room.

11

He was an uncomfortably bitter man, this Petter Hauge. Renate accepted what he said, that he had been a friend of her father's – colleague was probably a more appropriate word – but why had she agreed to him coming round to her apartment? Maybe she should be worried that his story was all an excuse, that he was just a dirty old man on the prowl. It was his persistence that had persuaded her; he appeared so brutally honest and determined.

When he arrived at her tiny home, she offered him some wine she had just bought at the *Vinmonopolet*.

'Thanks.' He took the glass and started sipping straight away.

'Tell me more about him. My father,' Renate prompted, as he settled into the armchair she had pulled forward for him.

'You know most already. We got on well. He was different – tall and blond, the typical Norwegian boy. By contrast, I am a bit of a runt. I've always believed I must have some Spanish Armada blood in me or something.' His voice tailed away. Renate sat in silence, watching and waiting as the old man collected his thoughts, sipping compulsively at his glass.

'Would you like . . . ?' She offered the already half-empty bottle.

'Yes, of course . . . I always accept a second glass,' he replied. 'I don't drive,' he added, primly.

'Please. Tell me more.' She stood and poured from the bottle, standing well back from him as if he might infect her.

'He believed in what he was doing. Of course he was scared. We were all scared. He wanted to stop. Particularly after you were born. But he had this personal drive. He believed it was important for us, for the West, to find out as much as possible about the Soviet nuclear industry. He was too well qualified for us at home base to allow him to give up. He knew his geography; he knew how to survive in the Arctic wastes. Did you know, one time, he almost died? Frostbite. He lost some toes. But he had talent. He had style. He could talk to the Laplanders like one of their own. It wasn't just that he was a good skier or that he had done the commando courses. He had this in-built ability to live through the worst of weathers, to get there and back. It worked. He did many trips in and out . . . too many . . . that year . . . 1966 it was . . . until the last one. He got out then too. We know he got out. We had absolute proof of where he crossed the Russian border . . .'

'Tell me,' Renate urged again.

Hauge appeared to hesitate, but it was largely for effect. He knew precisely what he was doing. He had his own agenda to pursue – through her. He deliberately took her over every detail of what the Russian reports, laboriously translated, indicated. Where they were unclear, he gave his own carefully-conceived interpretation. He explained that the KGB were very methodical. He kept the last report of all to the end. It covered the final days, up to the moment on the ferry when the termination happened.

The words of the report, addressed to KGBHQ, Moscow, were precise and almost emotionless.

Subject tracked from Kirovsk on the Kola peninsula to Murmansk. Immediately he left his contacts there, we pulled them in and interrogated them and their entire families. There was nothing to be gained further from holding them in captivity so they were all eliminated, without resistance. Ten men, four women, three children.

Under instructions, we did nothing to arouse the subject's suspicions. We wanted to identify which route and with whose help he made the treacherous crossing to Kirkenes in northern Norway. At any time of year it is a task of supreme difficulty. We needed all the technical means at our disposal to track him. We have to report that we were impressed. Do not misunderstand. He travelled on skis, totally alone and unaided, carrying minimal supplies. We cannot identify any help he had on a journey which would have defeated an ordinary person. Had it not been for your strict instruction, we would have picked him up while he was still within our jurisdiction, and interrogated him to identify what particular skills and fortitude he possessed.

Even inside Norway, he sought no official help. We would have known. He made his own way by public transport on the ferry supply route towards Bergen. Our operatives boarded the ferry at Ålesund. Their disposal method, given that the use of firearms or knives was deemed inappropriate, was Category Seven, which, it was correctly judged, would attract no attention and leave no trace of the body.

The mission was satisfactorily completed on Saturday 26 November 1966 at 1605 hours precisely. There have been no subsequent reactions from the Norwegian authorities.

When Petter Hauge had finished reading, he looked across at the girl. He saw that she had her head bowed, that tears were running down her cheeks. The sight gave him an almost perverted satisfaction. He reached his hand towards her as if to comfort her.

'Please, please don't move. Leave me. I'll be all right.' Renate backed nervously away from him.

'I shouldn't have brought up this past. I should have done as they told me at the Foreign Ministry. Let it lie.' Hauge's words carried little conviction.

'I'm glad. *Glad*,' she stressed. 'I wanted to know.'

'What else d'you want to know?' Hauge was watching her closely, analysing and savouring her every reaction.

'How did it happen? Why was he caught? Who was responsible . . . ?'

'Somebody was,' said Petter Hauge. His voice was vicious. He looked at her, through her, then, as if afraid of betraying the depth of his passion, stared down at his hands, waiting. He did not wish to appear too eager to divulge the rest.

'Who?' Renate breathed the word.

'It was a long time ago.' Hauge hedged.

'You wouldn't be here unless you wanted to tell me.' Suddenly Renate realized something of his game, and became angry. She stood up, tall, staring down at him. 'That's why you're here, isn't it? You've got some hang-up. You've got some deep grudge. You *want* me to know who it was. You want me to do something.' Her words came tumbling out.

The little man shrugged, then looked up with a defensive smile. 'Maybe,' he said. 'Maybe yes, maybe no. I was asked the same question at the ministry by the Deputy Secretary. I said I wanted the truth known. You must believe me: I really did like your father. I did work closely with him. His death has long gone unavenged.' Hauge stared at her, his eyes intense and brooding. 'That is surely wrong, isn't it? Those responsible, out there, are marked for retribution. Surely you agree? You *must* agree.' He stood up then, and continued to watch her and wait for an answer that was long in coming.

That was how it had been. That was how Renate Olafsen had discovered who was responsible for her father's death. That was how Petter Hauge had enticed, then hooked, then trapped her. She did not remember her father. Memories were a myth. But she could not forget the long years of aftermath: her mother's constant tears, the agonizing time of waiting, the speculation that he was in some prison camp. Then came the inquisitions, the attentive people who came to give them money and support and settle them into a new, much smaller, home. The authorities had been kind. They came round for a while. Then they forgot, because time moves on. For her mother it was the beginning and it was the end. Her mother, always dressed in dark clothes, always shuffling about, always gloomy, always waiting, always hoping, knowing there was no hope.

That was why, immediately her mother died, she had felt compelled to leave Norway, to get away from her past, to go off to Germany and bury herself in something that really mattered – the Green cause. And now, this coming home, this chance meeting, if it was a chance, with her father's friend, Petter Hauge.

'Why d'you tell me this,' she shouted at him. 'Why do you unsettle me so?'

'I did not look for you. We happened to meet.' He avoided her gaze.

'Have I to believe that?'

'You must. I had forgotten all about your existence.' Hauge stood up, his voice also raised, his anger real. 'Don't you understand?' he said. 'What really brought it all back was that, suddenly, we were offered access to the Russian files . . . files on their infiltration of the Norwegian Intelligence Service, Renate. That's my job, you know. Archives. I used to be important . . . Behind the scenes . . . They were even going to make me an ambassador . . . but then, well, I don't know . . . I don't quite fit. Never have. Do I look like a Norwegian Ambassador?' Hauge turned towards her and laughed emptily. 'No, I'm not the right type,' he said. 'That's why, at my age, I'm working in the archives. Weeding archives. Looking through sensitive papers to make sure they can be made available to a sensitive, scandal-hungry public. That's when I came across this file. That's when I came across your father's name. That's when I came across my own name. Can you believe it? I came across *my own name* in these Russian files. The ministry gave me a grant to have them all translated. That's how I know. D'you realize how many important people throughout Western Europe are trembling because Soviet, and East German, and Czech, and Romanian Intelligence files are now available? D'you know how many traitors could be unmasked if the right resources were made available to go through all the files, to find out who paid whom for what?' Hauge seemed deeply indignant. He stood up and, unasked, helped himself to the last drops of wine from her bottle.

'I'll go and buy some more if you like,' she volunteered, sheepishly.

'I don't want to drink. I used to do that too, you know,' Hauge said. 'I want to talk: talk to you.'

'You make me nervous, Mr Hauge. Please . . . sit down.' There was something increasingly malevolent about him.

'OK. Sorry. Look, I've heard what you're doing now, Renate,' he said. 'Temporarily working for the Nobel Peace Committee. It's a good job. I hope you get a full-time position there. It's interesting. You meet lots of interesting people, do you?'

That was how she realized at last that he had not met her by accident. It was how things had evolved. It was how he had urged her to turn anger into action. It was how she had learnt the name of the man who had betrayed her father. Hauge had been clever: he had judged precisely how she would react. He had everything ready. He put her in touch with people in London who hated the British system more than she ever could. That was why she had gone there, even her air fare was funded by him. Hauge was the avenging angel, and she had foolishly become involved in his cruel game.

Only afterwards had she realized how futile it had been; to punish one crime with another was madness. She had come to realize that folly, most of all when she had, impetuously, gone to the hospital and had seen an innocent young man, lying, body racked by bullets that she had caused to be fired. How she had wept with frustration and regret. Then she had returned to Oslo. To do more was madness.

And then, a month later, like an unwelcome shadow, Petter Hauge had come to see her once again. He seemed older, he was just as driven, he was even more vindictive. He would not let go. She was a strong, self-possessed woman, but on this she felt weak and vulnerable. Hauge recognized this. She would be his avenger. He used every device to persuade, told her that she was betraying the memory of her father. How could she give up now, let the guilty man off, a guilty man who was rich, and famous, and prosperous, and, above all, alive? He went on and on, using all the emotional blackmail he could muster, to persuade her into a change of mind. He succeeded in inspiring her again to seek out this man who had destroyed her father. This time he gave her a contact in New York. He again provided her with an air ticket, gave her money, told her how she must act. Deep down she recognized that she was under his spell, but, even within herself, she wanted to see and to know: who was this British diplomat? What was he like? How had he lived with his conscience for all these years? This time Hauge was more cautious. He knew Renate would not take the same route again, so he pointed to ways, other than violent ones, of seeking her revenge. Which was why she soon abandoned the hard man whom she had contacted when she had first arrived in New York, and started to hunt on her own, not with people who would shoot and maim, but this time armed only with her own resolve. She promised, not Hauge but herself, that she would seek out this man and confront him face to face.

'There are many ways,' Hauge sighed softly when he telephoned her from Oslo, and she told him what she intended, 'to destroy people without injuring them'. He quoted from a poem by Oscar Wilde – *The Ballad of Reading Gaol*. It was all about how some people kill with a knife and others with a smile or a word. Afterwards she could not quite remember the phrase he used, but it was something like that.

The minutiae of embassy life bored Sir Martin Milner. He had never relished the points of protocol, etiquette and *placement* which were part and parcel of an ambassador's social duties – the calls on other ambassadors, the making sure that the right people sat next to the right people to give a good balance to a dinner party. He recognized that the choice of guests was always important, but he showed little concern for the efforts that Lucinda put into how far above or below the salt they sat.

Lucinda was not there to make the detailed arrangements for a black-tie dinner he had to give one Wednesday evening, for a visiting delegation of British MPs in Washington on some fact-finding junket to do with prison reform. She was away in New England with David, for their postponed days of rest and recuperation or whatever. He closed his mind to all that and left it to Paul Fawcett to supervise the arrangements for the dinner itself. It was a small incident in the life of a busy embassy, but it did, he noticed, lead to one social oddity: Fawcett, unasked, had invited an unexplained girl to attend. Milner was of course briefly introduced to the extra guest; he could not have failed to notice such an attractive woman. But it was not until David Velcor came to see him the next morning to complain of his annoyance at having been told that his own wife could not come because of lack of space at the table, that Milner realized the girl was no more than a new-found friend of Fawcett's. It was not the girl's fault, of course, but he would have to take Fawcett to task. It also made him recall that when the girl had arrived for the dinner party and they had shaken hands, while he had smiled warmly at her, he had been thrown when she had stared so coldly back at him.

Sir Martin Milner had, in his library which he had always taken with him from post to post around the world, a wide collection of biographies, autobiographies and diaries of politicians and diplomats. It was his preferred range of reading material. Among them were one or two books written by eminent predecessors of his, about their time at the British Embassy in Washington. In the past, he had never felt the urge nor did he think he had the time or duty to keep a diary. But since arriving in Washington he had changed his mind. He now had the habit of an evening, when energy allowed, to scribble down a few thoughts on a piece of paper and drop them, methodically and in date order, into a locked drawer by his bedside. Sometimes the items in the diary were about the great issues of state or other important events of his day, which he would be able, if he ever felt so inclined, to mesh in with his official diary which his appointment secretary kept for him in her office. If he ever did come to write anything for public consumption, the two would fuse together, would match enough to remind him of what had actually happened. In consequence, these diary pages, brief though they were, were flavour rather than detail, impression rather than substance, ideas more than fact. Just occasionally he would write about domestic problems, for example touching on Lucinda and her current affair with David. But usually he would write about how he saw things in the wider world. His diary entry for that particular December day, for example, read as follows:

> *If who knows whom is still a dominant force in British life, it's very much the same here in Washington. The top two or three hundred know each other, intermesh, deal, fraternize, mix and marry. Outsiders are admitted with reluctance. I know most of those I need to know by now – it's part of my job. The Washington Establishment is not a club but acts as one. Even opponents at the top see each other more often than they do their camp-followers down in line. Most are men, though there is the occasional woman, the great society hostesses, the occasional woman politician or senator, there usually by her own right, though sometimes because it is essential to have* 'a good woman on the board'.
>
> *This afternoon I went and listened to some of the Senate debate about the situation in Eastern Europe. Dialectic used to rank with rhetoric as a great liberal art. Now all we have are politicians speaking in sound bites. I've seen it in the House of Commons; I see it here too. There was no debate, there was simply slanging or, to quote, I think it was Dr Johnson,* 'a sequence of contradictory assertions'. *Politicians spend their time speaking to their audience rather than arguing a case. Most of them seem not to know what they're talking about: they've had their speeches prepared by their staffers who, if you go on television as I've done at least three times this week, actually turn up at the television*

studio with their principals to rehearse the answers prior to them going in front of the cameras. Spontaneity is out; pre-planning is everything. Sometime I may get round to write a thesis on the art of debate, quoting Swift, who argued that so many individuals are only impatient 'to interrupt others' and are uneasy at being interrupted themselves. Why am I writing all this? I've got so many other things to do. I suppose it's to assure myself that I'm still capable of thinking, that I don't just have to decide about today's issues, tomorrow's telegrams, about when I'm going to have the next opportunity to sleep with Flora or what I'm going to do about the too obvious passion going on between David and Lucinda. (Does that matter? Is it bad for residence discipline? Why, after my own dalliance, should I worry about it?) If I stop thinking I am lost.

Tonight, for some reason, I am visited by memories. There are deep things stirring, things that I never usually think about, things come back to haunt me. I must force them out of my mind. They are dead. They are not to come back to life. They are of the past.

12

When Anders Berg, the big, solid, dependable Norwegian Ambassador, rang to say he would like to come round for a chat, Milner for once had a free evening, and suggested that his colleague come round straight away. The two men went to his study and, once the steward had brought them their drinks, they settled down in deep chairs by the fire. For the first ten minutes or so it was, as always, casual gossip about the current Washington scene and the ever-deteriorating situation in Eastern Europe.

'Norway is a small power,' Berg said, 'but we still feel we have a role in trying to reach settlements behind the scenes. Remember our brokering the Middle East peace? You've probably heard we've had the Ukrainians and the Russians in Oslo trying to sort out their difficulties in a neutral place. It's our humble contribution to . . .'

'You've got a good reputation for all that,' said Milner.

'We're too good for our own good, we Norwegians. We don't lack problems of our own, you know.'

Milner wondered where this conversation was heading. He had known Anders Berg for years and knew that it took him time to reach the nub of what he wanted to talk about. He was apprehensive. When it came, his anxiety proved justified.

'I've never asked you about your time in Oslo.' Berg folded his hands together in front of him as if he was about to pray.

'A long, long time ago.' Immediately Milner realized his visitor's agenda. It hit him like a blow in the pit of his stomach.

'We were all young. But then . . . some things, sometimes, come back to haunt us, don't they?' Berg looked across at his friend.

'Do I have to guess at what you're driving at, Anders?' Milner felt numb.

'I'm picking up a story out of Oslo.'

'Yes?'

'About you,' said Berg.

'Ah.' It came out more as a gasp than an exclamation.

'Someone's been digging through files.'

'Norwegian files? I don't think there can be much about me.' Milner tried to laugh.

'Not Norwegian files. A batch of stuff about Norwegian security operations, out of KGB archives. Our people have been looking for hints and clues, mainly for historical purposes, you must understand. We don't want to dig up long-buried dirt.' Berg frowned and sipped at his drink.

'What are you telling me?'

'Somebody seems to have found something . . . about you.'

'Not surprising. Three years liaising with your Intelligence people before I transferred and became a legitimate diplomat. I imagine there're reams of files about me.' Milner knew his words sounded false.

'About the death of Olafsen. You know the one.'

'I know the one.' His voice sank to a whisper.

'They indicate you had something to do with it.'

'I did.' There was, to him, a welcome pause as the residence steward appeared to replenish their drinks. 'I did,' Milner repeated at last.

'Is that all you're going to say?' Berg asked.

'Simply . . . yes. It's a long time ago. Even now, Anders, even to you, some things I don't talk about.' Again there was a pause.

'Well,' said the Norwegian Ambassador, gently easing himself to his feet. 'I just came to tell you . . . to warn you . . . as an old friend. I was not instructed to come. I don't much approve of such digging but then it depends what the dirt is, doesn't it?' He looked hard at Milner.

The British Ambassador appeared to have regained control of himself. He looked bored, almost uninterested. 'How right you are, Anders. How right you are,' he repeated, as he too got to his feet to show his guest to the door.

If he was perturbed by what Anders Berg had said to him, he did not let it show. Colleagues saw no change in him. In any event, as the political situation in Eastern Europe careered into a crisis over the next few days, with economic refugees in their hundreds of thousands trying to stampede across the borders to the West, he had little time for personal introspection. Many were reported killed in food riots in the streets of Moscow and relations between Russia and the Ukraine had reached breaking point over the future of the mothballed former Soviet Black Sea fleet at Sebastopol. Everywhere, sectional, regional and ethnic outbreaks of violence were spreading like a disease, one fire inflaming another. It was impossible to monitor everything, though NATO, for once united, had sent military reinforcements to contain the unrest within the borders of the former European Communist Empire. As ambassador he was kept long hours at his desk, reading the telegrams from Brussels and elsewhere that reported on the meetings of home and foreign ministers of the Community as they negotiated the building of a new Iron Curtain right across Europe. It was to follow the same lines as the former one, to ensure that a mass migration of starving East European immigrants would not overwhelm their prosperous Western neighbours. Border patrols were rearmed and Rhine Army bases, long abandoned by the British and the French, were being remanned as holding points for troops before they were sent to patrol the eastern approaches.

Of even more immediate consequence to Milner was, once again, the roller-coaster state of relations with the United States. At a European summit in Brussels, there were strident calls for America to contribute substantial numbers of troops to the defence of the new Iron Curtain. Congress and House of Representatives rejected such American involvement by huge majorities in each case. 'Let the Europeans fight their own battles' was the common cry on the floor of each House. Isolationism was rampant, the US President was running with the tide, and White

House sensitivities were high. So when, within only a few weeks of his apparently successful visit to Washington, the British Prime Minister gently chided the American lack of response in the House of Commons, their Administration reacted with unusual bitterness. The President went on television to condemn London's armchair warriors who expected the Americans to fight their battles for them. 'Every time there's a problem,' he said, 'they run whining to the US for help. My fellow Americans, we have sufficient problems of our own,' he went on. 'We have tensions enough in our own spheres of influence in South America and in the countries of the Pacific rim. Let the Europeans, for once, stand up for themselves. Let me be more blunt: it is absurd for the Prime Minister of the United Kingdom to complain when what he and his government have been doing for years is to ask America to reduce its commitment in Europe. They cannot have it both ways.'

Later that day the ambassador received a top-secret, highest-priority, *Flash* telegram, containing urgent instructions to seek a meeting, if possible, with the President. It was personal from the Secretary of State himself. It read:

1. The Prime Minister and I have been considering urgently what steps you should take to try to defuse the increasingly bitter tensions between the White House and ourselves. The Prime Minister had not wished his remarks to be taken so personally by the President; we regret he has reacted as strongly as he has. Once again he has shown how touchy he is in relation to any criticism, and from us in particular. We are especially concerned because the Prime Minister had felt, as I did, that relations had improved following the Washington visit.

2. You should now seek an urgent meeting with the President or, failing him, with the Secretary of State, to try to ameliorate the situation. You should point out that the Prime Minister was speaking largely to a British audience and regrets it if the President has

taken his words out of context. You should go on to stress, however, that the increasingly catastrophic situation in Eastern Europe requires the closest US involvement. All Europe would be grateful were the United States Government able, at least nominally, to strengthen its military commitment to Western Europe's frontiers.

3. You may, if you feel it would help, also mention the matter of the Confederate Flag . . .

Milner threw the telegram angrily aside. 'The Confederate fucking Flag, for God's sake,' he exploded. Only Fawcett was within earshot. 'What's that going to achieve at this point in time? Sometimes Foreign Office Ministers don't seem to be living in the real world. They'll be sending out morris dancers next.'

Milner knew all about the Confederate Flag. It was ancient; probably the first known example of the flag in existence; it was due to come up for sale at Sotheby's. The British Government had stepped in and agreed to buy it from its vendor; their intention was to present it, at some suitable opportunity, to the United States Government as an act of friendship. But now, for God's sake!

He had to kick his heels for two days waiting for his audience with the President. Eventually he got news of the time and place, happy not to be brushed off with a meeting with the Secretary of State. He took that as a positive sign. This time Velcor accompanied him as note-taker. He had rehearsed very carefully with his senior colleague what he was going to say, intending to keep closely to the instructions contained in the telegram from the Secretary of State, but fully determined to put his own gloss on matters, pointing out the incredible pressures HMG were under from their own backbenchers. He would ensure that the President understood; internal politics and catering to various wings of the party in power, led to swings in policy in the United States as much as it did in the UK. It would require all his skills as ambassador to get the President to see things from Britain's point of view. He would invite him to suggest what Her Majesty's Government should do. This was an occasion for asking for assistance and support, not for demanding. Milner was widely reputed to be an outstanding diplomat. This would prove him or break him.

He called in his Press Counsellor and got him to line up interviews with the *Washington Post*, the *New York Times* and a couple of the TV networks so that the right sort of background noises would filter through to the White House prior to his meeting with the President. The Counsellor was good at his job and within a few hours had fixed them all up, following this with a call to the White House Press Office to make sure it read correctly the friendly signals that were going to be hoisted by the ambassador.

Milner saw the two newspaper correspondents later that day, then went downtown to the television studios for the other interviews. For once the American media were paying a lot of attention to what was going on in Eastern Europe since a senior US businessman was currently being held in Moscow on spying charges. Their usual tunnel vision of the world had swung in precisely the right direction.

Milner played the TV interviews well. He began by sympathizing with the US Administration over the human-interest story of the businessman; the British had had a similar incident only recently. That got him listened to and widely reported. He then went on to praise the wisdom and determination of the President; flattery did not always win friends but it usually had more upside than downside. The White House Press Office would ensure that what he was reported as saying would reach the President's desk. He ended both newspaper interviews and the television sessions with the words: 'We recognize the constraints that may prevent the United States from deploying troops, but we in Europe continue to need their wise advice and guidance.'

The following day's headlines set the scene to perfection. The meeting with the President in the Oval Office was much less of an ordeal than it would otherwise have been. The President was in a good mood, greeting the ambassador warmly and calling him by his first name. He had the Secretary of State with him, and only a couple of staffers. Milner spoke as he had been instructed, but dressed it up by saying how much the Prime Minister wanted his advice and support at this difficult time. What would the President advise the British Government and its European allies to do? Might the President attend a summit with European leaders? Might he take up an invitation to visit London, Paris or Bonn so that, for the benefit of the outside world, he was seen to be involved, even though no American troops could, for understandable reasons, be committed at this stage? Having made his points, Milner sat back to listen.

The President began in reasonable mode. He said he was obviously flattered to be asked for advice, made the usual noises about working together with Europe and how America valued the closest co-operation with its European allies. He was glad that the ambassador recognized the difficulties he would face in committing American troops to defend the Eastern Approaches. He was not immune to what was going on over there and American diplomatic representatives in Moscow and Kiev were doing all they could to bolster the local governments in their attempts to keep anarchy off the streets. He was about to announce a further package of aid to Eastern Europe, though he realized that, however it was window-dressed, it was only, as he said, 'a piss in the ocean'.

Then suddenly and unexpectedly – it appeared to be a surprise to them too – he once again asked everyone else to leave him alone with Milner. The Secretary of State went particularly reluctantly, leaving the President and the ambassador alone.

'I want this entirely off the record, Martin.'

'Of course, sir.'

'Between you and me. Nothing personal, you understand.'

Milner sat in silence and waited.

'Right. Here it is. I cannot stand you fuckin' Brits lecturing to me. I blew my top when I heard what your Prime Minister said. I'm in it up to my neck without letting you has-beens tell me what or what not to do. It can't happen again, d'you hear?'

Milner was shocked by the coarseness and anger in his voice. 'I hear what you say, Mr President,' he said carefully.

'There you go. Typical diplomatic soap.' He mimicked: '"I hear what you say, Mr President."' He laughed bitterly. 'You guys really get my goat.'

'I ask again, why, Mr President?'

'I told you first time. You English are so fuckin' unreliable . . . and patronizing.'

'Is that all?' Milner knew he was on dangerous ground but it was now or never. He decided to provoke and see what reaction he got. 'By the way, we're not just English, we're Scots, Welsh and Irish. All very different.' He was deliberately pedantic.

'Don't lecture me.'

'Mr President. I'm just trying to get at the root of your dislike.'

'The root of my dislike is that you're a bunch of self-centred hypocrites. You think the world owes you a fuckin' living; you think what's good for Britain should be good for the rest of the world. You're arrogant. You once ruled and, for God knows what reason, you still think you've got a place with the big guys at the top. The world has moved on, leaving you miles behind.'

The President's angry and deep-held feelings were so intense and were expressed more by his body language and manner than by the words he used, that it actually insulated the ambassador, allowing him to think more clearly. Here was an extraordinary man with strong but simple emotions. Yet the underlying root cause still escaped him.

'I'm the first to realize there are some pretty old-fashioned attitudes floating around the British Establishment,' Milner moved cautiously. 'But whatever your personal views, it's not Britain that brought about the current East European crisis . . .'

'I know that too, Martin,' the President interrupted. 'Sure. You guys have a serious problem in Eastern Europe. The National Security Council, the CIA and the State Department are doing nothing much else but monitor the situation. I meant what I said about our ambassadors doing what they can behind the scenes.

That's a different damn matter from committing US troops. That would be political suicide.'

Milner listened in silence, wondering what else was to come. Then, suddenly, the President let it all out: 'I know you have been burning up the oil trying to analyse why I feel this way. I hear your latest theory is that it's because my mother run away with an English gink. I can tell you one bit of news for your files. He was a S . . . H . . . one T bastard, what he did to me . . . and her, I suppose, though it was her choice. She asked for it. Well, Martin, I faced up to that particular problem years ago and I think I've got it out of my psyche. Don't waste time on my hang-ups, Martin. They're not the big issue.' The President checked himself, breathed deeply, straightened his jacket, walked to the door, opened it and left the room. The meeting was at an end.

The truth about the ambassador's meeting with the President came in various forms; most were a long way short of the whole truth. But then the whole truth on anything to do with international relations is a rare commodity. The first version was the way the British media reported it. Clive Crick, ITN's Washington correspondent's report was typical, reflecting as it did, embassy briefing.

The much-discussed meeting between the British Ambassador and the President took place at the White House today in an attempt to defuse the increasingly acrimonious relations between the United States and Europe over East European policy. According to informed sources, the ambassador received assurances from the President that he was monitoring the situation carefully and that while no guarantee on the despatch of US troops was given, the President promised to keep the situation under urgent review. Once again the skills of the British Ambassador to Washington, Sir Martin Milner, have been put to the test. All in all a good day for British diplomacy. This is Clive Crick at the White House returning you to the studios of ITN in London.

The ambassador's telegram was less rose-tinted. It went *Flash*, top secret and personal for the Secretary of State and read:

1. I saw the President at the White House this morning. He was accompanied by the Secretary of State for the first part of the meeting. I am reporting on that open meeting separately.

2. Much to my surprise and that of his staff, he again dismissed them and I saw him on a one-to-one basis for about half an hour. He turned from amiable to aggressive mood and went through his bitches about the Prime Minister's remarks. I tried to explain that these were largely meant to appeal to a British audience, in particular right-wing backbenchers in the party. The President dismissed this out of hand, despite having many similar difficulties himself.

3. The President again spoke brutally frankly about his dislike for Britain and all things British. He has never been so blunt. He himself brought up his mother's unhappy relationship with a British army officer. I am reporting separately on this.

4. The President moved on to a totally new subject: he complained that he had recently received detailed evidence of how much the Conservative Party had helped his Republican opponent when he was running for office. He gave me a full list of names of Central Office staff who had actively worked against his candidature. He felt that this was outside the bounds of what was reasonable in relations between two countries. Such gross partisanship and interference by members of the Conservative Party reinforced his suspicion of us.

5. I tried to distance the actions of party activists and what they may or may not have done on a personal basis during the last presidential election, from current policies being pursued by HMG. The President

dismissed my argument out of hand. My conclusion is that we have a real and continuing problem; it will not go away without hard work on our part.

6. I raised the question of the Confederate Flag. To my surprise it actually seemed to help matters. The President was most grateful and said he would see to it that a suitably warm response was forthcoming when the gift was announced . . .

Rain threatened but the huge black umbrellas carried by the waiting footmen remained firmly rolled, as the guests, the men all in white ties and tailcoats, bedecked with orders and medals if they had them, the women in long gowns and dresses sweeping the ground, filed into Buckingham Palace. It was the annual diplomatic reception given by The Queen for ambassadors, high commissioners and senior diplomats accredited to Her Majesty's Court of St James's. Hundreds of them lined up for hours in the great state rooms, waiting to be presented, while British diplomats drafted in from the Foreign Office, members of the Royal Household and gentlemen ushers, paced elegantly around making sure all went smoothly.

Later that night, after most of the royal family had retired and the diplomats themselves were beginning to drift home, Trafford Leigh and Sir Caspar Rudd, the Secretary to the Cabinet, stood talking quietly in a corner of the White Drawing Room.

'What does Ivor think?' asked Sir Caspar. He was a balding, bespectacled figure with a quick, inquisitive look and a moderate smile. He had once been called the cleverest man in Britain. 'He knows Martin Milner better than most,' he added.

'He doesn't know all that we know, of course, but I thought we might put him in the picture. He should be here somewhere.' Leigh looked around the huge room. 'I got him an invitation after all his help with the French state visit.'

'There he is,' said Sir Caspar. 'I'll go and . . . no . . . he's spotted us. He'll be over like a shot.'

A moment or so later, Dr Mark Ivor disengaged himself from the discussion he was having with the Deputy Private Secretary to The Queen and advanced across the White Drawing Room towards them. 'It's been a long evening,' Ivor sighed, greeting them both. His order, the CB, dangled from its band just below his meticulous white bow tie.

'Well worth every penny. Does great things for the morale of the London Diplomatic Corps,' said Trafford Leigh grandly. An old Etonian, he looked the part, as if chosen by central casting for his role at Buckingham Palace that night.

'I was about to leave,' said Ivor. 'I have an early flight to Cannes tomorrow.'

'Ah the jet set . . .' smiled Sir Caspar wearily. He was not at all envious.

'Sadly not. Meeting one of my Arab sheikhs. He lives there. Back after lunch.' Ivor shrugged philosophically.

'Before you go. A word . . . about your friend and ours, Martin Milner,' said Trafford Leigh. 'I was saying to Caspar . . . I'm worried. Would like your advice. You know him well.'

'He's getting a good press . . . Any more intelligence on who shot his son?'

'Almost nothing. The Intelligence community is embarrassed.'

'Then . . . ?' asked Ivor. His antennae told him something was in the wind.

'Personal factors are making us worry . . .'

'I've heard the gossip about a new girlfriend. If that's what you're . . .' Ivor smiled. 'A bit soon after Annabel's death, I agree, but surely . . .'

'Nothing to do with that. It's a bit delicate, but since you know him, you ought to be more in the picture . . . We may need your help.'

13

The Georgetown house had become his refuge. He looked forward to going there, getting away from the cares of the embassy, unwinding. He did not mind that the gossips had started to whisper. He had been worried about David's reaction, but his son seemed not to know or did not care. He was a widower; there was nothing to throw at Flora Simons. He had an excellent excuse: she was painting his portrait. Everyone knew that. It was coming along well; she now always worked on it there rather than at the residence. He was flattered by the way she had picked out the strength of his features; the mouth was firm and confident; only the eyes still seemed hesitant, as if the painter was yet undecided as to how to make them come alive.

MacKenzie had become resigned to his long sojourns there and had taken to bringing books with him. He said he was thinking of studying for another degree. He got on well with Flora, which helped, since they were forced to spend a lot of time in each other's company, both linked, Milner idly thought, by the business of looking after his body.

That early-December evening, he lay in bed with Flora. A sheet was draped lightly across her, covering none of the parts where his attentions were particularly directed. He caressed her as they talked.

'Years of experience ... You've had years of experience ...' Flora whispered in his ear. She was at the same time relaxed and excited at the prospect of what was to come.

'It's you who brings out these skills in me,' he breathed, hand moving ever more intimately.

'And what else do I bring out in you?' She moved to caress him in turn.

The words came faster with his breath. 'You're the most sensuous woman I've ever met.'

'Me? Sensuous? All I'm doing is lying here, enjoying . . .' Her words ceased as he moved on top of her. Then there was no more talk until they had both slaked and spent their passion.

Later, they lay side by side, glistening with the sweat of satisfaction.

'I'm glad you still find time for me,' Flora said gently. 'I do realize . . .' She hesitated.

'Time . . . My life's biggest problem.' Milner gradually pulled himself back to reality.

'A real problem in everybody's life. Handling it is another fine art.'

'Ruled by my diary. If you knew how much trouble it took to find occasions like this.' Milner used a corner of the sheet to wipe his forehead.

'I cause you trouble?'

'I didn't mean that.' He turned to look at her, stretching out his hand to touch her hair.

'A president in the morning, a princess in the afternoon and a painter at night: three Ps. And the ever-present MacKenzie, like a guard dog, sleeping at your feet. Don't you think we could send him home? To his girlfriend . . .' Flora stopped herself. She had, nevertheless, spoken deliberately.

'He has one?' Milner took the bait. 'How does *he* find the time?'

'I gather . . .'

'Who?' he asked, looking at her again.

'No one you should know about.'

'You and Andrew have secrets from me?' Milner was amused.

'A little secret.'

He decided not to pursue it. 'He won't go home. Even for sex. Not until they find out who was out to kill me. They haven't . . . Doesn't that ever worry you?'

Flora shrugged her shoulders. 'Not any more. It's a million miles away from us, lying here together . . . though . . .'

'Though what?'

'It brings up something else I keep thinking about.' She lay on her back, facing the ceiling.

'What's that?'

'*You*, quite simply. You've had a life I know so little about; a past world I've only glimpsed, a history of which I know only a fraction. I've hardly even met your David, except once, formally, at some reception.'

'You'll meet him, I promise. When he's better adjusted.' Milner had been putting off what he knew he must arrange. It wasn't fair on any of them.

'So . . . All I have to go on is the here and now. You here and your body now.'

'You're in a strangely philosophical mood. Isn't now enough?'

'You say I live for the moment, so, yes, I suppose it should be enough. But . . . I'm curious. I'm curious about what disciplines you. I know how much self-discipline you need, like now, not to jump up the moment we've made love and use the telephone to make sure your empire is still working without you. You're good at disguising it, but how you long to get back to your desk the instant our moment is over.' Flora turned her head with a soft smile.

'Am I so obvious?'

'You hide it well. I suppose it's a normal male instinct. You want to get up and I want to go on.'

'I do find it relaxing with you.' She looked so peaceful, lying there beside him, yet he sensed that her mind too was fully active.

'I'm sure you relax more with me than you do most of the time. But you're still tense. Not the tension I massage out of your shoulders. Together we can get rid of that. It's . . . Doesn't anything out there worry you? Isn't there anything you're afraid of? These are the sorts of questions I'd like to have an answer to.' Flora half sat up, resting her elbow on a pillow.

This time it was Milner who rolled on his back and lay staring up at the ceiling. He was aware of the slight discomfort of the crumpled sheet under him, the stickiness of the sweat matting the hairs on his chest. He paused before he responded. 'I worry about events, about the unexpected. In work, as I suppose in life, I never quite know what's going to happen around the bend. A single action, a sudden incident, and one's entire life can change.'

'Fatalist?' She watched him in profile, willing him to turn and look at her.

'No. I don't mean the car accident sort of incident or a heart attack, though these are also possibilities. It's . . . it's that somebody, somewhere, can take a course of action which, coupled with other circumstances, can totally change the course of your own history. That is always worrying. Things entirely out of your control.'

'As I say – fatalist.'

'What will happen will happen. Turning points in life, like me meeting you.' He turned his head quickly and caught the affection in her eyes as she lay watching him.

'Or the death of your wife.'

'That too.' He fell silent for a moment.

'I feel . . . I've said it before . . . there's some shadow lying over you,' Flora went on remorselessly. 'It's not to do with the important, or at least perceived to be important, work that you do. You're always in the newspapers, on television, in the places where the great and the good live and work and exist. Something hidden . . .'

'We all have shadows. We're all selective with our memories. We put things out of our minds. If we lived with every worry and anxiety and misfortune from the past we'd go insane. You must feel the same . . .' Her questioning unsettled him. He did not like it.

'As you keep saying, I live for the moment. I don't let pasts haunt me. Have you a past that haunts you?'

'I have a son . . . shot up because . . . I have a suicide . . . These things will never go away.' He was brusque. He wanted her to stop.

'Guilt?'

'Of course. But if I didn't moderate that, it too would destroy me.'

Flora Simons suddenly sat upright on the bed and looked down at him. 'Now,' she said. '*Now*. If only I could paint your eyes as they are looking now, *then* I would have you. But, by the time I get you seated downstairs in a properly dressed condition, since if you went and sat on that leather chair in your present state even MacKenzie might be a bit shocked, they will have lost that spark I've been looking for.'

'What d'you see?' He stared back at her.

'I see confidence; I see strength; I see determination, but still, deep down . . . behind your pupils . . .' Flora checked herself. She recognized that she had, for some unexplained reason, gone too far. 'Come on . . . get dressed, will you, Martin? Play's over. We've work to do.'

Apart from Flora Simons's very private analysis, he was the constant subject of profiles in the British and American press. He was told he should be flattered by all the attention he received. Most of the articles were scissors-and-paste copies of each other, regurgitating stories that had been doing the rounds ever since his appointment in Washington. Variously described as an enigma, brilliant, effortless, superior, incisive and cold by *The Times*; if one read the *Guardian* essay, he could be secretive and devious when he had to be. The *Telegraph* shared the view of the *Washington Post* that, on balance, he was proving a success, not only having the confidence of his own government but that of the US Secretary of State and of the President. He kept the better of the profiles in a leather folder and decided that if the media were going to write about him so much, he should give them more substance to work on.

Knowing there would be press present when he was invited to make a speech to the British Universities Club of Washington, he worked hard on what he was going to say. Unusually, he showed it to no one at the embassy, and, on the night, delivered a small masterpiece that was amusing by being self-mocking. By quoting cleverly from these profiles he got his audience to laugh with him. He even mentioned the *Sun* exclusive; and, much to Andrew

MacKenzie's embarrassment, he dramatically pointed him out to a delighted audience as his resident Rasputin.

It was all part of a carefully formulated defence mechanism against allowing himself to take too seriously the criticism that did emerge from time to time. Sharing the popular views of himself with a wider audience was meant to show that he did not care. Only those very close to him recognized the ploy: he acted that way because he cared very deeply indeed about what people thought. Whatever the reason, on this occasion, his captive audience of prominent Brits who lived in Washington and pro-British Americans who valued their British education, was highly appreciative.

There was much serious meat in what he said. He treated them to a lively lecture on diplomatic techniques; it was all a great game, he suggested. Diplomats were deal-makers, brokering with words. While they too had feelings over what was right and what was wrong, they must not let personal convictions get in the way of the hard decisions they had to reach. Take someone in his position, he argued: his duty was to represent the interests of Her Majesty's Government in Washington, to make sure that British interests were well safeguarded, to improve relations between two great countries. If he made any contribution towards those ends then he would be well pleased. But he could not work alone. There were lots of current problems on the trans-Atlantic net, and he urged his audience to work with him, since they too were key players in the overall strategy of Anglo–American relations. They were all people of prominence; they too had to contribute, to ensure that, even if the special relationship was no longer valid, the underlying strength of the British–American linkage survived. He ended in rousing terms about the deep ties between two English-speaking peoples being secure, whatever the waves on the surface of public life might indicate. There is nothing like a well-delivered cliché. He got, as he expected, a standing ovation.

At the end of the dinner, as he was looking for an opportunity to slip away for a late-night rendezvous with Flora, a distinguished, white-haired gentleman accosted him and steered him into a corner.

'Simon Fitzgibbon, Your Excellency. Old English name . . . but ma' family's been here in the US of A for five generations. New College, Oxford, ma'self.'

'My college too.' Milner smiled vaguely and made other pleased-to-meet-you remarks. He had come across people like this on many occasions. At a guess he'd be a Rhodes Scholar and be more British in his tastes and habits than the British.

'Your speech. Good points; well delivered.'

'Thank you,' he responded automatically.

'Ah come from our President's home state. Where he was a boy. Where he grew up.'

'Interesting . . .' Milner was distracted. He wished Simon Fitzgibbon would get to the point if he had one.

'Interesting, yes. Knew him. Knew his family. All his family . . . Knew that English officer who stole his mother away all these years ago . . . Ah even know what his real name was.'

'I must . . .' Milner had glanced at his watch, not wishing to be discourteous, but then he stopped and listened, suddenly realizing the considerable significance of what he was being told.

'Ah don't want to keep you hooked to an old man's memories. Ah've never told anyone else, least of all the media.' Mr Fitzgibbon made a little grimace of distaste. 'Didn't want to do it,' he continued. 'But now Ah think it's my duty. There's a little bit of gossip Ah ought to tell you . . .'

First thing the next morning Milner sent for Charles Nairn.

'I want this totally off the record. Between you and me and only your most trusted people back home. Do you understand, Charles?'

'I hate giving blank commitments, sir. But yes.'

'You remember when the President was last in Britain we were required to have emergency drills set up in case he needed hospitalization?' Milner was particularly brisk this morning. 'We were given all his blood group and DNA registers, weren't we? Can you get hold of them?'

'Expect so.' Nairn was fascinated. What was the ambassador up to?

'Good. Then I'll tell you what else I want. Which may be a bit more difficult.'

Another part of an ambassador's life was having to get involved in the human tragedies that came to him via the several British consulates in cities right across the United States. Seldom did a diplomat as senior as he was get personally involved in the difficulties faced by British tourists or businessmen and -women but, just occasionally, prompted by a hysterical British tabloid media, he was forced to take account of the real-life dramas that confronted British visitors to North America.

One such happened three days later: the horrific murder of a whole family of British tourists outside Tampa in Florida. It was a small event in Anglo-American history, but not so in the eyes of the tabloids, which immediately drummed up a campaign to stop British tourists visiting the United States by giving graphic illustrations, sometimes real, sometimes invented, of the level of crime in the streets of metropolitan America. Tourist chiefs in Florida bombarded the embassy with protests at what they saw as the biased coverage of Florida's tourist industry. The British Consul in Miami was desperate. It was a horrific murder; there were real problems of crime and violence, but the tabloid reporting was way over the top. Something had to be done. The ambassador summoned the consul to Washington and, after consulting the State Department and speaking personally on the telephone with the Governor of Florida, he issued a widely reported statement, urging British tourists not to cancel their holidays. He added his congratulations to the Tampa Chief of Police, since his force had already apprehended the gang of youths who had almost certainly perpetrated the crime. As he issued his press release, Milner remarked dryly that, while there was a huge outcry over this incident, nobody protested at the fact that Americans cancelled their holidays in droves every time there was a bomb scare or other terrorist atrocity in Britain or elsewhere in Europe.

His mind was still on this consular matter when Paul Fawcett came in to see him. Some days ago, in much excitement, his Private Secretary had asked for special leave to take his new-found girlfriend to Florida on holiday. Now he came in looking rather shamefaced. 'In the circumstances, she says she'd rather stay here,' he said. 'I hope you don't mind if I delay, sir, and take my days off a bit later on?'

'I thought you'd choose a girl made of sterner stuff, Paul,' said Milner kindly.

'She is, sir. Very. She's made up her mind; she wants to be here, be around. I guess I best go along with it.' Fawcett looked subdued, but Milner thought nothing more of it.

That December day, shortly before Christmas, Milner worked on a draft submitted to him by the embassy's economic section, and finalized and sent off a *Flash* telegram to London on the subject of the Reserve Bank and its newly-announced interest-rate cut. He wondered why he was bothering, since the money markets tended to beat the embassy by days in their analysis of Federal monetary policy. Apart from the arrangements for the forthcoming embassy Christmas party, it was a busy morning in other ways too. The famous Confederate Flag had arrived by special messenger. Now it had to be made ready for display to the press when it was handed over; there was another party to be arranged for the group of British businessmen who had put up some of the money to buy the flag. He was glad Lucinda was around to handle all the arrangements. She and David had looked quite pleased with themselves when they had returned from their New England jaunt, but he had got little out of them on the detail, beyond her saying, more than a shade mischievously, that David was A1 in all departments. He himself had been invited by Flora to spend a few days skiing in Vermont, but was unable to leave Washington: the multi-layered mechanisms of diplomacy, telegrams, despatches, letters, faxes and the unrelenting pressures from the media demanding to know every detail of the latest state of play of Anglo–American relations, chained him to his desk.

Charles Nairn came into his office later that day. MacKenzie was sitting by the window reading a newspaper.

'A word, sir. Alone.' Nairn, who was holding a red top-secret file, stared pointedly at the inspector.

MacKenzie got up and silently left the room, with Milner, for the first time, noting the tension between the two men.

Nairn pointedly closed the door behind the policeman, then, opening the file, explained that MI6 had easily retrieved the details of the President's blood group and other medical indicators. He was still hard at work on the other task the ambassador had set him.

'We know the man's dead. We have the date, the cause, everything. It's difficult . . .' said Nairn defensively.

'Difficulties are what you're good at,' Milner snapped. 'Look . . . I realize the problems, but . . . hospital records? I need to know if there's a possibility of verification.'

'If it exists, we'll find it. Then what will you do with it?' asked Nairn, aware of the importance the ambassador attached to what was, in his opinion, a very long shot.

'Not necessarily anything. But knowledge is power.'

'We'll be as quick as we can. We've put our best people on to it,' said Nairn as he left the room.

MacKenzie slipped straight back in as Nairn left. 'Sir,' he began hesitantly, 'I know what you're working on . . . with Mr Nairn. I might have a lead that would help . . .'

Milner, alert to potential intra-embassy conflicts, was not going to get his priorities mixed. It was most unlike MacKenzie to interfere with his diplomatic work.

'Not now, Andrew, if you don't mind,' he said sharply. 'I'm pressed for time . . .'

That evening, he drank little at the reception, then dined alone with David. At around ten-thirty, after his son went up to an early bed as was still his habit, Milner decided to check up on the day's telegrams from the Foreign Office, since he'd had a telephone call from Alexander in American Department, alerting him to items that needed his urgent attention. Flurries of snow were falling, it was bitterly cold, and he walked quickly across to his office in the grey, unlovely Chancery building. He had warned MacKenzie he might go back to his office, but had faithfully promised not to leave the compound. His bodyguard had, consequently, taken a well-deserved evening off. Milner's feet slipped slightly on the snow, but then the clouds briefly parted and a shaft of moonlight lit up his route as he advanced up the short driveway. The security guard let him in to the Chancery building, and he took the lift to his office, unlocked the door, switched on the lights and, with a sigh of resignation, sat down at his desk. Piles of papers were neatly laid out for him by his staff: correspondence to sign, letters to read, the batch of Foreign Office telegrams. Here he was, still at his day's work, and it was well after ten-thirty in the evening. He was fifty-six; he wondered how long he should or would go on, yet deep down, he knew there was no alternative.

At top of the pile was one of the telegrams the Foreign Office had warned him about; it was to the point and explained why they were summoning him back to London for consultations. He was due to fly home in two days' time. Ostensibly the reason was that the American Government were again talking about sending an emissary to Ulster, but he knew that could only be part of it. The deteriorating situation in Eastern Europe and America's lack of response to it were still at the top of the real agenda. There were confusing signals to sort out and justify. His defence attaché had been reporting one line back to London; he knew that his opposite number, Hiram Suskind, at the American Embassy in London, was interpreting matters differently to the State Department and the Pentagon. This often happened in diplomacy, but things were getting too far out of step. The office needed him there to discuss the options face to face.

He left a number of handwritten notes for his diary secretary to attend to the next day; he dictated a few letters into his tape machine, following those up with some other instructions, including which flights he wanted to be booked on, in and out of London. Then he sat back in his chair and wearily looked at his watch. It was time to call it a day. Almost midnight: he would sit quietly for a little while longer and collect his thoughts. Absent-mindedly, he stood and switched off the main office light, then went and sat back down at his desk. A gleam of moonlight reflecting off the snow found its way through the shutters, casting momentary pools of light across the papers on his desk. He sat there for about twenty minutes. Perhaps he dozed off. Then, suddenly, he was fully alert as he heard a noise in his outer office; probably the security guard coming up to make sure he was all right. He heard a bang, something fell to the floor, and these sounds were followed by muffled laughter. He stood and quietly walked towards the door, grasped the handle, waited and listened for a moment, then pulled it sharply open. There was a very drunk Fawcett with his girlfriend. He was in the process of pressing her backwards across his desk as if attempting to make love to her. Her skirt was halfway up her thighs, but she was angrily pushing him away.

'What the hell?' Milner exclaimed angrily. The flush-faced Fawcett sobered up rapidly, straightening his clothes. Pulling her skirt down, the girl moved silently to one side.

'I'm terribly sorry, sir. I was just . . .'

'What the hell are you doing here in this office at this time of night, Paul? And your friend . . . ? You know the regulations.' Milner had to stop himself from shouting.

'Yes, sir. I was just coming up to see everything was . . .' The young diplomat's words were heavily slurred. Milner controlled himself in front of the girl, who, he was aware, was standing staring at him as if transfixed. She, very evidently, was stone-cold sober.

'I'll say no for tonight,' Milner said, forcing himself not to explode. 'Go home. I'll see you first thing tomorrow morning, Paul.'

He turned on his heel, went back into his office, switched on the light and rang down to the security guard. When the man answered he yelled: 'How dare you let Mr Fawcett into the building, with a woman, at this time of night, and in the state he's in? I want a full report on my desk by first thing. How dare you?' he repeated, slamming the phone down in fury.

Once he had cooled down, he walked home. Fawcett could not get away with behaviour like this. It was a serious offence; he would talk to personnel department when he got to London to see if he should not be recalled home. And as for the duty security guard – he'd discuss his future with Andrew MacKenzie. But, above all, as he carefully picked his way back towards the residence along the snow-covered path, he thought of the girl: cold-eyed, staring at him, through him, saying not a word, not a single word. Why would someone so strikingly self-assured waste her time with a fool like Fawcett?

14

He took the shuttle to New York and flew Concorde back to London, was picked up by official car at the airport, and driven straight to the Foreign Office. Because speed was of the essence and the Treasury would not pay for a Concorde ticket for Mac-Kenzie, the latter had seen him on board at Kennedy Airport and had arranged for Special Branch to look after him while he was in London.

His senior diplomatic colleagues were already in mid-meeting, waiting for him in one of the ornate conference rooms in the Old Indian Office building. The agenda was businesslike and incisive; all the familiar Anglo–US problems were revisited by the team around the table; he was glad he was able to be there in person to give them his slant on events. After an hour, a messenger came in: the Prime Minister wanted to see him. Straight away. He left his colleagues and walked across Downing Street to Number Ten, wondering, with some apprehension, what the urgency was.

'The PM won't keep you long,' said Francis Pierce, the Private Secretary who greeted him and ushered him upstairs to wait in a side office. Pierce was the Foreign Office appointment at Number Ten, a sallow, intense civil servant with tired eyes and an anxious expression. Milner wondered, looking at him, how long he would last in that powerhouse.

'Good flight?' Pierce asked, uninterestedly.

'Concorde takes the exhaustion out of a lot of things. I'm glad Treasury authorizes me to travel that way.'

'Treasury hate it. It's bad enough a grade-one ambassador being allowed to fly first-class . . .'

'The PM wants to talk about Ulster?' Milner asked.

'He's leaving you to talk on all that to the Northern Ireland Secretary. He wants to concentrate on the big issue,' Pierce said vaguely.

'His current thinking on Eastern Europe?' Milner was trying to prepare himself for what might come up.

'His thinking is what Foreign Office thinking is. Something has to be done to force the Americans' hands. You've seen the latest Intelligence reports. Major movements of refugees; squalid camps all along the borders, filthy weather conditions, fear of epidemics. It's looking worse and worse.' Pierce paused. He had a lot of work to do, but if Britain's most senior ambassador wanted to chat, he'd have to put up with it. 'The press are having a field day, attacking HMG's apparent weakness . . .' he continued. 'God are we sick of their "why, oh why . . ." holier-than-thou editorials. They're right on one thing though: what happens if the refugees try to force their way through? We can't have Western European troops shooting starving women and children.'

'How close to agreement is this idea of a new Marshall Plan for Eastern Europe?' asked Milner.

'An inter-governmental working group's burning the oil. Everybody thinks it's a great idea. But nobody's prepared to put up that sort of cash. Not when most of it will be squandered or syphoned off by the mafia gangs and the inefficient bureaucracy that passes for the new order in Russia.' Pierce wore a permanent air of cynical resignation.

'The Czechs and Poles aren't so bad,' Milner volunteered.

'The whole thing's spilling over them. The domino effect.'

'NATO meeting?'

'The Prime Minister hopes you'll attend,' said Pierce. 'The Defence Secretary thought it would be a good idea.'

'Looks a bit obvious?' Milner hesitated.

'Behind the scenes of course, not sitting at the table. We've got to make the Americans realize how important this is. I'm sorry . . .' Pierce interrupted himself, somewhat embarrassed. 'I'm telling you everything you know a lot better than me.'

Milner smiled politely. 'Germans and the French?' he asked.

'Sure, Sir Martin. Right behind us. You yourself reported that their ambassadors in Washington have been pressing the same line as you. But we still seem to stick a long way out in front.'

As he spoke, a red light lit up on the Private Secretary's desk. Pierce stood, went and opened a door into the next-door room, and reappeared almost immediately. 'The Prime Minister will see you, Sir Martin.' He held the door open and the ambassador was ushered into the Prime Minister's presence.

The latter did not get up from his desk. 'Sit down, Martin, sit down. Tired? How's your son? Anything new to add?' All three questions were shot at him in quick succession. He answered carefully, but the Prime Minister was not listening. He had already moved on to his next subject.

'Why is that bloody man so anti us?' he asked aggressively.

'I've reported all I've been able to find, Prime Minister.' Milner was only being a little economical with the truth.

The two men talked their way through the problem, then, just as Milner was leaving, the Prime Minister having thanked him for coming in, almost as an afterthought, added: 'You've got enough on your plate without this Oslo thing coming up after all these years.'

An icy chill seized him somewhere in the pit of his stomach. He turned and looked at the Prime Minister. 'Sir? I don't understand.' His shock could have been taken for genuine bewilderment.

'Haven't they told you yet? Damn it to hell!' said the Prime Minister, in sudden realization. 'Sorry about that. Damn it to hell!' He stalked furiously across to the door, yanked it open and bellowed. 'Francis! Why hasn't somebody told the ambassador about the Oslo business? Why wasn't I told he hadn't been told? Damn it to hell! Somebody's head is going to roll for this.'

Half an hour later the ambassador was sitting in the Permanent Under-Secretary's room at the Foreign Office. The other man, with Sir Clifford Pelling, was the deputy head of MI6.

'I'm sorry you heard about it that way,' said Pelling. He was as arid and distant as Milner had always found him. 'Unfortunate. The PM hadn't read his damn brief,' said the MI6 man, equally icily. 'It was as simple as that.'

'The Prime Minister had read his brief. He just didn't get to the bit about not telling me,' said Milner furiously. 'As I seem to be the subject, would you tell me what the hell's going on?'

'The Norwegians have disinterred some papers ... rather they've been given to them by the Russians. Files on KGB activities in Norway, during the sixties and seventies. It's all part of a deal: selling their old secrets in return for a Norwegian aid package. Everyone's doing it; a lot of people are shaking in their shoes.'

'And?' asked Milner. He could guess only a little of what was coming.

'Your name comes up.'

'My Norwegian colleague in Washington hinted that something was going on. So what? MI6 have long known all about what I did.'

'That was the old story, Martin. Forgotten and forgiven. To the Norwegians, it's all new, however. To be blunt, the reports in the files make it crystal-clear that by tipping off your friend and letting him escape to Moscow, you were responsible for the death of one of their key operators.'

'I've admitted it. I knew the man personally. They caught him on his way home from his last mission. In a way I was responsible. But don't forget; I also did it to protect one of our people – an agent I was running. I regret it. I always have. I admitted to it all, away back in 'sixty-eight.'

'According to the Russian files that have recently become available, however . . .' the man from MI6 paused ominously.

'Have you actually seen them?' Milner interrupted aggressively.

'I've seen the files. Copies of translations of them at least. I believe them to be genuine.'

'What do they say?'

'That's the problem,' said the Permanent Under-Secretary slowly. 'I'm sorry about this, Martin. We've got to take you through all this. It's a long time ago. We accept that. It's not immediately going to affect your position in Washington or anything like that.'

'What precisely does it say?' hissed Milner through clenched teeth. The word 'immediately' had struck a further warning note.

'It says that you were paid money to betray this man,' said the MI6 man softly.

'That's absurd. You know that's a damn lie,' Milner burst out in genuine, horrified rage. 'With hindsight and much mistaken loyalty, I tried to protect my man and help an old friend, that's all. That is *all*,' he repeated.

'We accept what you say, Martin. Nevertheless, the KGB files say you were paid.'

'Surely nobody in the British system believes . . .' Milner grew pale as the implications of what he was hearing began to sink in.

'Of course not, Martin,' said the Permanent Under-Secretary, in a somewhat less hostile voice. 'But we had to tell you. You'd have done the same. It throws a nasty shadow. The Norwegians may believe it.'

'I am appalled . . . How could anyone think I . . . ?' Milner was totally aghast.

'There's no corroborative evidence from any other source, if that's any consolation,' said the man from MI6 dryly. 'Maybe the KGB were covering up their own misuse of funds. It's happened. It's difficult to account for money paid to . . . spies.' He threw a glance at the Permanent Under-Secretary as he spoke.

'May I see the files?' Milner asked at length.

'We have them here,' said the MI6 man, proffering a bundle of photostats. 'Perhaps when you've read them, you could tell us if there's anything else we ought to know. Any little hint.'

'Why now? Who's driving what out of Oslo? Why after all this time?'

'We're not entirely sure. The Norwegians were almost apologetic when they told us. They thought we'd better know before it got out in any other way,' the MI6 man volunteered.

'Why should it get out?'

'Some man over there, you knew him once, I think. Petter Hauge's his name. He's been going through everything with a small tooth comb. He too was involved all these years ago. He's got some sort of axe to grind.'

'The name again?' asked Milner.

'Hauge. Petter Hauge . . . I'm not sure it matters. The thing is that the files are out. Have a look at them.'

Milner reluctantly took the bundle of papers. 'Hauge . . . yes . . . maybe I remember . . . This couldn't have anything to do with the attack on David, could it?' Milner shot a sudden hard look of enquiry at the MI6 man.

The latter shrugged. 'Would I know?' he said emptily. His response gave nothing away.

'You do know this is a complete and absolute fabrication, don't you?' Milner almost yelled the words. 'Any suggestion of my having been paid any money by the Soviets is totally untrue. You know and understand that, don't you?' he added, standing and looking down at the other two men. They looked back at him, coldly, without speaking. Now he realized that this was much, much more than just a shadow from the past.

Sir Martin Milner was driven back to the airport. He remembered nothing of the journey. He had not slept for nearly twenty hours and this added greatly to his feeling of impotence. He had always been able to cope with political crises; he revelled in his dealings with the President and the American Administration over Eastern Europe, but this additional personal accusation, coming on top of everything else, could, unchecked, eat into his soul. He would have to be on his guard; in its very magnitude, it could easily destroy his self-control.

The only good that had come out of his London visit was that, after his meeting with the Permanent Under-Secretary was over, the MI6 man had taken him aside and told him the results of Charles Nairn's request about the President and his blood group.

'We've got all the details. Exciting. The link is much more than just a possibility.'

'Well . . . ?' asked Milner, forcing himself to concentrate on what he was being told. 'How close a match?'

'The data are being analysed at a certain central London hospital at the moment. We've a small unit there that works for us from time to time. They're matching up the DNA and all that. We'll let you know.'

'Set the cat among the pigeons, couldn't it?' For a moment, Milner was distracted from his own problems by the excitement of his discovery. Talk about shadows from the past. 'Treat like top-secret?' he added unnecessarily.

'We know our business, Sir Martin,' said the man from MI6.

The Foreign Secretary's private office unexpectedly rang Dr Mark Ivor at lunchtime the next day. Could he please make a meeting at the House of Commons early that evening? Trafford Leigh would be in his room there, working on his forthcoming presentation to the Select Committee on Overseas Representation. But before that meeting, the Foreign Secretary wanted him to see some papers. No. They could not be sent round to Ivor's office. Could he please come to the Foreign Office to read them? This afternoon if possible.

Ivor cancelled another appointment, and after he had finished at the Foreign Office, he walked over to the St Stephen's entrance. There he cleared police security, and was shown straight up. Much to his surprise the Prime Minister was waiting there as well.

'Advice and help, Mark,' said Michael Wilson as soon as the door was closed. 'I've got to be quick. I'm meant to be hosting a reception at Number Ten.'

'You've been fully briefed on Martin Milner and the Oslo business?' asked Trafford Leigh in his usual remote manner.

'An hour ago. Not very nice, is it?'

'What d'you think?' asked the Prime Minister.

'I always said I'd tell you if it wasn't going to work. I'm his friend, but I said I'd speak honestly.'

'And . . . ?' said Trafford Leigh impatiently.

'Now . . . ? He'll have to go. He'll have to come home.' Ivor looked as unhappy as he felt. Milner had been his candidate, after all.

'Glad you agree,' said the Foreign Secretary. 'I, like you, was always his greatest supporter, but this was totally unexpected. No one could have foreseen . . .' Leigh's words tailed off. 'I'll write personally . . .' he went on. 'Send him the bad news. It's a pity we couldn't have told him while he was here yesterday, but we had just seen the papers from Oslo and needed more time to think it through.'

'No,' said Ivor, interrupting and addressing the Prime Minister. 'Don't write. Not that way. Leave it to me. I'll go out to see him in Washington. My responsibility to get us out of this. He's got to see it as *his* decision. Let him resign. Neater and more honourable.'

The two government ministers stared at Ivor in silence, then the PM nodded. 'OK. Go ahead,' he said quietly. 'Send us the bill for the flight. But not Concorde though, or Treasury will kick up a real stink!'

Sir Martin Milner was met at the airport not only by his driver and MacKenzie but by Charles Nairn. MacKenzie sat in the front of the Rolls with the driver. Nairn firmly closed the glass partition between them.

'Bring you up to date before you get to the embassy, sir. You met my boss, I gather,' whispered Nairn.

'Not altogether pleasant. You know about the Oslo accusation?' Milner knew enough about MI6 to know what the answer would be.

'As much as you do, sir. It's not my concern.' Nairn looked away.

'You've heard from your people about the blood groups, the DNA matching of the President and all that.' Milner forced himself on to the main topic.

'Sir.' Nairn nodded.

'Who else knows about it here at the embassy?' Milner asked.

'Me, sir. Me and me. That's all.' Nairn continued to keep his voice low.

'We'll keep it that way.' It was a statement by Milner rather than an order.

'I can't guarantee MacKenzie won't have heard something. By the way, I have to tell you frankly, sir, I'm not at all happy about his degree of access to things that don't concern him. It's not good for your reputation either, if you don't mind me saying so,' Nairn ventured. He guessed that the ambassador's days in Washington were numbered, but did not want to throw his weight around too much at this delicate stage.

'Leave MacKenzie to me,' responded Milner, checking his irritation.

Nairn read the signs, backed off and changed the subject. 'Because I'm interested in embassy security, I followed up on your complaint to the head security guard about Fawcett and his girl. My recommendation: he should go home soonest. Then . . . there's the girl.'

'What about her?' Milner asked. Not surprisingly, he had forgotten the incident.

'Just a girl, I thought. Then . . . well, I have to tell you, she turns out to be Norwegian . . .' Nairn paused to let his words sink in. Milner said nothing, so he continued: 'All my training says: don't trust coincidences. There are – at a guess – four million Norwegians. But in the circumstances . . .' Nairn left his sentence unfinished.

Milner was suddenly alert. 'Fawcett isn't a good-looker. He's overweight, has a bad complexion, is too full of himself and drinks too much. And she – I've only seen her a couple of times – is a stunner. I'd already wondered what it was about him . . . why somebody as glamorous as that would pick Fawcett up in Manhattan when he was up there with me?'

Nairn stared back at the ambassador. 'My own view too, sir,' he said, as the car pulled up in front of the embassy. 'I was sure you'd ask me to follow it up. So I am.'

Despite the background turmoil over the days that followed, an unwarranted feeling of normality settled on him. Life at the residence was reasonably agreeable. His diplomatic staff, attuned to his style, got on efficiently and effectively with the management of British relations with the United States Government. He had one or two problems to deal with in his relations with his son, David, who was getting increasingly fretful and was keen to get back to his City job, but these were minor. There was also the matter of Fawcett, a letter from whom had been waiting for him on his return. It was marked 'Personal and Confidential' and was, as he suspected, a long and rather pitiful apology for his behaviour. Milner put it to one side. It was not going to make any difference to the fact that the young diplomat's move from Washington was going to come up very soon.

On the political side, things also appeared to be going a shade better. In diplomacy, when in doubt, call a conference or set up bilateral talks. This, at his insistence, had happened, and there was now an Anglo–American Working Committee, composed of senior diplomats and military leaders from both sides, monitoring and reporting on all aspects of the breakdown of law and order in East Europe. Sharing the problems in this way was something he personally felt pleased about having negotiated. If it did not solve anything, at least it kept everyone busy.

The following Monday he got a phone call from his friend, Mark Ivor, to say that he was arriving in Washington the following Wednesday. Could he stay at the residence? Of course he could. It was always a pleasure to see Mark; indeed he was looking forward to it, since he was one of the few people to whom he could talk freely about life's problems.

Lucinda Forbes-Manning rearranged the ambassador's diary specifically so that he and his old friend could dine alone together. The steward served it in a little private dining room in the residence. He had thought of booking a table at a favourite Georgetown restaurant and inviting Flora Simons along, but as David was around and he was not yet ready to face that potential confrontation with his son, he decided to delay mixing the various strands of his life. It could wait. He chose the menu himself; a special claret was dug from the cellars. Ivor was due the very best.

After dinner he poured them both a glass of malt as they sat chatting in the great wood-panelled study. Outside, under a blanket of snow, Washington was peaceful and still.

'You used to be over here much more often,' Milner remarked, savouring his glass.

'Fax and E-mail has changed my life,' responded Ivor. 'This time round though, I need to see some of my clients personally, monitor their body language when I talk about my fees.' Ivor laughed mirthlessly and changed the subject. 'So . . . tell me, Martin, who's in and who's out in Washington, these days?'

'We'll get to that later.' Milner had his own agenda for their conversation. 'You're close to the PM. When d'you think he'll have his reshuffle?'

'Any day. He's getting all geared up. The press are being fed the usual stories by party headquarters, to warn and confuse.'

'What're they saying about me in London?' The question was as direct as it was unexpected.

It presented Ivor with the cue he was looking for. 'You've talked to everybody who matters,' he opened gently.

'Believe it or not, on my visit the other day, I only saw the Prime Minister, the Foreign Secretary and a couple of people at the office. Sounds grand but they're not the ones who really count. What is the Establishment saying?' Milner prodded for an answer.

'You get a good press.' Ivor sensed that his friend was deliberately prompting him. He did not want to rush things.

'Downside?'

'With the state of Anglo-American affairs, you're the fall-guy in between.' Ivor shrugged and held out his glass for another measure of whisky.

'So . . . Mark? You have a message for me?' Milner stood over his guest, whisky bottle in hand.

The other man was silent for a moment, then he said: 'You guessed?'

'I know you too well. I thought something must be up. I presume I can guess what.'

'They're thinking of replacing you.'

'Doesn't surprise me. After all that's happened. Why the hell didn't they tell me face-to-face when I was over? Why do they send you? Why do they think that anyone, say Vincent, will do better than me?'

'They don't. But, as always, when anything goes wrong they change the team. Same with the Cabinet reshuffle . . .' said Ivor, staring down at his hands which were clasped defensively round his glass.

After a while Milner asked: 'You're being totally honest with me, Mark?'

The other man did not reply.

'So you know?' Milner said eventually. He stood, went to the window, and stared emptily out into the wintry night.

Ivor gave an unnoticed nod. 'They showed me the files. The Oslo files.'

'You've come to tell me . . . drink the cup of poison, pick up the revolver, do the decent thing and resign?'

'Yes.' Ivor's voice had dropped almost to a whisper. 'Go before you're pushed, Martin. It's the best way.'

Late that night, as he climbed into bed, Milner found, to his surprise, that he felt relieved that everything was coming to a head. What form it would take he was not yet sure. They would not push for his early departure. After all, he had not even been in Washington for a year. That was very short. They would not want the move to look bad. He saw the threat to end his career as coming only from that distant Establishment, the senior people he knew and worked with in London. He could cope with them. He would rise above it.

15

In early February, there was a swing in public perceptions once again. The British media seemed to be trying to set the agenda, forcing HMG into taking a more anti-American stand. Telepundits and leader writers united in proclaiming that the British Government was wimpish in not forcing the Americans to face up to their responsibilities. One editorial read: 'The United States wants to strut the stage as the world's only remaining superpower and to preen itself as the great champion of democracy and capitalism – as long as this can be done with no risk to American blood or money.' The conspiracy theory journalists coupled this line with a rather spurious argument over interest rates, and the suggestion that the American Reserve Bank was holding the free world to ransom by keeping its interest rates at too low a level. Such armchair pundits argued that this was contributing to a lack of economic impetus in the British economy.

After reviewing the press at his morning staff meeting, Milner was enraged. 'They're all at it again. When in doubt, blame the Americans. What do we do about it?' He turned to his Press Counsellor.

'I'm briefing the British correspondents this morning, sir. You've seen a copy of the line I intend to take. Perhaps you'd like to talk to them yourself?' the Counsellor suggested.

'I'll think about it,' said Milner. 'What time are they coming in?'

'Twelve noon.'

'I'll see how my diary looks. How many of them?'

'BBC, ITN, *Telegraph*, *Times*, *Independent* and *Guardian*, sir. We may get the *Mail* along as well. I'm not sure whether the others – the tabloids – will bother. They would if they knew that you were giving the briefing. We certainly won't invite that *Sun* stringer.' He laughed cautiously.

'It's a good idea talking to them all together rather than picking them off one by one?' asked Milner. 'They prefer exclusives, don't they?'

'One by one is always better. But the pressure's on your time. If you do talk to them together the other danger is that they decide, when they leave the room, what they're going to report of what you've said. I've seen it happen again and again. One word too many or too few and, even if they misinterpret you, they'll send back identical stories. Whatever you think you may have said, their version of the truth sticks.'

'So?'

'It's the only quick way if you want to risk it, sir.'

'Twelve noon it is. They can come here. No, wait. They can come to the residence. I'll give them a drink. That'll soften them up.'

Only two of the correspondents were of the old school and took the alcohol that was offered. The rest sipped orange juice or mineral water. They sat in easy chairs in a semi-circle around the room. He faced them from an upright chair, his Press Counsellor beside him.

'I thought I'd get you all together to talk informally. If you don't mind, totally and absolutely off the record . . . Have I your agreement? Totally off the record?' A flurry of nods rippled round the group.

'I'll begin by saying that current Anglo–American relations are not as bad as some of you are painting them. There are lots of storms, but underneath, most bilateral issues are panning out well. Of course there are problems; but on the interest-rate front, for example, there's not much difference in the policies of the Reserve Bank and the Bank of England. When everybody thinks it's time to increase rates, it'll be done. In the meantime there's no point in blaming the Americans for everything that's wrong with the British economy.' Milner paused for a moment to see how his remarks were being taken. 'Now, Eastern Europe. The

Americans have their internal political brakes the same way as we have. A lot of people in the Administration would like to be right out there with us, contributing with arms and back-up. But the President has his hands tied. He's Commander in Chief but he wouldn't get away with it on the Hill or carry it through the House. You've got to give him that. It's not entirely his fault. Behind the scenes they've given us loads of moral backing and are doing all they can to bring some realism to the governments of Russia and the Ukraine. You can't blame them . . .'

'We can blame them for not putting their hands deeper into their pockets. Giving more aid might help stabilize the situation,' interrupted the man from *The Times*. He was not someone who was slow in coming forward with his views.

'Even American pockets aren't deep enough to do that,' said Milner coolly. 'They're thinking about what they *can* do . . . like drum up support for the proposed development plan, under United Nations auspices.'

'That's not going to keep their favourite East European leaders in power. Too long-term.' This time it was the *Guardian* correspondent.

'Right. Timing is everything. They show willing, though. They're not as isolationist as some of you suggest . . .'

'So everything in the garden's rosy. That what you're saying, Sir Martin? It's not what we hear from briefings at Number Ten or the Foreign Office.' The *Daily Mail* man had turned up and was determined to get his aggressive oar in.

'I'm not saying that. There are plenty of weeds in the garden,' Milner said expansively.

'Like the President's personal vindictiveness towards Britain, you mean?' the *Times* man suggested.

Milner hesitated. '*Vindictiveness*. . . that's far too strong a word.'

'Animosity does exist, you mean,' the *Times* man persisted.

'The President isn't a dyed-in-the-wool pro-Brit, if that's what you imply. I understand him. He has to think globally. The days of the Special Relationship are . . .'

'You're optimistic?' the *Telegraph* correspondent tried to be helpful.

'I'm not pessimistic.'

'The US Secretary of State?'

'I've very good relations with Antonio Delgadi,' said Milner, openly. 'He's shown me the most excellent courtesy. He's realistic.'

'More realistic than the President?' someone asked.

'Don't put words into my mouth.'

'What about the story that the President dislikes the Brits because his mother ran off with a British Army officer years ago?' It was the *Mail* again.

'I've no evidence . . .' said Milner cautiously. 'By the way, let me remind you that we agreed that this is all strictly off the record.'

'Your embassy people must have done a pile of research on that,' said the *Times* man. He was being particularly aggressive today.

'The story's been peddled over and over again by the British and American press a thousand times. You know that better than I do.' Milner shrugged.

'Did you know, Ambassador, we've asked the White House Press Office if the President would agree to brief British correspondents?'

The ambassador looked at his Press Counsellor. The Counsellor shook his head. No, he had not heard.

'Let me ask,' said Milner, turning the question back at them. 'Why would he give you a special briefing?'

'We want to get at what drives him,' one volunteered. 'We're due an explanation.'

'Keep me posted, won't you?' said Milner, getting to his feet. The meeting was at an end.

As the journalists left, Milner moved to a side room which had a window overlooking the courtyard below. He opened it quietly and listened as some of them, standing in a group, talked openly about him.

'Waste of bloody time,' one of them was saying.

'I don't know,' another said loudly. 'What more could he say?'

'Six out of ten for trying,' said a third.

'Maybe this is his swan song.' Milner recognized the *Times* man's voice.

'Swan song?' asked somebody.

'Heard on the grapevine: he's for the boot. Sometime soon.' The *Times* man sounded confident.

Milner closed the window and went back to his study, where his Press Counsellor was waiting for him.

'Well?' he asked his colleague.

'Very good, sir. I'm sure they all appreciated it,' said the Press Counsellor buoyantly.

'Don't lie to me, Terry,' said Milner.

After lunch Milner called in Paul Fawcett. It was a disciplinary matter, so he had the Head of Chancery with him as witness. He came quickly to the point: because of his behaviour, and he had been found drunk twice since the late-night incident in the ambassador's office, Fawcett was to go. Personnel had agreed. In the meantime he was to move from the ambassador's outer office. Immediately. Fawcett tried to argue, tried to protest, tried to apologize.

'It's too late for that, Paul,' said Milner. 'I'm sorry. We all make mistakes but I can't have that sort of behaviour. Our work here is too important.'

Later, Fawcett wept his heart out in front of a less than sympathetic girlfriend. She left him after that. He had outlived his usefulness. She would have to act quickly.

Flora Simons had demanded a session in daylight to finish off the portrait. With difficulty, Milner rearranged his programme and turned up at her house the next day shortly after lunch.

'You look a bit low.' She greeted him with a kiss on the lips. MacKenzie, as usual, looked the other way.

'Feeling my age,' said Milner as she led him by the hand through to her studio. MacKenzie took a book and went and sat in the living room, out of earshot.

'Andrew tells me he's getting hassle in the embassy from some-one called Nairn. What's that all about?' said Flora.

'Professional jealousy largely, I think.' He paused. 'It won't be for long . . . for either of us,' he added.

'What?' She looked intently at him.

'It's all coming to an end . . .'

'You're leaving Washington?' She looked anxious. 'Not yet, surely?'

'The way the wind's blowing.' He shrugged with resignation. 'I briefed a bunch of journalists yesterday morning. They seemed to have heard something too. It's how things happen at the top. When the going gets tough in international relations, it's time to shoot the messenger.'

'You're bitter?' Flora suggested anxiously.

'No. Resigned.' Right now he looked the part.

'Not like you to be defeatist,' she challenged.

'I've got a hell of a lot on my plate at the moment. And I've had to sack my private secretary.' He explained the background on Fawcett.

'If we were all held responsible for our actions that are driven by sex . . .' said Flora, trying to humour him. She saw she was going to fail so stopped trying. 'Go, sit in the chair,' she ordered. 'I want to work on your eyes.'

The session was not a success. She painted for a while, then they went up to bed. They made love, but it was mechanical; he realized he had neither given nor received the sort of passion that they had developed earlier. Soon they got dressed and went back downstairs.

In her studio, for the first time for some while, he went to the other side of the easel and studied the portrait closely. The face, the body, the posture: all good . . . no, much better than good. He liked the way she had painted his hands. Even the mouth was fine . . . but the eyes . . . They had gone through so many changes. First warm and compassionate, then cold and steely, and now . . . now there was something else. They had lost their life . . .

'I look like that? Are these my eyes? So empty?'

'Don't worry. It's a down day for both of us. They'll change again,' Flora said brightly.

'You're right,' said Milner, without conviction.

He had a free evening ahead, but did not even suggest to Flora that he would stay. Instead, though it was bitterly cold, he had arranged with MacKenzie that there would be no car waiting for them and that, wrapped up well in scarves and hats, they would walk back to the embassy together by the route Milner had taken on the first morning of his arrival in Washington. He kissed Flora goodbye, both knowing that something of their relationship had died that day.

It was early evening and already dark. The two men walked away from her house through the lamp-lit streets of Georgetown, and up towards Bretton Woods, the Parkway and Massachusetts Avenue. They had hardly gone a block when Fawcett's girlfriend suddenly appeared in front of them. She was about thirty yards ahead when Milner recognized her. MacKenzie too was suddenly alert. Without stopping in his tracks, Milner hissed, 'This is no coincidence.'

Though he had not discussed the girl with MacKenzie, the policeman would know about Nairn's suspicions of her Norwegian origins.

MacKenzie said nothing but casually moved his hand to open the buttons of his heavy overcoat, to give himself ready access to his gun holster. They walked on towards the girl. She stood on the sidewalk blocking their way. They were forced to come to a stop as they reached her.

'I wish to talk to you.' Her opening words were directed at Milner alone.

'Good evening, Miss . . .' He had never caught her name.

'Olafsen,' she said, in a voice devoid of emotion. 'Renate Olafsen, daughter of Jan-Erik.'

He took a sharp intake of breath. 'So,' he said softly. 'This is no coincidence.'

'Of course not,' said the girl, continuing to stare coldly at him. For the first time he took in how good-looking she was. Neatly dressed, like them, in a heavy overcoat, she had a Cossack-style fur hat on her head. She showed no hint of nervousness.

'I wish to talk to you,' she repeated firmly.

'Here, walk with us, or at the residence?' suggested Milner with forced politeness. 'I presume you want to talk about Paul.' He knew what her answer would be.

'No,' she said. 'No, I've heard from Paul. He's going home. I don't want to get involved in that. I wish to talk to you, here.'

'About?' asked Milner, needlessly.

'It's you I want to talk about,' said the girl. 'But alone.' She looked pointedly at MacKenzie. 'I want to talk about Oslo. Oslo, November, 1966. And about the death of my father, your colleague, Jan-Erik Olafsen.'

> It's still the same old story
> A fight for love and glory
> A case of do or die . . .

It came back like the blast of ice-cold wind that swirled along that Georgetown street. He remembered hearing 'As Time Goes By' sung relatively recently in that piano bar in New York, but much more vividly, he recalled, years earlier, sitting in the corner of a dowdy pub in downtown Oslo. He was waiting there, a glass of light Norwegian beer in front of him, when he heard what had happened. He remembered, with the words of the song, the pain, the sickness in the pit of his stomach, as his strange little Norwegian contact, Petter Hauge, had rushed in and broken the news. They had cried a little. Nobody had apportioned blame then. What had taken them so long? He had already been in Oslo for about eighteen months, as British Liaison Officer with the Norwegian Intelligence Services, when it happened. He had been recruited as a full member of MI6, and spent several years with them before he had transferred to the relative tranquillity of the regular diplomatic service. In those days that was a not uncommon occurrence, particularly if one's cover had been blown, as his had been by these events. He had worked with the tense and secretive Petter Hauge as part of the joint debriefing team, every time Jan-Erik came back in from his run behind the Curtain. For Jan-Erik it was his last time. He had had enough. Young Martin Milner sympathized. It was sufficient strain just waiting for people like him to come in and report, let alone suffering the nerve-racking intensity of fear at having to slip in and out, across the icy wastes, to pick up whatever pittance of intelligence their superiors felt was so crucial. He, Milner, had been a very little cog in a little machine that was part of the enormous Western espionage community.

His liaison job with the Norwegians had been a double cover. He was there to do that, but he was also in Oslo to run an agent of his own, someone totally unknown to the Norwegians; only a tiny number of people back in London headquarters knew about it. His roles were like the skins of an onion: nominally he was Second Secretary in charge of economic affairs in the embassy, then he had the covert Liaison Officer brief, while, in his deepest role, unknown even to his own ambassador, he ran this agent.

All had gone well for many months. The onion-skin existence could not have operated better. Then Jan-Erik, whose daughter now stood incongruously in front of him in peaceful, sedate Georgetown, picked up the fact that he was running the deep-cover action as well. The Norwegian did not like it; it could blow his own activities. Something had to give.

The story about Milner having tipped off a friend who was about to be arrested as a double agent was a further skin, embellished to add to the uncertainty. He, meanwhile, sought and obtained instructions from London as to what to do. He did not like it, but could claim that he was merely following orders. The rest was easy. He knew people who knew people who passed on the word in the right ear. The two Russian hitmen, their suitcases filled with bricks and joined with a thin piece of piano wire, did the rest. Like them, he was merely obeying orders. There was no question of money changing hands. There was never any question of his loyalty. It was an operational necessity.

It was an incongruous scene: Her Britannic Majesty's Ambassador to Washington, His Excellency, Sir Martin Milner KCMG, standing in an almost deserted Georgetown street with a tall blonde Norwegian girl, Renate Olafsen, who knew that in some way he had arranged to have her father killed. They talked together in cool, emotionless terms. Two or three paces away, Inspector Andrew MacKenzie shivered in the cold and waited, alert for danger, ready to counter any sudden move on her part.

She confronted Milner with the story as she knew it. At first she spoke coldly, without passion, about how she felt. He answered by attempting to justify his actions. She waved him to silence and he soon realized that it would be an impossible task trying to persuade a woman so bound by her inherited burden of emotions. She would not listen. Why should she listen? Here he was, the guilty man. She had tracked him down. How could he live with his conscience, she demanded? He had sold his soul. He protested, but his words were feeble. He had made nothing out of it, he said, neither money nor in career terms. He had not even been praised for what he had done. He had been a small part of a dirty but essential system. In that process many got hurt.

'You killed my father. You betrayed him . . . and look at you . . . with your gilded, glittering life. How can you live with yourself?' Renate Olafsen hissed the words.

He tried to break off their conversation. 'I have nothing more to say to you,' he said eventually. 'You know the story. You believe you know my part in it. Yes, I took action to protect my agent. But it is a lie that I took any money, that you must believe.'

'*I* . . . believe *you*!' she exclaimed with a sudden outburst of rage. MacKenzie moved a protective step forward at her words.

'Don't worry,' she turned and sneered. 'He is physically safe.' Renate Olafsen turned again towards Milner. 'You lied then. You lie now. I have seen what it says in the KGB files.'

'There are lots of examples,' he pleaded, willing her to believe him. 'That Russian double agent, Gordievsky, even explains it in his book – about the KGB claiming to have recruited high-level Western agents, claiming to have paid out money that actually went straight into their own pockets. I want you to know that is a lie. Otherwise . . . I'm sorry,' he said lamely. 'I'm sorry about your father . . . about Jan-Erik . . . But that's how the world was thirty years ago.'

'Thirty years of not having had a father.' The words poured like a torrent from Renate Olafsen. She did not need to raise her voice; he could not but be enthralled and horrified by the intensity of her feelings. 'When I came back from Germany a year ago I was told about you. About the information from the KGB files. How I hated you then. How delighted I was when the people I contacted in London tracked you down. Identified you.'

'Tracked me down?' Milner stopped and looked at her. For the first time the girl hesitated.

'Who were they?' Milner demanded.

'What does it matter? Ex-IRA people. Anarchists. Terrorists.'

'Terrorists . . . David? Was it you?' he shouted in turn.

MacKenzie, who had continued to hold back, came up to them. 'You all right, sir?' He guessed most of what was going on. 'Can't we go back to the embassy?' he pleaded. 'Work things out in the warmth.'

'Not now, Andrew. Keep out of this, will you?' Milner barked.

The girl, for the first time, looked towards the ground. 'It wasn't me. At least not directly. It got out of hand. Horrifically. I'm sorry. About your son, I mean.'

In his turn Milner directed his fury at her. For a moment he was about to order MacKenzie to seize the girl, have her arrested, take her away, do what the hell he liked with her. Revenge and vengeance shook his whole being. Then he paused in sudden realization of the truth.

'How dare you? How dare you accuse me of anything when you . . . you personally engineered such a horrible thing? Have you seen what you did to my son?' He shouted out the words and MacKenzie again started forward as if to restrain him. Milner again waved him back. 'Leave it, Andrew. Let me sort this out.'

They all stopped talking for a moment while an uninvolved American couple wandered past, arm in arm, turning and staring curiously at the unlikely trio arguing in the dark Georgetown street.

'I'm sorry; truly sorry. I went to see your son . . . in hospital.'

'You . . . the weeping woman,' Milner burst out.

'I didn't mean to harm him. But God, I would love to have harmed you. Even in New York, there was a professional. Then I changed my mind. I changed my tactics.'

There was a long silence. 'New York . . . You changed your mind . . . Look . . . I'm not going to prolong this conversation,' said Milner, turning away.

'I'm not going to let go,' the girl threatened.

He turned to stare at her again, wondering what she was going to do next. 'You're going to try and harm . . . ?' Milner raised his voice. 'Mr MacKenzie . . .'

The girl made a dismissive gesture with her hand. 'Have me arrested if you will. It won't do much good. I can prove I was in Oslo when the shooting happened . . . No, I'm not going to harm you physically. Not any more. But, whether or not you charge me, I'm going to ensure that you are destroyed.' Her last word was said with huge vehemence. 'God help you, you pitiful, evil man,' Renate Olafsen whispered viciously, then she turned on her heel and walked quickly away into the darkness.

MacKenzie came up to the ambassador. 'And that was, sir?' he asked.

'That girl . . .' Milner began, then he thought better of it, shrugged and said: 'Nothing. Trying to threaten me over sending Fawcett home.'

'You know something, sir?' said MacKenzie steadily. 'I don't believe you.'

16

The next month presented him with an ironic mixture of triumph and tragedy. On the public front, everything he turned his hand to seemed crowned with success. The *Observer* published a profile of him, calling him the most accomplished diplomat ever to have filled the post of Ambassador to Washington. That same Sunday, he drafted a top-secret and personal telegram to the Secretary of State, Trafford Leigh, finally tendering his resignation from Washington as soon as a successor had been identified. By return came a message, a personal one from the Prime Minister, praising him for his efforts, but saying that, in the circumstances, HMG agreed that it was time for a change. Pre-warned by Mark Ivor, they knew he had agreed to resign, and Milner presumed that as they thought the Oslo story might break, they would all be greatly relieved by his going. With the present slim state of the government's parliamentary majority, they did not want skeletons like him coming out of the cupboard.

First thing on the Monday morning, Charles Nairn turned up with disappointing news. Milner greeted him coolly. He knew from London that, on top of everything else, Nairn had been trying to have Andrew MacKenzie recalled.

'We've drawn a blank,' said the MI6 chief. 'We had identified the blood group and the DNA analysis. It looked exciting but then we drew a blank. There is no recent trace of the British officer. No social security, tax or Health Service records anywhere. Very odd. We've got people still working on it with Scotland Yard and Special Branch, without them knowing the background of course, but I don't hold out much hope.'

'Thank you, Charles,' Milner said dismissively.

'By the way, sir. Fawcett's girl . . . We've found out that . . .'

'I know all about her. All I need to know.' Nairn watched uneasily as the ambassador moved to his desk, sat down, picked up some papers and, pointedly ignoring him, set to work. Then he turned and left the room.

Later that morning, after a brief Chancery meeting, Milner's bodyguard came in unannounced. 'Sir, can I suggest we go for a walk?'

'What are you on about, Andrew?' Milner could scarcely conceal his irritation. He had enough to worry about without MacKenzie acting out of character.

'I said: we should go for a walk. I need to talk to you. Away from walls with ears.'

'If it's about the Norway thing, you can talk here.' They were standing facing each other by the window of his office.

'Not that, sir.' MacKenzie stood his ground.

'Then? Oh, it's Charles Nairn, is it? Look, I know you're having trouble with that man. Surely you're big enough to handle it on your own. I realize a lot of people in the embassy are a bit jealous . . .'

'Nothing to do with that, sir. I'm able to stick that sort of aggro. It's the other thing . . . the one you've been talking to Nairn about.' MacKenzie kept his voice low.

'How the hell d'you know about that? You haven't taken to eavesdropping?' Milner erupted.

'I'll ignore that accusation, sir. But I know he's drawn a blank. I knew he would.' MacKenzie spoke firmly but undramatically.

'*You* knew he would . . . What the hell are you getting at? Is this some sort of battle with Nairn? If it is, Andrew, you're out of your league.' Milner hissed the last few words, so taken aback was he by MacKenzie's behaviour.

'You want to go for a walk, sir. Out of earshot. You really do. Trust me. Then we'll see who's in what league.' MacKenzie was not to be swayed and, in the end, with the greatest reluctance, Milner agreed to his request.

MacKenzie began talking only when they were well away from

the embassy compound. As they had done on many occasions since their arrival, they walked up past the Observatory and over towards Georgetown.

'You've probably heard ... I'm being withdrawn.' Milner broke the uneasy silence.

'Yes, sir. Me with you, of course. Mr Nairn will be pleased.'

'Stuffy embassy attitudes aren't getting too much for you, are they, Andrew?' Milner looked at the other man with brief but genuine concern.

'They could do. If I'd had to stay longer. Relative status is a load of sh—, but I'm not going to let them,' said MacKenzie with a toss of his head.

'So ... You wanted? Go on, talk! And quickly. I have work to do.' Milner pulled them both to the business in hand.

'Well, sir. You know that over the last hundred years or so a large number of famous British families intermarried with Americans ... usually, but not always, for money.'

'This a history lesson? I know you studied US ...' Milner turned and looked curiously at the policeman.

'Sir. Just this once: listen to me. It'll be worth it.' MacKenzie paused as a pair of joggers ran past them. 'The Marlboroughs, Churchills, Cunards, the Guinnesses, the Dukes of Manchester ...'

'You're beginning to irritate, Andrew. If I didn't know you so well ...' Milner interrupted.

'For every famous Anglo-American family link, there have been thousands of anonymous ones. Ordinary men and women – think of all the GI brides, for example. My father, he was sort of the same. He died a few years ago. He'd had a dissolute life. Not a particularly pleasant man. I think I told you ...'

Milner stopped in his tracks. 'I'm not going any further, Andrew. You're giving every impression of having flipped your lid. What are you driving at? What's all this about your father? And the American connection?'

MacKenzie ignored the interruption and went on with his story. 'My father was by all repute very bright, but rough and ready.

He got a field commission during the war . . . and a DSO. Something to do with the SOE. Anyway, soon after he met my mother, he was posted on exchange duty over here to the States. There were a lot of US–British service secondments, liaison officers, during the fifties and sixties. I suppose that's one of the reasons why I studied American history. It's certainly why I manoeuvred . . . why I jumped at the opportunity of coming over here with you, sir.'

'There has to be a purpose in all this, Andrew,' said Milner. To his surprise, his irritation had evaporated, to be replaced by growing curiosity at what the normally sober MacKenzie could possibly be driving at.

'There was a film I saw recently, you may have seen it . . . where this prosperous businessman keeps trying to admit to some horrific murder and all his friends laugh at him. They don't believe him. They think it's some sort of sophisticated wind-up. It's too absurd. They refuse to take him seriously. I'm just about to test your credulity too, sir. In a bigger way.' MacKenzie paused to collect his thoughts.

The two men walked on together, talking in low tones.

'Let me try to get to grips with what you're leading up to, before I have you taken away by men with white coats . . .' Milner prompted.

'It couldn't be simpler, sir. Captain Tony Barr, DSO, of the Highland Light Infantry, was posted to the States in the early fifties, leaving his Glasgow girlfriend, my mother, behind him. She eventually reverted to her maiden name – Mackenzie. He was sent to a small training base in an even smaller Southern town. There he met a girl – she was already separated from her husband – they had an affair and she had a son by him. Later she ran off with my father, leaving her child, my half-brother, with her legal husband, who thought the child was his, and the grandparents.'

'You're out of your . . .' Milner at last began to see what MacKenzie could be driving at.

'I am in *total* control,' the policeman said with vehemence. 'I have . . . I am almost certainly alone in having all the facts, all the birth and marriage certificates, the medical records, everything. Before his last illness, my father, wayward though he was, was a very methodical man. All his papers were carefully recovered from all over the place and filed, then placed by him in a safe in his solicitor's office in Dumbarton. I have photocopies of everything with me. You will see that they match, very precisely, the material already obtained by Mr Nairn. I have the missing links. You can verify everything when we return to the residence.'

'MacKenzie . . . what are you saying . . . ?' Milner was almost speechless with disbelief. Both men had stopped walking and were facing each other on the path.

'The name is *Andrew*, sir. Remember. What I'm saying is that I have every proof possible, DNA matchings, the lot, that I am the half-brother of the . . . I've never said this out loud before . . .' There was a long, a very long silence, '. . . of the President of the United States of America.'

The British Ambassador, Sir Martin Milner, let out a bark of something like laughter. 'If it wasn't so absurd and ridiculous, I'd make a riposte that I'm a king or something . . .' He paused and stared hard at the other man. He felt himself shaking with a mixture of fascination and disbelief. 'You're not joking, though. You're deadly serious, aren't you, Andrew? How can I possibly believe this?'

'You'll believe the truth when it's proved to you. It may be a quantum credibility leap, but, on the other hand, it's very simple. Too simple. I realize it would all have been easier for you to swallow if it was some other guy and not me, your mere minder.'

'Come off it . . .' Milner began to rationalize. 'How could a truth like this possibly have lain hidden? The media, the Ministry of Defence, MI6, your police friends, the lot.'

'Think how many secrets about so many past American Presidents have remained hidden for years. Eisenhower had an English mistress throughout the war and she was his army driver, for God's sake. Look at the mating habits of the whole Kennedy clan. Some girl who had been with Clinton at Oxford tried to claim she was made pregnant by him. Given his reputation for womanizing, would that be unbelievable? And this hasn't all lain hidden. The President, the media, found out quite a bit about his mother's affair with a Brit. They tried to find my father when the President started running for office but he had hidden his tracks well so that the US part of his family couldn't find him to claim paternity payments or whatever. In any case, by that time he was ga-ga, his mind totally gone. There was no story to follow up, no proof let alone accusations of dubious patrimony, and, with my mother dead, the only evidence, given that the President's mother, for obvious reasons, never gave the game away, was in the family legal and medical papers which I alone have. No one has seen them but me.'

Later that night, back in the study, the two men talked quietly and guardedly. The ambassador had studied the birth certificates, the medical records, blood groups, the lot. Reluctantly he came to the conclusion that it was . . . possibly . . . the truth.

'Why the hell didn't you say something earlier?' Milner asked.

'I tried to once, but you cut me short. In any case I had to be very sure, particularly with Charles Nairn and his guys busy ganging up on me. Look how hard a job I've had convincing you, even with all the proof. Before . . . you really would have had me taken away, and certainly sent home.'

'What more did you want to find when you came over here?' Milner questioned the other man further.

'I don't know. I wanted to see what the President looked like. I was planning to come over, and you gave me the opportunity. I had to fight hard to get the job as your protection officer. Now I've seen him in the flesh when I've been with you to the White House. He looks OK, but . . . At one time I thought of going public, making myself known. Then I realized that, like winning twenty million in the lottery or something, what a living hell that would immediately dump on me. I would be treated as a nutcase, then as a joke, then, if they eventually believed me, I'd never again be a private citizen, able to do my own thing. They would probably . . .' MacKenzie laughed suddenly, 'give me my own Secret Service minders. Half-brother of the President! No way.

Look what happened to some of the distant family members of Kennedy, Carter, Reagan and others. Hell on earth. Life changed out of all recognition. The media would massacre me. And what good would it do him, the President, knowing? No. Only you, sir . . . *only* you know.'

'So why do you now tell me this huge secret – I still half-think it's absurd – if I can't use it? If you don't want it to be used?'

'But you can, sir. You are free to use the half of it. You can use all the evidence, if he doesn't have it already. He may, of course, have been told something by his mother, or guess – which would explain his anti-British hang-ups in a big way, wouldn't it? – that his father really was a British Army captain . . . Captain Tony Barr, DSO.'

'I still cannot grasp . . .' Milner muttered, half to himself.

'Then wait till you *can* take it all in, sir. And then . . . one more thing . . .'

'Yes?' Milner asked.

'If, by any chance, he *does* know of my existence,' MacKenzie allowed himself a half-smile, 'you can tell him that, by my choice, that particular secret is very safe with me.'

Some several weeks later, as far as the outside world was concerned, Sir Martin Milner's final meeting with the President of the United States could not have gone better. It was an unusual occasion since, shortly after the ambassador arrived, the President agreed to walk with him in the rose garden of the White House, out of hearing of any recording devices. When they returned to the Oval Office after about twenty minutes, both men, the President's staff noticed, looked surprisingly tense and strained. The ambassador left immediately. The two men did not shake hands.

Afterwards, the public perception of the call was a triumphant one. Milner was again hailed as the great conciliator because, within a few days, the American President, in a long-delayed but exclusive briefing to British journalists accredited in Washington, announced that he would, after all, and despite strong domestic opposition, allow a nominal number of American troops to join

NATO forces in their defensive strategy against the turmoil in East Europe.

Clive Crick, ITN's correspondent in Washington, summed it up:

> *Here at the White House, it has been a most extraordinary day. The British Ambassador, Sir Martin Milner, whose recall to London has, ironically, just been announced, has scored a major diplomatic victory in personally persuading the President to reverse his previous decision over allowing American troops to serve defensively on the Eastern borders. The President told British correspondents today that the first detachment will be leaving early next week. The reasons for this volte-face are far from clear. Senior members of the Administration claim to be as baffled as everyone else is as to the President's change of mind. The British, German and French governments have warmly welcomed this new development. The ambassador will leave in a blaze of glory. This is Clive Crick, at the White House, Washington, returning you to the studios of ITN in London.*

At a private level things were very different for Martin Milner. Renate Olafsen had lived up to her threat. After a brief twenty-four-hour visit to Boston to inspect the Consulate General there and to deliver a lecture at Harvard, Milner arrived back at the residence to find a large package, coated in bubble-wrap, waiting for him. The security guard at the door said: 'We've had it checked, sir. It appears to be a painting.'

Milner placed it against the wall of his study and, before examining it, tore open the envelope that was attached to it. It was a note from Flora Simons. It was very brief. It read,

> *I am sorry it has to be like this but now I know more about you and about your past, about how you once*

> betrayed a colleague, it is for the best. Perhaps I never
> knew you. It is as if I have tried to paint you in a
> dark room, and that, no artist, least of all me, is
> capable of doing. I am leaving Washington for some
> time. You will have gone by the time that I return.
> You may have the painting. I do not wish to be paid
> for it.

And then the one word: 'Flora'. Just that; nothing more.

He tried to call her house but the phone rang on unanswered. Only then did he turn to unwrap and examine the painting. It was the same portrait: the same mouth, the same posture, the same forehead and nose, the same hands, clasped powerfully in front of him, but the eyes had been repainted; cold and hard, they stared accusingly back at him. Bitterly he picked up the painting with both hands and turned it to face the wall. Then he went in search of MacKenzie. Instead he was stopped by Lucinda Forbes-Manning. She looked far from happy.

'I've been trying to find you everywhere, Ambassador. David,' she said anxiously. 'He's very upset. He's left messages for you, and me. He's moved out. He's decided to return to London.'

'He's what . . . ?'

'He's gone. He's on his way back to London. He's asked me to arrange to have his effects packed up.'

'David's done what?' Milner was shocked into speechlessness by this unexpected flood of misfortunes.

'He said to tell you that you would realize why. He said that he'd also discovered and read some of your diary – you must have written about you and me and that upset him more than somewhat – he was livid with me. It all happened after Paul Fawcett's girl-friend came to see him. You know the Norwegian girl? I don't understand. He's gone off to think about things, he said. He hardly said goodbye, even to me. After all that I . . .' Lucinda had tears in her eyes.

'God in heaven. Right . . . Where's MacKenzie?' Milner tried to pull himself together.

'He's packing. A message for him came while you were both up at Harvard. He muttered something about the security alert on you having been cancelled. He said he'd be in touch before he went,' Lucinda added, dabbing at her eyes with a handkerchief.

'He said he'd be in touch . . . ?' snarled Milner, a huge but desperate fury welling up inside him.

'That's what he said, sir. Will there be anything else?' Lucinda was staring at him.

Milner looked through rather than at her, eyes blazing. Then, suddenly, he felt drained and deflated, collapsing from implacable self-control to absolute vulnerability within a few seconds. He turned away without looking at her. 'No, there'll be nothing else,' he said softly.

'Shall I have some supper sent up to your room?' He could hear the concern in Lucinda's voice.

'Why don't you do just that,' responded Milner, then he turned and, head bowed, climbed slowly away up the long winding staircase.

Renate Olafsen had been back in Oslo barely a week when, early one evening, the doorbell of her apartment rang. She opened it cautiously and there, in the doorway, stood Petter Hauge. He looked much older than she remembered him, very tired and drawn, with a deathlike pallor about his skin.

'I've come to find out what happened,' he began hesitantly.

She blocked the doorway, determined not to let him in. She had done what she had to do, but now she did not want to explain herself or have anything more to do with him. She refused to relive the whole range of feelings she had gone through in the process of destroying Sir Martin Milner. Why should she reveal to this embittered old man the turbulent mix of emotions she had experienced afterwards? She did not want to have to explain that she felt no satisfaction, no sense of elation, no feeling of justice, in the retribution she had delivered. If anything, she felt guilt, uncertainty and a deep unhappiness, not least because she had seen the damage she had done to innocent people – especially to the ambassador's girlfriend, Flora Simons, who had broken down in front of her. Then she would always remember the haunted look in the eyes of his son, David. She had already caused him to be physically wounded; now she knew she had damaged him emotionally as well. She thought he might have attacked her when she told him the story, but he too had only crumpled and wept. And to what real end?

'Go away,' Renate said. 'I don't want to talk to you.'

'I need to know what happened.' Hauge stood his ground.

'Go away. You'll learn soon enough.' Renate tried to shut the door on him.

'I need to know now. I'm dying,' Hauge pleaded.

'Dying?' She was taken aback for a moment, then his face and his haunted, pallid look proclaimed that he could be speaking the truth.

'Cancer. I could barely make it here. I need to know,' Hauge whispered.

'*Why* do you need to know? All that matters, surely, is that you've done – I've done for you – what you wanted. I've destroyed him.' Renate Olafsen had to force herself to speak these last few words.

'Then that will have to do,' Petter Hauge said, and turned away.

She thought of calling after him, explaining more to him, looking for some reassurance that she had done the right thing. Instead, she closed the door firmly behind him and locked it. She never saw him again, but she saw his death notice in Oslo's *Aftenposten*, a bare three weeks later.

17

A lantern in a ship's stern casts light on the wake, illuminating the route that has been travelled. That light, that perspective, was now clear to him. What remained in total darkness was the course ahead. But today he had to cope only with the vast irony of the present. Here he was, standing in the Robing Room of the House of Lords, while people fussed around him, placing and arranging the red and ermine robes on his shoulders. Beside him stood the two distinguished Lords, old colleagues of his, who were to act as his Supporters as he took his seat in this most august of establishments. How could he, a mere three months after leaving Washington to such a storm of public acclaim and of private humiliation, be standing here about to be sworn in as a Peer of the Realm? It was the oldest of old stories: the Establishment covering up its sins and omissions; the Establishment protecting and rewarding its own.

'Time to go,' said that most exquisite knee-breeched gentleman, Black Rod. 'We mustn't keep the Lord Chancellor waiting, must we, gentlemen?'

The events that followed were a blur. Later, when he sat on one of the padded leather benches listening to their Lordships elegantly debating the present state of tension in the streets of Moscow, he fell into a deep reverie. 'Public success; private humiliation': the words repeated themselves again and again. A peerage: something he might once have dreamed about but, in the process, he had lost a wife, a son, a lover and every last shred of his self-respect. Only Andrew MacKenzie and Mark Ivor had stuck by him; they had sat together, watching from the gallery of the House of Lords, as he took his seat. Even the manner of his seizing his brief diplomatic glory had been underhand and deceitful. It was, after all, a small secret, a minuscule secret in the great rolling history of the world, that a President of the United States had not just had a mother who had run away with a British Army officer, but that a President of the United States, by every test of blood and DNA analysis, was illegitimate, and had had that British Army officer as his father. It was a secret that would never get out because so few on both sides of the Atlantic were aware of it. It was a secret too dangerous to know, one that the First Citizen himself admitted he had only recently discovered. In this enlightened age, the illegitimacy of a President would have been no cause for resignation, but it would have explained to the world so much about his policies and antipathies and would have given rise to so much mockery, consternation and humiliation, that it was best never told.

Milner had not attempted to blackmail the President; that would have been foolish and dangerous beyond belief. He had merely informed the President – at their last meeting at the White House – of what he knew. That and nothing more. The rest was history. That the President had, thereafter, changed his stance and attitude to Britain was none of the ambassador's doing.

Towards the end of that evening of his elevation to the peerage, after the House had risen, after he had had a superficially jovial dinner with Dr Mark Ivor and his supporters, after he had drunk rather more than he would normally do, he returned to the spacious but bleak flat he had rented in one of the great gaunt blocks of apartments behind Victoria Station, and there he threw himself on his bed and wept.

Then, some time in the middle of the night, he got up and went through to sit in the gloomy sitting room that was filled with half-empty packing cases containing all his possessions that had been sent on to him from Washington. There, in the corner, leaning facing the wall, was the portrait that Flora Simons had painted of him. He stood then, and in some vague hope of expunging the past, he seized a screwdriver with which he had been opening the crates and cartons, and, in great fury, he gashed and tore and hit and ripped the portrait until it was an unrecognizable shredded scattering of bits of painted canvas strewn across the faded carpet. When every single bit of the portrait was unrecognizable, with great physical strength he broke up the heavy, gilded frame. Then he went and got some large black plastic refuse bags and plunged all the bits he could find into them. Like a thief, he took the bags and sealed them, and left the apartment in the middle of the night, and dumped them with the dozens of others lying on the pavement awaiting garbage collection the next morning. When he had done that he felt in no way better, certain then that the world of his ambitions had passed away for ever.

The following pages contain an excerpt from

THE UNION
Michael Shea's new political thriller

AVAILABLE IN HARDBACK
ISBN 0 00 225474 3

'Michael Shea knows all about political intrigue . . . his
fiction bears a disturbing resemblance to fact.'
Sunday Times

1

The State of the Nation

Today is the fourth anniversary of Scottish Independence. But
who is celebrating? Look out of your windows. Where are
the Bravehearts, once so vocal? Where are the bands, the
flags, the parades, the bread, the circuses, the proud speeches
from our nation's leaders? Where, indeed, is that feeling of
nationhood? We believe it exists but it has been buried deep
beneath what has happened to Scotland in the last four years:
the strikes, the poverty, the unemployment and the civil
unrest. The opposition parties accuse the Government and
above all the Prime Minister, Keith Sinclair, of a failure of
leadership. But that is the easy option. Surely we all must
share the guilt and the blame.

Editorial in the *Herald*, St Andrew's Day

Clydebank, Scotland. A rhythmical spiral of water poured from
a fractured gutter tight under the grey slates. It made little
impression on a century and a half of engrained grime as it hit
the projecting lintel above the doorway. Most of the water
drained away in rivulets down to the flagstones but enough was
retained to provide nourishment for the bright green crops of
moss that flourished along the crevices where sandstone fitted
unevenly against rotting doorframes.

Aided by the teeming rain, the heavy grey of the clouds, only
one shade lighter in tone than the surrounding buildings, blurred
into uncertainty the line where rooftops met sky. Each surface
was decaying and slimy to the touch. The rain, rather than
cleansing and refreshing as it fell, became immediately infected

by its new environment. Running among the cobblestones to the blocked drains by the curb, it encouraged the polluted pools to stretch out and form a barrage across the street.

The high walls of the squalid tenements provided an all too effective trap for the small band of marchers. That wet Saturday morning was both St Andrew's Day and the fourth anniversary of Independence, which was why Clydebank's Republican contingent was making its sodden, tartan-bedecked way through the deserted backstreets to meet up with the main procession for the big rally in George Square.

Constable Wright, brought in by bus from his rural beat in the Campsie Hills to help a hard-pressed City Constabulary for the day, was one of the regulation handful of police escorts. He would submit his incident report later. He was an honourable man, always well turned out; his style was unpolished and unimaginative but he missed little of the detail.

The party faithful were far fewer than in previous years. The organizers comforted themselves by telling each other that the rain had kept people at home and that Celtic were playing away. But they knew in their heart of hearts that twelve percent unemployment and the general strike meant that not many had the passion for celebration.

But there were still sufficient numbers for the march to fall into disarray, particularly when the marchers had to ford the flooded street. The three pipers at the head of the procession neither faltered nor broke step, but those who came after them were less resolute and the procession ground to a halt while discipline was reintroduced in the ranks. The police escort took advantage of the delay to find a moment's shelter in a doorway. PC Wright, reluctant immigrant to Scotland that he was, privately cursed the weather, the squalor and the stridency of the pipe music with equal vigour. The respite was brief. The procession moved hesitantly forward once again. Pulling the collars of their capes up around their necks, the policemen returned to their duties and to the rain.

By the gates of an idle, deserted factory, the marchers turned a corner into another anonymous street lined with boarded-up shops. For a moment the rain and the misery obscured their view. Then the Republican leaders saw the men waiting for them: a crowd of some three hundred Reunionist strikers, spread across the street ahead, standing silent, black and yellow industrial helmets glistening in the rain.

The police sergeant in charge shouted an order. PC Wright spoke urgently into his radio. At Constabulary Headquarters alarm bells sounded.

By now only fifty yards separated the two groups, the Republicans outnumbered by at least four to one. The Reunionists were not there by accident; they would not willingly clear a path. Both knew their enemy; it had happened before.

'Keep on,' shouted the procession leader, a dedicated man in his fifties, in an ancient, well-used kilt. 'Keep on. We've a right tae march. The polis will see we're a' right.' The man's look belied the confidence of his words. Half a dozen policemen would not go far.

Ten yards separated the two groups before the procession hesitated and juddered to a stop. The pipers continued to blow resolutely, marking time, awaiting instructions.

PC Wright, flanked by his colleagues, moved forward in an attempt to clear a way through the motionless wall of men. Tension was at breaking point, but the pipes played on. High above, a few anxious female heads watched from tenement windows.

'Move along there. This is an authorized procession.' The sergeant addressed the strikers through his loud-hailer. No one moved at first. Then, unexpectedly, with some shuffling, a narrow but orderly path opened up ahead. PC Wright muttered hopeful words of commentary into his radio. At Headquarters the alarm bells continued to ring.

The small group advanced deep into the crowd, pushing its way along a reluctant path between the silent men. The policemen were a few steps ahead. The pipers kept manfully in tune. Even the rain seemed to ease a little.

When the procession was about halfway through, PC Wright heard from his left a shrill, deliberate whistle cut in above the sound of the pipes. At once the strikers closed in. The music died instantly and a set of bagpipes flew incongruously through the air. Wright raised his radio to his lips but strong hands grabbed him from behind, a sack was thrown over his head, and he felt himself carried like a child through a mass of surging bodies. He heard muffled shouts, a scream of intense male agony close at hand, and the clattering of steel-capped boots on cobblestones.

Wright realized he was being born away from the main crowd, but with arms and legs expertly locked by several pairs of hands, he was unable to resist. He felt one of his captors stumble, he heard a door slammed somewhere, then the sound of shouting became fainter.

'We've got no great quarrel wi' the polis.' A deep voice penetrated through the sack. 'But move and ye'll get the same as they Republican scum.' Thrown roughly onto the floor, Wright felt his hands being bound behind him. Further whispers followed, then there was silence.

He sensed he was alone. Gently he tested the ropes. He had been hurriedly and unskilfully tied and he easily worked himself free. He reached up and cautiously pulled the sack from his head.

The bare room was empty and almost in darkness, though a little light filtered in from a skylight above the door. At a guess he was in what had been a coal cellar. He felt for his radio but it was gone. He stood up, shaking, and as he did so, his foot scraped against something metallic: the crushed remnants of the radio lay on the dirty stone floor. He abandoned it and moved towards the door. Jammed rather than locked, it gave easily when he ran at it with his shoulder. He emerged into what was the close of one of the tenements and from there into the street.

Blinking in the dull light, he arrived back on the scene at the same moment as the first of the squad cars. The sodden street was littered with bodies and broken banners. Not a striker was to be seen. Wright stumbled towards his colleagues as they emerged from their shiny black cars. On his way he accidentally trod on a set of abandoned bagpipes which let out a low moan of sound. At last the rain had stopped.

The police were slow to recognize the scale of the Clydebank riot, otherwise they would have insisted that the Prime Minister leave by a rear door after his official lunch with the Chamber of Commerce in Glasgow's Merchants' Hall. The Reunionist strikers, kept well back from the Republicans' St Andrew's Day rally, were better informed; they had, after all, planned the ambush. Their blood was up but there was a sinister lack of heckling as Keith Sinclair emerged from the building at the corner of George Square and started to make his way, escorted by police protection officers, towards his official car. Beside it, his official driver, Ingram, and his Private Secretary, Robert Guthrie, stood waiting. Around him, the Prime Minister could sense that the police, many of them in full riot gear with helmets and visors, were tense and apprehensive. Why were the strikers so silent? It was as if they were waiting for some signal. Then one young constable who was standing closest to the Prime Minister suddenly looked up and over the heads of the dense crowd. The missile, thrown with great strength and accuracy, followed a graceful, curving trajectory against the background of the steel-grey clouds. The constable shouted a warning, *Look out, sir. Behind you.* But it came too late.

Abel Rosenfeld had also been at the lunch in the Merchants' Hall. The forty-one-year-old New Yorker was Strategic Director of the mammoth US multinational Unity Corporation, and he had gone more out of duty than enthusiasm to hear Prime Minister Sinclair speak about how his Government intended to deal with the economic problems currently facing Scotland. It was, as he had expected, a subdued occasion. Gone was most of the nationalistic bombast he had heard on previous St Andrew's Days since his dynamic and highly-demanding chairman, James Fulton, had first sent him over from Manhattan to Scotland. Rosenfeld had been charged with setting up a Unity branch office in the big castle they had bought north of Perth, a strange assignment to give a Jewish boy from the Bronx. He had never even been to Europe before and had not been sure where to find Scotland on a map when he had first been given his mission. He had demurred slightly when Fulton summoned him to his New York penthouse office and told him what was intended. But you didn't both argue with Fulton and stay with Unity for long. Abel Rosenfeld was a free agent with no family ties, he liked his job, liked the huge salary hike even more, and had come to Scotland – God, almost two years ago now. It was a challenge, he kept telling himself, and, above all else, Rosenfeld loved challenges.

Rosenfeld also loved conspiracies. He was in many ways a latter-day Machiavelli, who manipulated his carefully-tended network of influential contacts with polished cunning. A dedicated professional, he knew who to speak to and on what terms. Secretive to a fault, he seldom consigned his thoughts to paper, strongly believing in the flexibility of choice, action and opinion that not having things confirmed in writing gave him. He believed in being particularly pliant with his superiors, which some of those who worked closely with him called sycophancy, or worse. In fact, Abel Rosenfeld always knew exactly where he was going and what he wanted from life. He was a man for all seasons. Some saw him effortlessly smooth and overridingly ambitious. If he was the latter, his ambition was less to do with money than with the excitement he got from influencing those more powerful than himself. He had a need to win. He schemed and conspired with purpose and that purpose was, for the time being at least, to do James Fulton's every bidding.

The moment the Prime Minister left the Hall, Rosenfeld pushed through the crowd of fellow guests and darted out after him. Before the lunch, he had taken the precaution of finding his way around the building. He knew exactly where to go. Now he raced up a flight of stairs to the next floor and entered the empty office he had discovered that overlooked the corner of George Square, by the Queen Street Railway Station. He arrived just as the Prime Minister emerged from the main entrance and so had his intended grandstand view of what happened next.

Portable telephone in one hand he was already talking into it. 'OK,' he yelled. 'What the hell are they waiting for? It's now or never.' He rang off immediately but wished he had not, because, as he did so, he spotted the solitary brick come from the depths of the crowd and sail soundlessly through the air until, arching downwards, it struck the Prime Minister with great accuracy on the back of the neck. He saw Sinclair's body fall forwards and witnessed the subsequent pandemonium as police and others crowded around the body.

'Shit,' Rosenfeld swore to the empty room. 'This was just a frightener. Last thing we need is a fuckin' martyr.' He tried to get through on the number he had just called but this time there was no reply. He pressed his face against the window pane trying to get a better view. At that precise moment, the Prime Minister's Private Secretary, Robert Guthrie, waiting for the ambulance to force its way through the ugly, rioting, chanting crowd, looked up on some instinct, and glimpsed Rosenfeld surveying the bloody scene. For some reason that briefest of visions became firmly locked in Guthrie's memory. . .

The Heart of Danger

Gerald Seymour

'Unmissable' *The Times*

In a wrecked Croat village, a mass grave is uncovered and the mutilated body of a young Englishwoman, Dorrie Mowat, is exhumed.

Her mother, who loathed Dorrie in life, becomes obsessed by the need to find out about her death. But with civil war tearing apart the former Yugoslavia, none of the authorities there or in Britain are interested in a 'minor' war crime.

So she turns to Bill Penn, private investigator, MI5 reject. For him this looks like a quick trip to safe Zagreb, the writing of a useless report and a good fee at the end of it. But once there he finds himself drawn inexorably towards the killing ground behind the lines, to find the truth of the young woman's death and, perhaps, the truth of himself.

Penn's search for evidence that could, one day, convict a war criminal in a court of law becomes an epic journey into a merciless war where the odds are stacked high against him.

'It's impossible to find fault with this book, which builds relentlessly to its climax. It has an intense feeling of authenticity and it's well written'

NICHOLAS FLEMING, *Spectator*

'Vivid stuff. I write a fortnight after finishing the book and some of the scenes of pursuit and mindless cruelty still return to me'   DOUGLAS HURD, *Daily Telegraph*

ISBN 0 00 649033 6

The Fighting Man
Gerald Seymour

'It's time for Gerald Seymour to be recognized as ranking right up there with Graham Greene'   *New York Times*

Thrown out of the SAS for insubordination, Gord Brown now lives in disillusioned exile on a failing salmon farm in the Scottish highlands.

Yet to the three Guatemalan Indians who track him down, he represents the last hope of freedom. They have come to recruit a fighting man to lead an uprising against the brutal military dictatorship which is killing their people.

Gord flies with them to Cuba, then on with a small band of men to a rough landing strip in the rain forest of Guatemala.

As the ragged army marches through the jungle and across the high mountains towards Guatemala City, a hopeless dream becomes a burning reality. But the forces pitted against them are formidable.

'Unstoppable momentum'   *Daily Telegraph*

'Moving and gripping. Seymour's characters are all beautifully drawn. The dialogue is so real you can hear it and the plot is as tight as a drum. It is tempting to say that Seymour is at the height of his powers . . . He just gets better and better'
     Today

ISBN 0 00 647714 3

Provo
Gordon Stevens

Two women. One war. No rules.

Catcher
is the codename of Cathy Nolan, working undercover for
MI5 in Northern Ireland, fighting against not only a major
IRA threat, but also the internal politics of her own side.

Sleeper
is the perfect assassin, put in place years ago, unknown even
to the top-ranking members of the Provisionals' Army
Council.

PinMan
is the target of this, the ultimate coup. Now there is no way
of stopping the mission.

Provo
is the novel that redefines the modern thriller. From
Whitehall to Belfast, Hereford to South Armagh, it is
an adrenaline-pumping, white-knuckle ride behind the
headlines to a land of danger and betrayal.

ISBN 0 00 647632 5

Faith
Len Deighton

Bernard Samson returns to Berlin in the first novel
in the new spy trilogy, *Faith, Hope and Charity*

Bernard has known that he is not getting the full picture
from London Central ever since discovering that his wife
Fiona was a double agent.

Werner Volkmann has been cast out by London Central as
untrustworthy. Yet Werner still seems able to pick up
information that Bernard should have been told . . .

'A string of brilliantly mounted set-pieces . . . superbly
laconic wisecracks'   *The Times*

'Like lying back in a hot bath with a large malt whisky –
absolute bliss . . . superbly combines violent action with a
strong emotional undertow. The plotting in *Faith* is
masterly, the atmospheric descriptions superb . . .'
                                            Sunday Telegraph

ISBN 0 00 647898 0

Hope
Len Deighton

The second novel in the superb new Bernard Samson
trilogy, *Faith, Hope* and *Charity*

Bernard is trying hard to readjust his life in the face of
questions about his wife Fiona, and her defection to the
East. Is she the brilliant high-flyer that her Department
seems to think she is? Or is she a spent force, a wife and
mother unwilling or unable to face her domestic responsibilities? Bernard doesn't know but is determined to find
out.

Bernard's boss Dicky is certainly not anxious to reveal
what he knows, as he jostles for power with Fiona herself
in London Central, and takes to the road with Bernard on
a mysterious mission to Poland.

'As fresh and brisk as ever . . . a feast to be wallowed in'
Sunday Express

'It speaks volumes for Deighton's skill as a storyteller that,
years after the Berlin Wall came down, he can still set the
nerve-ends jangling with a thriller set in the Cold War . . .
His sense of pace is extraordinary, as is his sense of mood'
Sunday Telegraph

ISBN 0 00 647899 9

Dark Rose

Mike Lunnon-Wood

It was a nineteen-year-old civil engineering student who raised the alarm, drew attention to the first invasion in western Europe by outsiders since the Turkish siege of Vienna was broken by a mixed rescue force of Germans, Prussians and Poles in 1592.

Before anyone knew it, Ireland had been taken over, the surprise pawn in a stunning new game of Middle Eastern politics.

But if the invaders thought they would get away with it easily, they were wrong. As the truth dawns, an extraordinary collection of soldiers, farmers, students and expatriates gets together a Celtic resistance force and heads for a titanic confrontation . . .

With a great cast of characters, packed with action, excitement and suspense, *Dark Rose* is a fascinating portrayal of a world event that couldn't happen . . . or could it?

ISBN 0 00 647591 4